THE smoke, the flame and the death of war was over. Men were coming back to a world of peace; a world of which they had dreamed for six long dark years; a world, which they felt they, and those who were not coming back, had helped to remould nearer to the heart's desire.

That was where Ewart Brookes left his characters at the end of his best selling novel *Proud Waters*.

But the immediate years of peace were of the stuff of which dreams are made; tenuous, fragile. The years found cracks in the fabric of some of them; others found disillusionment.

That is the framework for this novel.

Temporarily deserting the sea, Ewart Brookes shows the same power to draw in characters with fine etched lines, shows the same ability to create a scene and sustain it to its logical end. In this, as in his other books, the appeal is not only in the major characters but in the minor roles, who are so carefully and faithfully drawn that they make up a large background before which moves the author's story, yet they are characters which live in the memory long after the narrative has left them behind.

EWART BROOKES

THE GLASS YEARS

178-202 GREAT PORTLAND STREET
LONDON, W.1

First published by Jarrolds Publishers (London) Ltd., 1957
This edition 1958

This book has been set in Bembo type
face. It has been printed in Great Britain on
Antique Wove paper by Taylor Garnett
Evans & Co. Ltd., Watford, Herts, and
bound by them

TO

All those who went over during the heat and burden of the day and never reached the Glass Years, and, above all, to a lovable Irishman who once came back to help me in the dark of the night, so that now I am here to write.

The eyes of the gods were turned away the day I tried to repay, but I steadfastly believe he knows that, and understands, the Darlin' Man.

For the glass of the years is brittle wherein
We gaze for a span. . . .

SWINBURNE

AUTHOR'S NOTE

Shortly after my first novel, *Proud Waters*, was published, and I was still basking warmly in the quite incredible notice it received, I was taken out to lunch by a famous author (a lunch for which I paid, incidentally), and among other gems of advice he gave me was this one: 'Never *ever*, my boy, write a sequel. It's fatal.' I treasured that pronouncement because I am at least ten years older than he is, more than for its content.

At the time I wrote *Proud Waters* I was extremely unhappy, not for any one cause but because at the time it was the period of the lean years. In the six years of war I had dropped far astern in the promotion race in my chosen profession; I came back to find new faces, new outlooks—in brief, to find that I was more or less forgotten except as someone who had once been around.

Gradually I began to build up a picture of what it must have been like for many, many others. The office boy of 1939 who came back with a decorated chest, a tight-lipped look and a knowledge of what it means to be 20,000 feet up and alone with his God, and fear, and another man up there anxious to kill him. The picture included the youngster who went away as a midshipman in 1939 proud of the fact that he had got his school colours just before a raving Austrian megalomaniac plunged the world into a mad round of killing—and came back after achieving the rank of Lieutenant, R.N.V.R., and First Lieutenant of a frigate.

In the still watches, when the tempo of the world begins to run down and sleep refuses to come, often I sat thinking back to the years which had had their fears, their losses, their heartaches—but also had their glorious moments of comradeship when a friend counted not the cost of giving, but gave freely.

The next step was but a short one. It was to recapture those moments on paper.

So *Proud Waters* began to take shape. The first steps were stumbling, hesitant, and for long periods the embryo novel lay neglected, hidden away. It was enough that in the writing, so far as it had gone, I had re-lived some of those hours when values were, shall we say, of more sterling worth. Finally I completed it, and finally it was published. How near the manuscript came to lighting a stove is a story for another day.

To the many thousands who have read it, and to the hundreds who have written to me, I say, 'May Allah always smile on you, may your vine be fruitful and may your tents be always full.' A man can wish another no more.

Perhaps we who came back, so that age could wither and the years condemn, expected too much. Possibly we wanted to step from the long shadows into a world of idealistic gilt and ever-shining light. It wasn't there, and never had been there, except in those dreams we had during the grim years.

On the other hand, as somebody once tritely but truly remarked, 'There is nothing cheaper than a returned fighter once the fighting is over.'

How true!

All this, of course, is working up to an alibi for writing a sequel.

There were the years after. For some of us they mellowed, and were more kind. In this story I have tried to follow the lives of but a few of the characters I created in *Proud Waters*. They achieve no

2

towering heights, neither do they drop to abysmal depths.

They just came back, not gifted with prophecy nor ability to control and decide events. There is at times disillusionment, even cynicism. It was there at the time; it is here in this book.

It is just a story of some men who came back to face up to the twisted, warped years of immediate post war. The saddening years, some of them; the years when dreams and ambitions crumbled apart in men's hands like dust. The brittle, glass years.

EWART BROOKES

1

THE wake trailed astern as straight as a ruled line, a ship's width of creamed water reaching back for a couple of miles, offering temporary evidence that a ship had passed this way, temporary for just as long as it took the sand-laden, dingy yellow waters of the Thames Estuary to mingle and erase all sign of it.

High in the blue, cloudless sky a solitary aeroplane scribed across the heights an equally straight, even whiter, line. The faint drone of its passage could be heard only occasionally.

Sub-Lieutenant Bolt, R.N.V.R., First Lieutenant of H.M. minesweeping trawler *Arandite*, screwed up his eyes as he watched it for a few moments.

'One of ours, would you say, sir?' he queried, the faint smile giving the lie to the serious question.

His commanding officer, Lieutenant-Commander William Haley, R.N.V.R., D.S.C., played along in the serious vein for a few moments.

'Could be, but on the other hand—— Perhaps you had better go to "action stations", Number One.'

The faint smile on Bolt's face expanded.

'If I buzzed the alarm now that lot would die of heart failure, or jump over the side in sheer terror,' he chuckled, jerking his chin towards the group of ratings lying about the fore deck in complete and contented relaxation.

'Or storm the bridge and commit mayhem,' amended Haley.

The two officers drifted into silence, each following the association of thoughts.

A few short weeks before, the drone of a plane would have brought the ship to a point of trigger-fingered tension so taut that a seagull planing into an angle of sight might easily have been blasted to pieces in a short burst of concentrated flame or sheer reflex action by a gunner.

A few short weeks before, Field Marshal Montgomery had laconically ordered the humiliated representatives of a well-beaten nation of war-makers 'Sign . . . or else,' and they had signed.

And there was peace.

And now men were going home, going home to pick up the threads where they had dropped them.

Arandite, war weary, slightly battered trawler, was going home, or would do after the guns had been removed.

Sub-Lieutenant Bolt, who had claimed only one war ambition, "to come out of it alive", had succeeded, he was going home.

The relaxed, sun-bathing group of ratings—they, too, were going home.

"So am I," Haley mused as he moved to his favoured corner of the bridge. He searched for and found with his shoulder the solidity of an upright behind the painted canvas, let his shoulder rest there—as it had done a hundred times before in the past five years.

Bolt, wise in the other man's ways, recognized that Haley wanted no conversation; he knew that the Old Man was off into one of his long, introspective moods. He rested his forearms on the bridge rail, allowed the sun full play on his face and let the wind caress it. Quietly, scarcely above a whisper, he murmured to the youthful signalman, 'Ginger up that steward. Tell him we want some tea on the bridge, then get your own. I'll call if I want you.'

The signalman departed, his rubber "daps" making scarcely any sound.

"So this is peace?" cogitated Haley. "This is what we fought for and paid for."

It was something strange, something as yet indefinable. A transitional period in which the sound of a plane at night would bring them keyed to above concert pitch.

"High or low? E-boat or plane? Bombing or laying mines?" A second elapsed before there came realization that there was going to be no more bombing, no more laying of mines, no more sudden roaring surge of an E-boat out of the blackness.

6

Haley snuggled his shoulder into the corner. In an hour, two at the most, he would be in Sheerness. He would call down the voice pipe, "Finished with engines and wheel, cox'n," and would hear the musical jangle of the engine-room telegraph. He would call down it for the last time, because it was peace. He and *Arandite* were going home.

Some would not go home. War had demanded its price, had made it a high price, had set the ransom at taking the best, and had been paid.

Regan. Haley stirred slightly as an old hurt reasserted itself. Time had softened the rending pain of the loss of his great friend, but the scar would always be tender. He could think of it now without a clenching of the finger and a tightness of the throat. He could dwell on the loss and pass on to wondering what they would have done had they both lived through to the end.

Often had they talked it over, planning as they sat at ease in each other's wardroom. Regan had refused to consider anything other than life in Ireland. He had a job in a bank and was but a few hours away from the riding and fishing he loved.

Haley had worked it out. He would buy another little cruising yacht, a five-tonner. He and She Who Had to be Obeyed and the Boy would make it a holiday cruise each year to Belfast. "And I'll. . . . And we'll. . . ." "Then we'll. . . ." Many hours of wardroom conversation had started with just those phrases.

Now Regan lay with his ship twenty fathoms deep. It was the price demanded; it had been paid.

Vaguely, through his absorbing thoughts, Haley was conscious of the steward placing a cup of tea on the flat of the bridge front.

'Tea, sir.'

Haley stirred to take it. The cup and saucer jumped six inches, disappeared over the front of the bridge. There was a dull metallic clang. The ship lurched and the officers staggered forward to gain their balance. Haley brought up with a jerk against the front of the bridge. He saw the bow climbing slowly as if labouring up an advancing sea, and as slowly it

7

twisted like a boxer turning a shoulder to take the weight of a blow.

An ear-piercing, strident, scream of rending metal followed on from the dull clang, as if the first impact had set the note for the twisting, tortured plating to continue.

As Haley gasped for breath, following the thud of the bridge against his chest, he had a quick vignette of the fore deck. Three or four men were scrambling aft, two or three others were hanging to the edge of the hatch combings or ring bolts as the fore deck climbed to the perpendicular. As he watched two slid inert, without movement of limb, down the steep deck and into the water.

Of those still alive all were looking up at the bridge. From there would come an explanation, from there would come orders to bring right to this screaming, breath-taking chaos.

'A floater, by God!' gasped Bolt with his first breath.

'Mined.' For five years Haley had expected it, lived through it in nightmares, had rehearsed in his mind what he would do, rehearsed and rehearsed until the orders which now flew were instinctive, and right.

The engine-room telegraph jangled an urgent "Stop engines." Haley listened for a moment, heard the faint tinkling reply which told him that the engineer had stayed at his post.

Bolt, slithering down the lurching bridge, stopped an almost panic-stricken rush of ratings with a staccato string of full-blooded oaths and a few orders.

Haley watched the fore deck narrowly as the ship wallowed once more back to a relatively even keel. The bow, as far back as the forward end of the gun platform, was a twisted, shapeless tangle of rent plates, gaping holes from which twisted thinning spirals of smoke.

The wallowing decreased; the angle of the deck, usually tilted upwards towards the cocked-up bow, sloped the other way as water rushed into the forward compartments. But gradually the movement identified itself in an uneasy pitching motion which lifted the shattered bow a couple of feet out of the water, showed it suspended for a second, then slowly

8

dipped it under again. It was as if the sea, in malignant mood, was saying, "Look, this is what has happened. See?" then hid it again like a mischievous child alternately concealing and showing some simple trophy.

Each time the bow lifted, dripping and red, some tortured piece of metal started a low-pitched moan which rose to a grating scream and was cut off abruptly as the water closed over it again.

Gradually, through the tempo of the rise and fall of the scream, Haley could hear a lower toned, muffled scream accompanied by a series of thuds. Before he could identify it he saw Clay, his gunner and leading hand, scramble across the wreckage of the gun platform, axe in hand, and start swinging powerful blows at the jammed doorway in the mess-deck hatch. As the door fell away the yelling became sharp. It had an animal tone about it, a senseless, hideous howl. In a scurrying rush three men shot up from the now open hatch. Their eyes were wide open in terrified hysteria; the screaming came from the second one out of the hatch and as he reached the deck he continued his howl.

Clay shifted his axe to the other hand, propped the man's chin up with a short clip then hit him hard with a second punch. The screaming stopped as the man folded up in a heap at Clay's feet. Haley saw the leading seaman grasp one of the others, shake him vigorously and point to the now unconscious stoker.

Then Clay disappeared down the shattered hatch.

In a few minutes Bolt was back on the bridge with a terse report.

It must have been a "floater", well down. The bow was gone to well below the water line, but the one bulkhead was holding and was being shored up.

As Bolt reported Haley gave an engine-room order for "Slow ahead", enough for steerage way, turned to Bolt and asked, in a voice little above a whisper, 'How many?'

'Four. Two got it when the gun platform collapsed on them and two were in their bunks against the forward bulkhead.'

9

Haley moved his head slowly and ran his fingers through his hair. Then Bolt continued briskly to more important matters.

'She's not making much water. I think we can hold it. I wish—wish that screaming would stop as she lifts. It sounds like hell down below.'

Already the metronomic noise was becoming part of life for them. They waited for it, braced themselves for the nerve-jarring, low-pitched start, followed its crescendo and if it did not go beyond top pitch were assured that things were as before, that nothing else was giving way.

The wireless operator's message came to a staccato end. From below decks Haley could hear dull thuds as Bolt and his party strengthened the shoring against the bulkhead.

High overhead the plane droned away, its white line lengthening from a pin-point to a woolly trail. It had taken it but a few minutes to cover nearly the entire arc of the sky. It had taken roughly that time to turn H.M.S. *Arandite* from a rugged, fighting-fit veteran of nearly six years of minesweeping into a twisted, pathetic wreck.

So this was being mined?

Haley finished his rapid mental assessment of the damage, the possibilities of saving the ship, probed into all he had absorbed of damage control, fought his shaking limbs to a standstill and stood at the fore end of the bridge apparently cool and collected.

Occasionally seamen scurrying around on a variety of jobs looked up, saw him standing there, and from him drew comfort and assurance. If the Old Man could take things easy, then it was going to be all right.

Always it had been like that, always when things had become tough. There was the Old Man, unflurried, cool—and things had turned out all right.

Always it had been some little order, or gesture, completely incongruous, which would raise a low chuckle and would turn their minds momentarily from the crisis.

Those gestures and commands had, more often than not, been quite unconscious on Haley's part. Had he ever attempted to analyse them he would have recognized them as being his own effort at whistling in the dark.

One such gesture came from him now. He saw a couple of stokers and a seaman struggling to move a piece of twisted gun platform. They wrenched away and eventually moved it clear. Their immediate task completed, they were at a loss.

Haley leaned over the front of the bridge and said levelly, 'Throw it over the side.'

They did. With the wreckage went a rack of shells.

'We won't want them—until the next war,' Haley added, a faint smile, so faint that they could not see it, momentarily creasing his face.

The men chuckled; it was perilously near a giggle.

'If you see the steward, tell him I didn't drink that tea he brought me. I would like another if there is any going.'

A light blinked furiously from a ship vaguely visible in the heat haze.

'Trawler *Perseus*, stand by to tow.' The signalman lowered his lamp.

Perseus, aided by a tug which took over the last part of the tow, made light work of moving *Arandite* into a berth.

As she snuggled down alongside the pier the weight of the ship rested momentarily on the twisted bow plates. The tortured scream they had heard every minute or so during the tow, was prolonged. Instead of being cut off by a slow descent into the water it trailed off to a thin sound as the bow eased off the pier—then stopped.

Haley found himself waiting for the next rising wail of sound. It did not come, and the absence was almost as much a torture to his jangled nerves as the sound itself. Alone on the bridge, he watched the shore party secure the ship, then stand in idleness scrutinizing the shattered bow of the ship.

Haley had once heard an actor use the phrase, "A tab line", the sentence used a moment before the descent of the curtain.

It was Clay, begrimed, bleeding from a scratch on the face, who provided the perfect tab line.

As he climbed through the broken mess-deck hatch one of

the shore party asked the inevitable inane question people ask after road accidents.

'What happened, chum?'

Clay looked levelly at the curious one, surveyed the shattered bow, returned his gaze to the man on the pier, flexed his muscles and shook his head reprovingly.

'Tck, tck. Temper again! Don't know my own strength.'

Haley climbed wearily down from the bridge for the last time and sat on his settee. The reaction was becoming almost physically painful.

A sharp knock at his door, a double rat-tat, sounded like a thunderclap and his nerves jumped and jangled, radiating from a spot between his shoulder blades until he felt his finger tips tingle.

A rubicund, brisk commander, R.N.R., entered, shook hands with Haley, helped himself to a cigarette from the tin on the table and sat down. The way he seated himself was in complete harmony with the character of the man. He sat bolt upright, hands resting on his knees, elbows bent out slightly, head erect. "All he wants is a Rugby ball between his feet to make him look like the centre figure in the front row of a school team," thought Haley. And he had to gnaw his bottom lip to stop a slightly hysterical giggle at the incongruity of the thought.

'Bit of bad luck, eh, what?' The commander, R.N.R., started off briskly. 'An odd floater—probably been drifting around since last winter's gales, covered with seaweed, no doubt. Eh, what?'

Haley nodded. 'We didn't see a thing.' In the same second the guilty thought flashed across his mind that they had not been looking out for anything, either. Two officers gossiping on the bridge, a calm, flat sea, cloudless sky and buoys every two miles did not call for any high-quality look-out work, especially as they were within almost hailing distance of their destination.

'Well, well, just one of those things, eh, what? We'll have to patch her up, move her into dry dock and stick a new bow on her. Pity she didn't go altogether. Would have saved a lot of trouble. Eh, what?'

Haley listened fascinatedly. He found himself waiting for the "Eh, what?" at the end of almost every sentence. He realized that it was not really a query. It was more in the nature of a final flourish, the completing crack just as a circus ring master flourishes his whip flamboyantly winding up with a double crack of the lash.

'I've had her for more than five years,' he answered mildly. 'I would have hated like hell to lose her like that. I've seen worse patched-up and sent to sea again.'

'No doubt, no doubt of it all.' The reply was brisk, the words skittering through the conversation like a flat stone skimming water.

The commander's eyes were on Haley's breast where the D.S.C.—by now a grubby ribbon—nudged a couple of other ribbons.

'You been on her all that time, eh? Don't often keep C.O.s on one ship so long. Would have thought they would have shifted you to something bigger.' The gaze had dropped down to the two-and-a-half rings on Haley's sleeve. 'Two-and-half, and a gong, is a bit heavy for a trawler, eh, what?'

Haley ran his hands wearily through his hair. He could have embarked on a long explanation of how he had refused a larger command, why he had preferred to stay with the *Arandite*, but shrugged it away. Instead, he sought refuge in a more technical channel.

'Were we coming here to de-commission, or for a job of work?' He poured out two drinks as he spoke.

'Most of your crew would have gone, you included, but we were going to use her for odds and ends of jobs. Chin-chin!' A slight pause while the drink was half disposed of. 'But now we'll swap her for a couple of balloons, or a windmill. You know, "any, any any old iron"?' The commander stood up and poked Haley in the ribs. 'Still, you couldn't care less, eh, what?'

He moved towards the door, becoming suddenly brisk again. 'First thing in the morning we'll start the hand-over.'

A full moon hung, startlingly large and white, in the sky

13

as Haley leaned against his favourite pillar on the bridge. To-morrow was the start of the hand-over, not a long job. Bolt had everything neatly tidied up for a quick check. Tomorrow he would step ashore and his responsibility for *Arandite* would cease, sharply, like the swift cut of an axe.

It would not be like going on a short leave with the know-ledge that he was merely thrusting the problems to the back of his mind for a week. It would be final.

For five years—five long years—she had occupied the forefront of his mind, she, those who sailed in her, and what she did had been his life. And now it was all over.

Haley squinted along the path of the moon over the water as it drew a wide, yellow track out towards the dark estuary of the Thames, and a little smile crept round the corners of his mouth.

It would be a long time before romance and the moon ran in double harness for him. He would find himself peering into the dark verge on either side of the reflection, wondering if that contrasting darkness held an E-boat or two, wondering if he was a silhouette in that revealing path.

His thoughts tracked backwards, without regard for chrono-logical sequence, over the past five years, back over events most of which had their connecting thread to the ship.

He turned towards the chart table to light a cigarette, then remembered that it was no longer necessary to shelter behind its covering sheet of canvas for a quick smoke. The flame lit up his face for a moment or two as he got the cigarette going.

Somewhere, deep in the ship, a door clanged as a stoker inspected his fire; it was a noise which had been an integral part of the ship for years. Haley waited for the next phase, the sharp clang as the stoker dropped his heavy steel slice.

So many times, as he had snatched a brief doze at the back end of the bridge, that clang had been the first note of an over-ture to a rapid, heart-jarring nightmare; had brought him upright, sweating and shaking.

And the actual mine explosion had been something of an

14

anticlimax; it had been a surge rather than an ear-splitting explosion.

A hand touched him gently and he started and spun round. Clay, his gunner and leading hand, stood there with a cup of coffee.

'Saw somebody light a cigarette up here, sir, and guessed it was you.' Clay's teeth shone white in the moonlight as he smiled. 'Thought you'd like a last cup of real coffee on the bridge.'

'Thanks. I wonder how many of them I've drunk in the past few years?'

There was silence between them for a while, a silence which Clay broke as he moved to the front of the bridge.

'Bin a long time—seems a lot longer than five years——'

'Yet it seems only yesterday that you gave me a cup of coffee my first night aboard. There was an air raid on——'

'And *Solan* got herself a German plane. I remember, sir.' Clay was silent for a moment or two. 'Good ship, *Solan*. We never had another chummy ship. Wouldn't have seemed right, would it?'

Haley shook his head slowly. Nobody could have replaced Regan, *Solan's* commanding officer, in his affections. To other ships and to other commanding officers he had erected a slightly frigid barrier.

'Most of us go to barracks tomorrow—then it's us for civvies. I was asking a petty officer about me taking on. D'you know what he said? DO YOU KNOW WHAT HE SAID, sir?' Clay laid emphasis on his point by heavily accenting the query. 'He said, "Listen, matlo, we'll have more REAL sailors around than we'll know what to do with. You take your bowler hat and gratuity and let's get this Navy tidied up."'

Clay drove his fist into his palm.

'We was in a pub, and THAT's what he said,' as if the place of utterance added sacrilege to the words.

'What happened?'

Clay blew softly on his knuckles.

'Me and Bluenose Ross and Skelton was together; couple

15

of others came in later.' He moved towards the ladder from the bridge, collecting Haley's empty cup as he moved. 'The picket in this place ain't so hot.'

From a man who had waged fierce warfare with pickets for five years it was a devastating criticism.

'I hope——' Haley started.

'They never knew what hit 'em,' Clay said flatly. 'More coffee, sir? Pity to waste it.'

'I think I would.'

He met Clay at the bottom of the bridge ladder as the man returned with the second cup.

'I'll take it in my berth, Clay.' The man followed him through the door and placed the coffee on the small desk.

'What's the trouble? Can't you sleep, either? Why are you around and about?'

Clay smiled, a small, embarrassed smile.

'I—I—I was having a sort of last look round on me own, sir. You know, without any other stupids there to ask a lot of silly questions. I've bin on this ship for more'n five years—seen a lot of things happen. Bin a lot of good blokes come and go, one way and another. We got a good lot now.'

Haley stirred his coffee and allowed the man's statement to circulate freely in his mind before replying.

'Quite so, Clay, but we were gathered together to do a job. The job is done. Now we go home.'

He offered a cigarette to Clay.

'Home is the sailor, home from the sea
And the hunter home from the hill.

That is written on R. L. Stevenson's tomb and about sums it up, doesn't it?'

Clay nodded. 'It does. We done plenty of hunting, we bin hunted—and damn' nearly didn't get home.' His interpretation was literal.

He moved towards the door and turned with his hand on the knob. 'Pity the old girl had to get it like this, just at the last minute. Still, we got her in.'

16

Haley's lips twitched at the collective claim. Clay had done the work of half a dozen men when the mine had struck.

'We did,' he answered gravely. 'And in a few months she'll be back at her peace-time job of fishing. You'll be back at yours and I at mine. You'll probably become chairman of the local branch of the British Legion.'

Clay snorted. 'Not me. Join a tin-hut boozer, open when the pubs are shut and carry a banner once a year? Not me.'

Haley felt there was an answer somewhere to the man's inadequate dismissal of that excellent organization, but he found no wish to expound. Instead, he turned quickly to his wine locker, poured out two stiff whiskies, and offered one to Clay. They lifted glasses silently and drank.

'Good night, sir.'

'Good night.'

"And for that I could be court-martialled," Haley mused when he was alone. He poured out another stiff drink and tossed it back.

In the past couple of months he had found it was the only way to get off to sleep; the only way to bridge that half-conscious period between wakefulness and sleep, that period when thoughts, free and untrammelled, soared away to join forces, only to return just as sleep arrived, thoughts concentrated into a sweating, shaking nightmare.

He realized that it was like knocking himself on the head with a hammer to achieve a mild form of unconsciousness, but had found it brutally effective, so he continued to do it.

Wide awake, and busy with the tasks of the day, he could cope with the fears which flooded in on him, a fear that there was one mine somewhere with the ship's name on it, a fear that it would strike and a fear that he. . . . Wide awake, he could deal ruthlessly with the thoughts; sleeping, they had their way.

As the double nightcap began to take effect he found his thoughts drifting inexorably in that direction; he found himself tensing himself, waiting for the bang. . . . He shrugged himself down into the bed-clothes. It had come—the BIG BANG was over—it had done its worst. . . it. . . .

'Ar' pas' seven. Tea, sir.' The steward carefully placed the small tray on a ledge at the side of Haley's bunk, pulled aside the porthole curtains and flooded the small room with morning sunshine.

'Bacon and eggs—and sausages—and tomatoes for breakfast, sir.' He brought each successive announcement out with the air of a conjuror surpassing each trick with another slick movement.

In fact that seemed to be the tone for the day. Everything went with well-oiled smoothness. Permanent stores, loan clothing, ammunition—everything was slipped ashore with rapidity to the satisfaction of a Wren petty officer who spent her time marking off lists with Bolt, and occasionally rewarding him with an arch glance.

It was late in the afternoon when Bolt tapped on his door. 'Shore party have taken over, sir. The crew is lined up ready to march to barracks. Would you like. . . .'

Haley took one last look round the room. Nothing of his remained; his personal effects were in the cases on the quay waiting alongside the Wren-driven light van.

'I would.'

They were lined up, three deep, a little group of inarticulate men, feeling probably the same as Haley felt. Wanting to say something, but not quite knowing the words to use.

He slowly moved down the short lines, catching each man's eye for the length of two breaths. Some of them had been on the ship for only a short while. Others had been on her when he took over years back.

Haley reached Clay, standing head erect, chin out. Alongside him was Noisy, the ship's cook. A cadaverous, toothless, undersized old man, a genius with fish to fry and a living lie. He had lied and cheated his way into a hard-pressed service at the beginning of the war and had followed his humble but vital bent until the end.

Haley stopped by him. The watery, faded blue eyes engaged Haley's and twinkled.

'What's become of your pet?'

18

The eyes opened wide, the twinkle increased.

Noisy's pet was an Army Bren gun, acquired during the Dunkirk evacuation and nourished and cherished by the old man from then onwards. It had been part of a game, almost a ritual, for Haley to pretend that he knew nothing of its existence. At captain's rounds each week, for five years or so, a complicated series of manœuvres had been carried out to ensure that Haley did not sight it by accident.

Time and again during air attacks Haley had seen a stream of tracer bullets flying from the galley porthole or skylight.

Noisy, whose voice had never risen above a husky, grating whisper, replied softly. Clay leaned forward, listened a moment, then stood erect.

'He had some gear in the forepeak, sir. It went when the mine hit us.'

Haley nodded.

'Good thing too. Guns are dangerous things in the hands of youngsters.'

A ripple of laughter flowed down the ranks.

Poor stuff, but it took the strain off aching muscles at the back of the throat.

Haley stood in front of his crew; slowly his eyes travelled down the ranks.

'I should make a speech. I can't. I—won't easily forget any one of you. If I am ever in difficulties in civil life and can find anyone like you to stand at the back of me—I will be content. Good luck.'

He saluted. A crisp-voiced petty officer rattled out commands, the small body turned and swung away in a rolling march.

Haley held out his hand to Bolt.

'You, too—good luck.'

'Good luck, sir.'

They exchanged salutes, the smooth Naval salute, the exchange of salutes between fighting men.

Haley put his cases into the vehicle and climbed in alongside the girl. Pointedly he kept his eyes away from the ship, settled himself in the seat, smiled at Bolt and nodded to the girl to drive away.

She swung the car expertly down the quay, round the end of the jetty and back along another parallel to the one they had left. As they drew level with *Arandite* the girl slowed down for a lorry. Haley felt his eyes drawn irresistibly across the small dock.

Arandite looked small, shabby, rust streaked; the twisted, shattered bow seemed to dominate the rest of the ship. Haley's head turned slowly to keep her in focus as the girl slipped into gear again and accelerated.

Then *Arandite* was gone, out of sight.

The girl hummed quietly to herself. Haley listened to her for a moment; a catchy tune, with a somewhat sad downward slurring finish.

'What is that tune?'

' "Smoke Gets in Your Eyes." '

Haley took his cigarette case out, lit a cigarette and looked the girl full in the face as she turned towards him with a smile.

'It's as good an alibi as any.'

She nodded. 'Gets in my eyes sometimes.'

Later a grey-haired captain, R.N., added a few lines round his eyes when he crinkled his face into a smile.

'Damn' bad luck, Haley. To run the full course, then rap a fence almost at the end is the outside edge. I took a look at her this afternoon. I see you've collected quite a bag. Without a doubt the balance is to your credit.'

'Yes, sir.' Haley smiled back.

'Anything we can do for you?'

'I think everything is being done, sir. My crew has been——'

'They'll slip through the machinery here without a snag. Cigarette? Personally, I never could bring myself to part with a ship's company without feeling that I was saying good-bye to part of myself. Probably was, too, when you come to think of it. For the length of a commission a captain had to make every man just a little bit of himself, sort of project a fragment of himself into every man. Otherwise the ship would become just a—a—bum boat.'

20

'I see what you mean, sir.'

'I'm a small-ship man, Haley. Destroyers remained my constant love. It's a good many years since I first trod on a bridge in command, but I remember every one of them, their problems, which were my problems. How I learned from each one something to give to the next.'

Haley studied the man in front of him. For more years than Haley had lived he had reigned in almost supreme command of complex little communities as complicated as a small township. Had been guide, philosopher and judge carrying the responsibilities of half a million pounds which could be reduced to scrap iron by one wrong decision and order, had held the fates of a hundred men in the hollow of his palm.

"And industrialists send their executives away for six weeks to learn personal psychology." Haley thought. "The way to fine a man—and the answers—is to be in command of a ship."

'Did you say something, Haley?'

'No—no—no, sir. I was thinking.'

'Look, Haley, I have a couple of young officers dining with me tonight before I hurl them back into a cruel world. Join us. They are about your weight. Seven o'clock? Fine!'

Haley stood up.

'Sir, there is one thing—I—we—the men who were killed on my ship. Could I just see where——'

The captain pressed a bell push. To the petty officer Wren who answered he said, 'Lieutenant-Commander Haley would like to visit—the place at the end of block E. See that a messenger shows him the way.'

'Yes, sir.'

'Thank you, sir,' Haley said.

'No trouble, my boy. Seven o'clock it is. And, Haley, a word of advice. Let the dead bury the dead. You have nothing with which to reproach yourself. Seven o'clock as ever is.'

The messenger made the necessary introduction to the corpulent seaman at the entrance of the small, red-brick building.

'Yes, sir. We only got the four in now. Mind, I've seen 'em

in here lying four thick when the raids was on. There was one day when——'

'Yes, yes, later.' Haley stopped the garrulity with a raised hand. He heard the door click behind him. He was alone with his men.

Four silent figures, blanket-covered, lay on raised stone slabs.

For a while he stood there. Somewhere beyond the still silent figures were the answers to all questions.

He came to attention and saluted.

In an almost soundless whisper, 'Good-bye. Speak well of me to those you will meet.'

The corpulent seaman was waiting for him.

'We'll hold 'em a couple of days until the relatives decide whether they want 'em home, or to have 'em buried down here. Down here is better. Barracks puts on a good show, gun's crew, firing party, buglers—the lot. I think the blokes in there would like it, if they was asked. You know, the old bit of flannel. And the P.O.'s Mess always asks the relatives to the Mess for a bit of a feed afterwards. I always think—oh, thanks, sir.'

A carefully designed little dinner party climbed from initial shyness to ultimate hilarity, sweeping Haley along with it. When finally they stood framed in the lighted doorway saying good night Haley would have admitted without demur that he was slightly lit.

'Good-bye, sir. See you in the next war.' A round-faced lieutenant held out his hand.

The captain took it. 'I hope I will be on the side of the angels. You, I've no doubt, from what I've heard from time to time, will be a temporary acting with a forked tail and a trident.'

'Yes, sir, rely on me. I'll stir 'em up.'

'You've had enough practice this past five years or so. Good night, and good luck, all of you.'

'S-s-s-alt of the earth.' The rubicund one had slight difficulty with his sibilants.

'Most of them were,' Haley said, thinking of Mahoney who had been his senior officer for long years. 'The few exceptions merely proved the rule. When you think of it, we jumped into their navy, which had been their lives. We did everything wrong time and time again. Their patience was inexhaustible.'

'Well, now they've got their navy back,' another officer submitted. 'They can be ship keepers until we want it again for the next war.'

'Who are we going to fight, for God's sake?'

'Oh, anybody. Let's have a bash at America.'

'Be like fighting a vast machine,' Haley said. 'And why America?'

The round-faced one slipped into a maudlin stratum.

'Damned G.I. barged in and she left me flat.'

'On that basis France, Belgium, Denmark and Norway should declare war on you personally,' the other officer suggested solemnly. 'That is, if we accept that all wars are based funda . . . funda . . . you know what I mean. Sex starts wars.'

Haley swung away. 'For God's sake! Can't you talk about anything but war?' He hesitated. 'Sorry, chaps.' And he walked off into the night.

'Touchy, eh?' The fat-faced young lieutenant watched Haley disappear. 'Ah, well! Did I tell you about the girl in Ostend? When she first saw me. . . .'

2

LIEUTENANT-COMMANDER OWEN MEREDITH, R.N.V.R.,
lowered his head to meet the wind-whipped rain. There
seemed to be a malevolent quality about the wind. It waited,
lurking, malignant at street corners, waited until Meredith
stepped clear of the sheltering buildings before raising a
gusty snarl which whipped the rain before it in grey, glistening
sheets.

Already he was soaked. His blue naval raincoat was sodden,
carrying more than it could hold. It shone, sleek and black like
an oilskin, and the surplus water ran down his trouser legs and
into his squelching boots.

He hunched his shoulders round his ears more in an unconscious gesture than in any defined form of protection.

Rain and a driving wind ashore was a filthy business. At sea
he had not disliked it. In fact there had been occasions when he
had welcomed it. He had stood on the bridge with the rain
whipping his bare head, the rest of him adequately covered by
voluminous oilskin and seaboots, with a rolled towel in the neck
of his coat to stop any errant rivulets of water. It had been clean,
invigorating.

But ashore it was filthy, soot-laden while in the air, and
turning the streets into liquid mud.

Meredith reached a crossing above which gleamed, like a
shining orange, a Belisha beacon. Briefly he eyed the street each
way and crossed the road, skirted the small square of grass
above which waved the bare arms of towering plane trees. The
grass was a startling, unnatural green, bright, vivid, like the
grass in a cheap postcard, as it reflected the blue-white light
from the vapour street lamps. It was six long years since the
street lamps had been dimmed and put out. Six long years. . . .

Now it was Christmas Eve, the first peace Christmas. Shop
windows flaunted their new radiance, although it was merely

a temporary concession lasting over the Christmas, flooding the wet pavements in pools of light. Motor cars hissed past, flinging misty clouds from their wheels, they, too, adding their quota of light after the six years of darkness.

Meredith turned from the main road into a side lane, a cobbled mews flanked by wide-doored garages and above them wildly expensive flatlets and maisonettes, bijou homes formerly the modest quarters of coachmen and later chauffeurs.

From a narrow door which gleamed redly as it hung nearly open Meredith heard a trill of laughter, rising and joining with a childish voice. Behind, there was a background of music.

> Peace on earth and mercy mild
> God and sinner reconciled.
> Joyful all ye nations rise
> Join the triumph of the skies

In a million homes loudspeakers would be blaring the carol.

> Peace on earth, and mercy mild.

A sound, scarcely articulate, almost a groan, forced itself through Meredith's lips. He thrust his hands down deeper into his raincoat pockets.

'Oh, God! You did it. Find me the answer. Tell me! Tell me! Why?'

His head rolled slowly as he walked, as a boxer's head rolls when he is near the knock-out, still on his feet and moving by sheer instinct, without conscious effort.

Meredith reached the end of the mews where it opened out on to a main road again. A main road flooded with wet light, full of people. He hesitated, half turned and looked back along the dark mews, lighted only by the gleam from curtained windows.

But along the mews was:

> Joyful all ye nations rise,
> Join the triumph of the skies.

He shook his head, looking first at the crowded street then back along the mews.

There was no way out either way. His train was not due to go for more than three hours. The train in which he hoped to rest his aching head against the padding, in which he hoped the rhythm of the wheels would help him to sleep, would provide something tangible on to which he could fasten his mind.

'Hullo, dearie. Going my way?'

Meredith searched the shadows from beneath his peaked cap and finally located the speaker, but only when she stepped from the partial darkness of a deep doorway.

He took half a step towards her and invitingly she moved to one side to allow the doorway to accommodate both of them.

'Looking for some fun, sailor?' The woman peered up at him calculatingly from under a close-fitting hat. Provocatively she swayed towards him. 'Wouldn't have a cigarette, would you, dearie? Mine fell out of my hands and. . . .' A gesture completed the story.

Meredith groped for his cigarette case and offered it. As he struck a match she shot a shrewd glance at her prospect. It lasted no more than a couple of seconds, but was enough to show her a dark face, black eyebrows drawn in a line above deep-set eyes, eyes which seemed to have a curiously opaque look about them, as if they lacked life, as if there was nothing for them to mirror. The glance was long enough to show her a mouth compressed into a straight, thin line.

'Going to a party?' She pulled heavily at the cigarette until it framed her face in a momentary pink glow.

He shook his head.

'How about it, sailor? I'll give you a good time.'

Again the cigarette glowed and again the face was tinged with pink.

A sudden incongruous thought flitted through Meredith's mind.

"Flash red every five." The sort of legend written against hundreds of buoys. "Flash red every five seconds." A constant warning, and ignore it at your peril.

A short, sharp laugh escaped from his lips without any accompanying relaxation of his face.

She groped for the meaning, searching it for any sign of acceptance.

'I've got a nice room, sailor. It's just round the corner. Two minutes. You can stay as long as you like.'

"Flash red every five seconds." The cigarette glowed.

Suddenly Meredith shrugged his shoulders.

'C'mon. I'll buy you a drink. You must be frozen.' He took her elbow in his cupped hands. 'What you want is a large rum and lime mixed with hot water.'

She fell in beside him, her heels making little clicking noises on the wet pavement.

With the vague conception that constant pressure will weaken even the sternest resolve, she snuggled against him and said softly, 'What I want is a boy friend. I've got a nice room. It's my own. We could——'

'Will this do?' He paused outside the public house where three doors each bore a different notice in red lights. "Public Bar," "Saloon Bar," "Lounge."

As they stood the door to the lounge opened and two people stepped out on to the glistening pavement.

'Cripes, it's comin' down like stair rods,' the man said and bowed before the rain. Before the door could close Meredith stopped it with his toe.

'All right?'

'Sure, baby, I often use this house. We'll have a little drink first, eh, sailor?'

Inside the door Meredith paused, his eyes wrinkled and half closed against the bright lights. The room was more than half full. Against the short service bar stood a line of people all engaged in animated conversation which built up into a blur of meaningless sound. He found he had a choice of two places. In the far corner was a short red-covered settee faced by a chromium and red table. Nearer the door and in the middle of the room was another vacant table with spindle-legged chairs, also of chromium, standing empty and inviting.

Meredith made his way towards the settee, the woman at his side. She seemed to be known to several in the room and exchanged words with them.

Most of the women had seen the best of their lives. They sat nursing glasses of stout or beer, their features set in inflexible resignation, most of them pale and looking under-nourished after six years. The ones to whom the woman spoke gave Meredith a swift, shrewd glance, then turned to her.

'Hullo, Mais. Things all right? Merry Christmas.'

'Same to you, ducks. Not so bad, considerin'. Isn't the weather awful?'

''Orrible. But it's nice to see the lights.'

'Wotcher, Maisie. World treatin' you O.K.?'

'Not so bad, considerin'. Merry Christmas, Lil.'

Meredith absorbed all this in a curiously detached way, as if he were sitting in the back row of a cinema seeing all from a long way off. He shook his head slightly and blew softly and shortly through pursed lips. He had learnt that for a brief moment these two actions seemed to give him a mental clarity, a fusing of mind and body, like shaking a bottle of medicine to obtain the full effect until the component parts separated again. He lifted his head inquiringly.

'I'd like a whisky, if you can get one. P'raps they'll have a bottle or two as it's Christmas.'

Meredith looked puzzled. Why shouldn't there be whisky, two glasses of golden forgetfulness provided he put the money down? He had disposed of a number of bottles of it in the past few months. Ever since they had told him, he had found that whisky had helped. All he had to do was say, 'Steward, put another bottle of whisky out for me.' Sometimes not even that. Not even that when he had realized that his officers were looking slightly askance, watching him through half averted eyes, knowing through the grapevine telegraph which threads through all ships that he was drinking more than a bottle of whisky a day. He, Meredith, the man who had maintained that a man at sea with a whisky under his belt was more than half way to being only part of a man. It was then that he had started

28

cheating. It was then that he had saved up an empty bottle and filled it with cold golden tea and left it about as evidence that he was drinking only a little. A subterfuge which lasted not more than a couple of days and made the eyes more averted, the looks more askance, and the doubts loom larger.

Why shouldn't there be whisky?

He thrust a shoulder between two men at the bar and caught the eye of the brassy-haired, big-bosomed woman who presided.

'Two large whiskies, please.'

She laughed, a short, sharp metallic laugh suiting the colour of her hair.

'You gotter hope! Two large ones! If you say two singles you'll stand a chance. Two singles?' She moved towards a solitary bottle which stood at the back of the bar.

'Blimey, chum, don't you know there's a war just ended?' Meredith turned to the speaker, his chin slightly out-thrust.

'Only bin over six months. And 'cos we won it we has to go short on the props of life.'

The man lifted his eyes to the badge on Meredith's cap.

'Navy, eh? I was Commandos. You swobs shoved me ashore a coupla times. In Algiers—lumme! That was a picnic. An' again D-Day. We went in on Juno beach. That bit——'

'Here y'are. Two singles. An' many's the time I've said "Thank Gawd we have a Navy." I knew a Navy boy. Bomb Disposal, he was. Used to feel around bombs an' make 'em helpless. Practised on me, he did.' She climbed up on the last sentence to a laugh which made her almost totally exposed heavy bosoms shake like huge jellies. 'Five bob, ducks, an' five for the glasses. Wot a lad! Many's the time he's showed me how he searched for the fuse——' The laugh soared again.

'Five bob for the glasses?'

'You fool, them's doubles,' the ex-Commando whispered. 'Slip it over quick before the boss sees her.'

Meredith handed over a pound note.

'Was you around D-Day? We——'

'I've been out East.' Meredith clipped it out, briefly, shortly.

'Bloody Japs, eh? I would 'a' liked to have a basinful against them bastards. Monkey men, they calls 'em. We was——'

'. . . an' ten bob makes a pound. Have a nice time, ducks. Christmas only comes once a year.' The barmaid looked across at Meredith's companion, winked at her, winked at him, and turned to a new customer.

'Three bitters, two stouts and a mild and bitter. Yessir. The bitter's nice tonight.'

'I reckon our outfit would 'a' given them yellow bastards somethin'. I remember once, when we was ordered to take a bridge. . . .'

Meredith moved away with the two glasses in his hand. Remember. Remember. Everybody wanted to remember. Everybody wanted to delve down into their memories, to keep them burnished, to bring them out for almost continual inspection and display, like a proud woman with a wealth of silverware.

His companion was engaged in deep conversation with a faded woman at the next table.

' "What I do with myself is my business," I says to her. "I never bring a friend inside your door," I says. "An' I'm as respectable as them tarts of typists you has here," I tells her straight. "So long as I pay my rent an' keep to myself that's all you're entitled to," I says.' Her listener kept time to the words with a slowly nodding head, her lips pursed up into a tight little bunch.

Maisie looked up as Meredith arrived with the drinks.

'Oh, you were lucky. You got doubles, eh?' She slipped from the ordinary conversational tones she had used when talking to the woman alongside her to a mincing voice, allowing her face to take on as arch a look as she could manage. 'You must have a way with you.'

The faded woman diplomatically leaned away as Meredith sat down.

'Merry Christmas, Mais.'

'Same to you, love, an' many of 'em.'

She sipped her whisky, with little finger delicately raised,

30

placed the glass on the table, crossed her legs so that Meredith—or anybody else interested—could see the sheen of nylon stockings, touched her little hat, adjusted her hair and produced from a brightly garish handbag a small mirror.

'The rain's played Old Harry with my face,' she simpered. 'Excuse me, while I put it right.' She embarked upon a complicated adjustment of flaring lipstick which involved heavy grimaces into the small mirror and some touching up with a little finger.

Meredith studied her, his elbow on the table, the weight of his head on arched fingers, one finger beating a light tattoo on his forehead.

She was young, not more than late twenties, nothing obviously hard about her. Meredith found that the tapping finger somehow helped him to concentrate, to co-ordinate his mental processes into a steady channel. There was nothing about her, nothing to distinguish her from many of the other women who were in the lounge.

She was slim, fair-haired, without any obvious physical attributes to be emphasized. Two blue eyes concentrated into a stare into the small mirror and it was when he reached the eyes that Meredith felt he had found something which made her different. They were age-old, with a mixture of weariness, glass-hardness and wariness. At the corners were small crow's feet. She lifted her eyes and engaged Meredith's with almost an audible twang. It was too late for him to look away.

'That's better,' she said. She leaned forward to reach for her drink, cleverly throwing open her coat so that her low-necked blouse beneath sagged enough to show the slight curve of her small bosoms.

'Like me, sailor?' she whispered. 'We could have a good time. I know a club we could go to—afterwards—— The drinks are all right there. Then we could——'

Meredith looked at his watch.

'I have a train to catch in two and a half hours.'

The look of weariness in her eyes increased.

'You'd have time——'

31

'How much?' Meredith clipped it out, cutting the words off short with a snap of his lips.

Swiftly she assayed him. Here was a sailor, an officer by the look of him, sunburned and just home. All officers had money.

'What time is your train, dearie?'

'Midnight.'

'Where from?'

'Paddington.'

'Oh, that's only a little walk from here.' The tip of her tongue went round her top lip once. With almost a touch of delicacy she said, 'Would three pounds hurt you? And if you like me and decide to lose your train—five pounds.'

She made it almost a gesture of unbridled generosity.

Meredith rubbed his palm slowly across his forehead and screwed up his eyes. How was he to tell this woman, this woman of the streets, that he wanted nothing of her but her presence, just to be with her? Merely to have one individual upon whom he could concentrate, whom he could listen to—without hearing, somebody who would be with him so that he would not have to look at people in the mass, would not have to be alone, alone and afraid because alone he would have his thoughts, and that deep cylindrical cloud which at times seemed to envelope his whole head, at others diminishing until it was a pin-point whirling into the distance, only to return bringing with it the shadows, and the thoughts, the memories.

'You see, dearie, I have a living to get.'

Her voice came to him from a long way off. He sat up.

'All right.'

She clicked into another routine with practised ease.

This was a reluctant hero. This was a man to get to point A as swiftly as possible, point A being a bed. This was no man flaring with bottled-up animal passion who would demand unceasingly for half the night, snore for the other half and with the grey cold ashes of passion around him in the morning quibble about the price.

A subtle air of alertness infused her simper.

32

'Shall we go, dearie? It's not far. Only a few yards. I left the gas fire on, so it will be nice and warm.'

Point A loomed.

Meredith stood up wearily and she followed, fastening her coat about her.

'Goo' night, dearie,' she said to the faded woman. 'Have a nice Christmas.'

'Wot hopes,' the woman replied. 'An' me with the old man inside.'

As they passed the bar Maisie said, 'Pity, we might have bought her a drink. Her old man's in the jug. He nicked a box of fruit to flog in the black an' they picked him up. He got a carpet.'

Meredith looked puzzled.

'Three months. An' in over Christmas.'

Meredith stopped at the bar and caught the barmaid's eye.

'The lady in the corner—could she have a single? And one for yourself.' He laid a ten-shilling note on the counter.

The barmaid beamed expansively. 'I'll fix it,' she grinned. 'Same size singles?'

Meredith pushed open the door and stepped into the night.

The barmaid carefully poured a dark stout into a glass, dropped the last drop from a height so that the drink climbed into a frothy and deceiving head and handed it to the ex-Commando.

'Shove that over to Maudie. With the sailor, tell her.' Negligently she caressed her ample bosom with the other hand and the man admiringly watched the ten-shilling note disappear. He placed the drink in front of the faded woman with the news that she had been bought one by the sailor and returned to the bar. He stood on tip-toes and looked down the deep valley between the barmaid's bosoms.

'It doesn't show,' he grinned. 'An' I call it smart. Nobody's hurt, 'cos Maude doesn't drink whisky.'

Their eyes met. He went on. 'Blimey, to think that I would be jealous of a ten-bob note.'

She leaned forward to give him a better view.

33

'You needn't be.'

The blood pounded behind his ears and his fingers flexed. 'Roll on, ha' past ten.'

'Eleven, ducks. I have to clear up. But it's a long time to breakfast.'

'We'll skip it an' wait for dinner.'

Her moist eyes met his. 'I got a little chicken.'

'So have I,' he breathed. 'An' I'll provide my own sauce.'

Her ample bosom heaved in one tumultous breath and the pounding of the blood became almost unbearable behind his ears.

'Um, um. . . .' It was almost an animal noise from her slightly parted lips. Then service was demanded. 'Two bitters and a glass of half an' half. Yessir. The bitter's nice tonight.'

Outside the door the tinny sounds of music battled with the loud conversation.

'. . . Peace on earth an' mercy mild
Gawd an' sinners reconciled. . . .'

A voice wrestled against the tinny music in a reedy tenor.

'. . . Joyful all ye nations rise
Join the triumphs of the skies.
'Ark the 'Erald Angels sing
Glory to the new born King. . . .'

The landlord of the public house stiffened as the first stanzas threaded through the loud buzz of conversation. He lifted a flap in the counter and thrust his way to the door. When he opened it forcibly the reedy, cracked tenor seemed to acquire power.

'. . . to the new born King.'

'Hop it. Take yer catawauling somewhere else. Go on, hop it. Or I'll put the cops on yer.'

A wizened old man with a battered banjo looked up at him from lack-lustre eyes, his finger stilled but just above the strings. Alongside him was an equally wizened man wearing an overcoat several sizes too big.

34

'Jes' tryin' to get a coupla coppers for Christmas, guv'nor,' the player whined.

'I'll get the coppers for yer, in blue. Now hop it.'

They shuffled away and the landlord, after a shrug and squaring of his shoulders, allowed the door to swing to and turned once more to the bar.

'It's a perisher outside. Coming down in sheets. Gawd help the sailors on a night like this.'

'From what I see they can help themselves on any sort of night.' The brass-haired barmaid finished it with a cackle. Her eyes swept over to the ex-soldier for a brief moment.

'Wait till you've met the Commandos, then you'll have something to talk about.'

A man with a fighter pilot moustache wheedled the landlord 'Just one more single, old man. Festive spirit and all that. What about a spot of Drambuie? Yes? Whacko! Bang on!'

When he was served and the landlord had moved away he said quietly, 'Hard-hearted bloke. When he read *The Christmas Carol* he thought Scrooge was the hero.'

'If he can read,' answered his unhappy-looking companion, unhappy because he was faced with a liquor he didn't want on top of beer he had wanted.

Maisie fumbled in her handbag and found a key. The hall was dimly lighted, barely furnished. Shiny lino covered it from wall to wall. A thinner strip of the same material ran up the stairs; her feet made sharp little clat-clat noises as she climbed. Another key opened a door on the first floor and although the room was in darkness a wave of warm air met them.

'Don't—don't put the light on. Just leave it as it is.' Meredith stopped just inside the door. The glow from the half-turned-on gas fire was just enough to throw highlights from the furniture, to show a sagging bed in one corner.

'As you like, dearie. But I'll have to find a shilling for the meter. I always put one in, turn the gas on and let it burn itself out.'

Meredith held out a handful of silver. 'Take one from that.' She bent down by the fire and pawed over the silver.

'I've taken two in case it goes out. Don't want to be cold, do you dearie?'

The meter whirred as she put the two coins in.

'Take your coat off, dearie. You must be sopping. I know I am.' She sat down on an armchair, kicked off her shoes and rolled down her stockings. Her costume coat followed and she stood up to cope with the fastenings of her skirt.

Meredith stood still.

'C'mon, dearie. And you can't wear your wet trousers and muddy boots on the bed, now, can you?'

'Look, I don't want—— Please believe me, I——'

Maisie had a routine ready. A certain note sharpened her voice.

'You haven't been having me on? I have a living to make. I've been with you now for nearly an hour. There are clients. . . .'

Meredith fumbled in his inner pocket, pulled out his wallet and extracted some notes. Three? Four? He didn't count. He held them out to her. As she counted them, shooting him some sidelong glances, he moved towards the fire and leaned his crossed forearms on the small mantelpiece. There was a rustle as she put the notes away.

Maisie went carefully into another routine.

'If it's some funny business you want—well, I don't like it. But as it's you, I would for another pound. An American friend of mine always gives me two over the odds. Are you feeling all right? Don't want to be sick, do you?'

She'd known men who had drunk too much and found the dual strain of alcohol and passion too much at a critical point.

A low moan, almost a tremulous sigh, escaped from Meredith. With his head resting on his arm he said, in a muffled voice, 'No, I'm all right.'

Maisie had exhausted her routines. Her money safely hidden behind a cushion, she could afford to let events take care of themselves for another half-an-hour or more. She skirmished into the practical.

'There's clouds of steam coming from you, and you're dripping water on the fire. Take your coat off, sailor.'

Meredith allowed her to help him to remove the raincoat,

36

which she draped over the back of a chair where it continued to drip. He sank wearily into the armchair and allowed his arms to hang over the sides.

Maisie sat on a bulbous, lop-sided pouffe.

'Got a cigarette, dearie? I've only got these dreadful Turkish things.'

She pulled at the cigarette, rested her elbow on her knee and blew a thin, long cloud towards the ceiling. Meanwhile, from half-lowered lids she watched Meredith. Sometimes men with a skinful of whisky acted this way. They had the ideas, but the whisky beat them. Then they wanted their money back.

Meredith took a deep breath, his eyes on the fire.

'I wonder if I can explain. I just want to stay here for an hour, talking to you, listening to you, until my train goes. I couldn't face crowds, anywhere. Been to a cinema—no good. Couldn't stay in a club—just wanted one person to talk to. . . .'

Maisie brought feminine intuition to her aid. This was easy. This was a man who had been given a kick in the kisser. Maybe his wife had run off with a Pole or a Yank. Funny business was off, that was obvious. Soon he would want to talk, would want to know how she had come to take up such a life.

She tossed off an opening gambit.

'Going on leave, dearie?'

'Sort of.'

'For long?'

'Few days. I'm due to be demobilized. Have to be at—at—Earl's Court in a few days.'

'Oh, I know. They'll give you a new suit, a funny pork pie hat, a pair of brown shoes in a cardboard box and—Bob's yer uncle. You're out.' She leaned forward confidentially. 'Some of the boys don't like the suits and things, and flog 'em. If you like, I'll introduce you to a friend of mine who'll make you a bid for the lot, raincoat and all. He gives a fair price and chucks in some coupons for you to buy your own suit.'

Her voice droned off into the distance as she entered a side stream, the iniquitous price of coupons. It was just a background of feminine chatter, not requiring a reply.

Meredith felt a mild sense of relaxation. This was what he wanted. This was more or less restful. This was how it had been when She would chatter as he read, or stared into the fire.

The feeling of relaxation went from him with a jerk and was replaced with the old, familiar aching pain.

Always before the war he would sit half listening, not expected to reply, unless one was specifically called for as She expounded her news of the day, or audibly debated some point upon which She had already decided.

Restful, wonderful.

'. . . so I says "I'll walk about in my bare skin sooner than pay that for coupons, you bleedin' spiv," I says. And off I goes. . . .'

When he had gone off to war, leaving Her with four young daughters, there had been a smile, a brave smile untinged with tears until he was out of sight. Then, when he had been stationed in Dover, he and Haley and that wild Irishman, Regan, had found a farm on one of their walks. And in less than no time the family was installed with the childless farmer and his wife. Just an hour away from Dover, with frequent day or overnight leaves when he could sit and listen as she talked on, with gurgles of laughter, and the tempestuous daughters had revelled in the life.

'. . . a girl like me has got to look after herself. A pound is a pound these days, but there must be a limit. I know there are girls who will do anything. But. . . .'

Just a background, meaningless, but feminine.

From Dover had come promotion and wider seas. Finally the Pacific, in command of a new ship, second S.O. of the group.

Her letters came at wider intervals, but were longer; were full of news. He would retire to his room and read them over and over again until they became her voice, until almost every line was committed to heart and he could supply fragments of background at any time and make it sound, inwardly to him, like her voice. In one she wrote:

38

And the Boss [the farmer] *has found a cottage for us, not big, but big enough, only half a mile from the farm. I've pulled some of the furniture out of store, found a school for the girls—Lorna is in the middle of a heavy crush on our chinless curate.* [He had grinned at that. Lorna was twelve and was her mother all over again.] *I have an idea or two for after the war. The Boss says. . . .*

And so she had planned and he had planned with her, thousands of miles away but hearing her talk.

Maisie's voice crept through.

'In the black-out it was terrible—never knew who was going to speak to you. There was a girl in Shaftesbury Avenue who thought she was. . . .'

Then one day the chaplain of the base came on board.

'Out sweeps,' Number One had chuckled. 'Sinners one pace forward. That means you and me, sir.'

The chaplain had placed an arm lightly on his shoulder and had said, 'Could I speak to you alone, Commander Meredith?' Number One had got in his second broadside. 'I knew your past would catch up with you, sir. You should have left that French girl in Mauritius to me.'

'Meredith, I'm afraid I bring bad, sad news. It will be a shock. All I can offer you is the comfort of the word of God, the words of Christ when he, too, was stricken. "Father, forgive them, for they know not what they do." '

Meredith had frozen.

'You know, of course, that there has been heavy bombing back home. Some new sort of thing, a flying bomb. I'm afraid one of them has fallen on your home. . . .'

Meredith's heart had given a great, pounding leap. For seconds he had found it difficult to breathe, his throat had been tight. Then:

'Were they badly hurt? My wife? My. . . .'

Something in the padre's face had told him all.

'I'm afraid they were all. . . .' A gesture had finished the sentence. 'I have received a letter from the vicar. It was a direct hit. It was mercifully swift. They didn't feel anything.'

39

Meredith vaguely remembered the padre's hand on his shoulder, vaguely remembered some words. . . . 'God's pattern is difficult to understand, difficult to bear. Take comfort, my son. . . .'

Then he had been alone.

For a week a harassed senior officer ashore had fought off a taut-faced Meredith, a Meredith whose eyes had seemed to blaze with a cold, diamond fire.

'I don't want to kill Japs. I want a transfer back to home waters. I'll drop a couple of ranks. I'll take a trawler, an M.L. Anything so long as I get my hands on a German. I want a GERMAN.'

Finally a higher senior officer had brought him to sanity.

'You'll stay here; you'll do the job you have to the best of your ability. A million have died and a million want revenge. You'll stay. That's an order.'

'Yes, sir.'

'Meredith.'

'Sir?'

'I understand more than most. My wife was killed in the bombing in '40. In another week my son would have been born.'

'Yes, sir.'

For weeks his ship had been commanded by a man who lived in a small world of his own, a world which revolved round one thought, a single thought which hammered away during every waking moment—and they were many. Outwardly he seemed frozen, inwardly he seethed and raged. When merciful sleep did come it was soon broken by dreams in which he saw them again, as at the last time he had spent leave with them. They had been grouped near the door as he had climbed into the village taxi, an ancient Austin saloon, waving until it was out of sight.

Then he would wake up and the gulf between dreams and the awful reality would bring him, shivering and wide-eyed, upright in his bunk. It had been about then that he had started drinking whisky. First a strong tot to steady himself. And like a drug, before granting effect it had demanded greater use.

40

'. . . I was a good girl until then. It was awful. I lost my hat and one shoe and the grass was wet. But, mind, he looked after me. Until one day he found out that I had gone with an R.A.F. man for a pound, then he. . . .'

Meredith lifted his head, pulled himself back from his torturing reverie. She sat opposite him, hands locked, arms straight over her knees looking into the pale gas fire. Vaguely he was aware that she had been talking for some time.

'I didn't start in the business until long after that. But one thing came after another. You know, dearie, how it goes. And boys would ask me to go off for the night, so I. . . .'

Meredith ran his hands through his hair. 'One thing after another. That's how it goes.'

The Jap submarine had had no right to be where it was. That area had been considered 100 per cent Allied. An overwhelming rescue force of American sea and aircraft were on the spot in a matter of an hour or two and had turned the sea into a mile-square cauldron of death, a cauldron in which the Jap sub had died without a chance.

But it had caught him napping. It had blown his bow into a mass of steel rearing up in fire-blued accusing arms, trapping more than thirty men.

For thirty hours he had nursed her along, at first stern ahead until Number One had reported all shored up. Then, with bow rising and falling like a fractured limb, they had crept to safety at bare steerage speed.

'My, oh, my! Such a soulful biff on the snout. Twenty feet farther aft and you would have been indenting for insect powder, for wings, use of.'

The engineer commander at the major base had been humorous. Meredith had stayed frozen until Number One had reported that all the bodies had been recovered and had been removed to the hut ashore which did duty for a mortuary.

Meredith had gone over in the dead of night and had looked in on the treble row of prone figures. Somehow he had laid the blame on his own shoulders, assuming that had he been awake it would not have happened. After standing inside the hut for a

41

few minutes he had returned on board—it had been golden in a glass, a really stiff one big enough to dispel shadows and thoughts.

And so Number One had found him slipping into forgetfulness, had listened to a slurred voice. He vaguely remembered Number One saying, 'There's not a man on the ship who doesn't believe you did a wonderful job getting her in, sir. You ought to hear the Yanks rave about it. What could you have done had you been on the bridge? Kicked it away with your foot? It was just one of those things. Let me give you a hand, sir. . . .' And sleep came. Troubled sleep, full of dreams.

'. . . I would have gone straight, for him. The times he asked me to marry him. But his bomber didn't come back. Just one of those things. So I. . . .' She droned on.

The ship had been in the hands of the incredibly organized American Naval Base when a vast cloud of smoke had climbed into a gigantic mushroom over the Pacific, bringing a bewildered end to the fighting.

Meredith had been given command of a scratch crew on a weary ship for homeward passage. Most of the crew were of the "first in, first out" group. He had listened to some lying on the fore deck as they steamed through the Red Sea nights.

'Wot you going to do when you first get home, Nobby?'

'After that I'm going to give the kids a bob for the picshurs an' have another go. Then I'm goin' to. . . .'

A surge of laughter had drowned the ribald pre-construction of homecoming. They were going home to somebody, to somebody who waited; divest the thoughts of the crudities, and the elementals were there. They would return to somebody who had waited.

The ache had become unbearable.

'This Old Man can belt it back. I went into his berth and he was sitting in his chair, high-class, top-line stinko. Eyes like gob-stoppers.'

The young sub-lieutenant had not realized that he was leaning near the voice pipe from the bridge to Meredith's room.

42

'Sure can. And when he's around the bridge he acts like he's lost somep'n.' The other sub-lieutenant had lived with American forces for nearly four months.

"Of course I've lost something. I've lost everything," Meredith had raged inwardly. "I ought to go on the bridge and flay the hides off them. What do they know? What do they care?" He had splashed another strong tot into a glass, had thrown it back in one gulp before calling up the voice pipe.

'Forebridge. . . . Bridge. . . . Seems to be a lot of talking going on up there. Usual night orders. Call me if anything—anything. . . .'

Vaguely he had heard a voice. 'Yes, sir. Yes, sir.' But not the whispered query, 'Do you think he heard me?' And the answer, 'Who cares?'

'I found I didn't dare any more. And men were willing. So—well, here I am. Are you all right, dearie? Thought you were asleep. Sometimes I think I'd like to give it all up and go back to live in the country. But what would I do? Pity we didn't think of getting a bottle of gin. I know a club where we could get one. . . .'

Meredith looked at his watch.

'Time I was going. How long will it take me to get to Paddington?'

She helped him on with his sodden raincoat.

'You can walk it in ten minutes. You might get a taxi. If you shout like a Yankee they'll always stop. You know, shout it through your nose. Like this: "Hey, ta-a-a-xi!"'

The rain had stopped as she stood by the half-open door. The next day, Christmas Day, faced her, empty and alone, empty because middle-aged, frustrated men were making the best of what they had, and young, virile men were tangled up in parties with plenty of amateurs on tap.

'Have a nice time, sailor. You could stay if you wanted. We could go to a party tomorrow—that nice boy I told you about—the one with the coupons. . . .'

'Good-bye.'

And the street was his, and his alone.

43

Paddington was a seething throng of people who from choice or by compulsion had left their travelling to the last minute.

'Pla'form three, train's in now. Gor'any luggage?' The porter shrewdly assessed Meredith.

Luggage? Somewhere along the route he had left his canvas grip. It didn't matter. He was going somewhere, in a train, somewhere so that the steady beat of the wheels would give him a basic rhythm and help him to sleep. What was at the other end concerned him not a bit at the moment. He had just a hazy idea that he would go to the places where he had met Her, walk the same lanes, climb to the same cliff tops. . . . After that? Possibly the beckoning sea which he had feared, and loved, would provide the answer.

And suddenly there was the noise. A cloud of twisting white steam rose from the engine. It roared, shrieked, drowned every other sound, tore his nerves to the surface, bombarded every one of them. The steam had shrieked like that when the torpedo had struck. He could hear the thin-edged, rising scream from the men, trapped and doomed. A young fireman on the engine turned from the shining wheels and handles before him to face a mouthing face at the level of his feet. A face twisted into sound-less curses. Then it was gone.

A petty officer in the R.T.O.'s office slewed round to face a porter.

'Whad'yer want, chum?'

'We got a Naval officer on number three. He's cryin' drunk. Lummy, what a jag! The engine lifted her safety valve an' that set him off. Can't get no sense outer him. Cryin' pints.'

Meredith vaguely remembered a respectful petty officer, a bright, warm office, then a lieutenant with the red piping of surgeon on his sleeve. Somewhere in the disordered, broken picture he remembered an ambulance, its purring engine, an orderly white bedroom, and somehow he was in bed.

'Drink this, and we'll see about things in the morning.'

Meekly he had obeyed the voice. The drink was bitter. It had crept upwards from his feet, soft, relaxing, peaceful, until he breathed deeply once—almost a sigh—and was asleep.

44

A soft-footed petty officer sick-berth attendant peered round the door, listened and almost closed it.

'Right off, sir, dead to the world,' he reported to the surgeon-lieutenant. 'He must have been on some blind, sir. How much had he had, do you think?'

The surgeon looked up from his writing.

'If he's had three drinks, that's all. And he's been carrying a load for a long time, far too long. Keep an eye on him. If he wakes up, another dose of. . . .' He embarked on technicalities.

And Meredith slept, deeply, a drug-infused, dreamless sleep. The first for months.

3

MARJORIE HALEY hummed softly to herself as she trimmed
the edge of the tart she had just completed. It represented the
culmination of a neat bit of wangling on her part. She smoked
very little, so two packets of Gold Flake had gone in exchange
for sufficient fat and sugar to enable her to make just the sort
of tart that He liked.

From the moment the telegram had arrived it had been one
scurry, but now all that remained was to slip the tart into the
oven.

A soft smile joined the gently hummed tune as evidence
that for her the day was nearing perfection. The smile was
really born of her recollection of the arrival of the telegram.

She had answered the doorbell, and her heart had given a
thump, then caught up its laggard task by pounding heavily as
the telegraph boy handed her the buff envelope. A dozen times
in the past five years she had answered telegraph boys, and each
time her heart had given that convulsive leap until she opened
the envelope and read the message inside. There had always been
that dreadful half second, until her mind had taken in and
translated into relief the first word or two. Always it had been:
Home is the sailor. Arriving . . . and a time given. But always
she had dreaded that the first words would be, *The Admiralty
regrets.* . . .

The war was over. Finished in the East and in the West.
She and a friend, Sheila, had sat glued to the radio set until the
official announcement had been made in the dispassionate voice
of an announcer.

Having arranged for someone to keep an eye on the boy,
she and Sheila had gone out into the streets in the evening and
had given way to a little of the hysteria which had caught the
crowd. Somebody had torn down a wooden hoarding and started

a fire, others had contributed the fencing round a ruined building. It was celebration of the new peace. Strangers and friends linked arms and sang, danced and kissed. Even now she blushed slightly as she remembered the ardour of an American soldier with a one-track mind and a degree of determination to match.

Then came the few minutes before she went to bed, the few minutes when she realized to the full that the war was over, that her man had come through it, a little more lined, a little graver than of old, but safely.

And this morning had come his latest telegram; this morning her heart had given its usual great jump; this morning the telegram carried the same message, with a significant addition embodied in two words. *Home is the sailor. 4.20 p.m. For Keeps.* There was no signature—there never was; one was not needed.

The tart finished and in the oven, she leaned against the table and watched The Boy. He sat on the rug on the floor engaged in a complicated game which involved a battered baking tin, some wooden blocks, half a bicycle bell and one tiny slipper. (Why does he always get his left slipper off and embroil it in any game he has in hand?) Finally he leaned back with a satisfied miniature grunt. The construction problem, whatever it was, had been ended. Then a dimpled, swinging hand demolished it, the structure, bell and baking tin combining to produce a satisfying clatter before the half bell rolled away to stop between her feet. The dimpled hand reached for the half bell but she covered it with her toe. A quick glance upwards assured him that play was on. This was fun, a grown-up joining in. He released a ready smile, then set about recovering his possession, which he was allowed to do after a mild struggle with a firm toe.

He signallized his victory by clashing the half bell on the baking tin and met mild disaster. A chubby finger got in the way and took the force of the little blows. He dropped the bell and a little pucker took possession of his face. 'Ups, dearie! Mummy kiss it better.' She caught him in her arms and sat down with him on her lap, and there followed one of those miracles of instantaneous healing which only mothers and children comprehend. Finally she took from her apron pocket the telegram and opened it.

'Let's read it again shall we? What does it say? *"Home is the sailor. 4.20 p.m. For Keeps."* You read it. Do you know what it means?' She lifted the child until he stood stoutly on her thighs. 'It means Daddy is coming home, to stay home.' She clutched the child to her with a delighted laugh. 'No more farewells, no more six days' leave. It says, "For keeps". Isn't that wonderful?'

He indicated complete agreement on all points by a noise which sounded like "glynch" and began to tear the telegram with his teeth.

She stood up and whirled him round in a few steps of a dance, and his laughter joined hers.

She examined the tart in the oven with critical eyes. Today of all days it had to be just perfection. A minute or two too long would make it just another tart. She shared her calculation with the ticking clock and gently closed the door of the oven.

Just an hour to go.

On the floor again the child had renewed work, with a wooden spoon, on the baking tin, a combination warranted to produce a satisfactory noise. Momentary rebellion clouded the boy's face for a brief flash as his mother removed the tin. Then he started to beat the floor with the spoon, again producing an adequate noise once he had moved the centre of the impact from the deadening rug to the more resounding lino-covered boards. After a spell of that she picked him up again and was preparing to sit down when there came a double rat-tat at the door. Her eyes flew to the clock, unconsciously establishing that it was still ticking, then with the child in her hands she answered the knock.

'You'll have to keep that boy quiet, Mrs. Haley. The noise gets on my husband's nerves something cruel.'

The speaker at the door was an undersized, small-faced woman with sunken mouth, black beady eyes, a look of perpetual complaint a constant ingredient in her expression.

48

'But Mrs. Madden——'

'It's bin nothin' but stampin' and hammerin' all the after-noon, and him suffering cruel with his nerves. It'll have to stop, Mrs. Haley.'

She ran the words together like a well-learnt lesson and at the conclusion her shrunken mouth pursed in until the lips were not visible except at the flaccid corners.

'I assure you, Mrs. Madden, that there has been no noise except for a little time——'

'All the afternoon! I can believe my own ears, Mrs. Haley. It'll have to stop.'

It was a frequent gambit, losing nothing by the frequency of its use. She felt—in fact, she knew—that were she to take her courage in both hands she could demolish the thin-faced harridan before her in a couple of sentences, but it would reduce life to the standard of constant sniping, unceasing guerilla warfare.

'Very well, Mrs. Madden.' She kept her voice modulated and started to close the door. Mrs. Madden, of the breed which must have the last word, considered it a spoil of war to speak her piece even if it was against a closing door.

'Mind you do, then. Or we'll have to do something about it. My husband——'

Marjorie flung the door open swiftly. Mrs. Madden had given her an opening which she instinctively accepted.

'Perhaps your husband would care to discuss it with mine? He's coming home today—and will be home for some time. I'm sure he would like to meet Mr. Madden again.'

The sting lay in the last sentence. Not long after Marjorie had moved in to what she hoped would be only a temporary haven, after being bombed out and accommodated for a time in a friend's flat, Bill had arrived home on a short leave. Madden, a wisp of a man with bleary eyes and a few heavily discoloured teeth scattered about in his mouth, had almost forced himself on them on some pretext—smelling heavily of drink—hoping to celebrate the homecoming of Bill by cadging a few drinks. In his social circle a leave meant lots of drink—on the homecomer.

Haley was tired, but polite for a time, then he had firmly pointed out to Madden that they had no desire to take part at that moment in a complicated social engagement, neither had he any intention of producing from his suitcase a bottle of gin or whisky. In short, Haley pointed out, his primary wish was to get to bed.

It was a fatal suggestion to the half-drunk man. His lascivious mind fastened on what he considered was the obvious and he proceeded to dilate upon it.

Haley's patience cracked with an almost audible sound, the fracture being accentuated by the blush which flooded Marjorie's face.

Madden had found his arm taken in a firm, almost painful, grip and he was hustled to the door and ejected. His discomfiture was complete, as he struggled for a teetering balance on the landing, by the presence of Mrs. Madden, who had arrived home, found her husband missing and had partly conjectured aright. He was visiting; he was in on something she was missing. She arrived in time to take a small, non-speaking part in the final scene.

'Get out—and stay out. So long as we pay you rent—and enough, God knows—keep away from my flat. Is that clear?'

He had slammed the door and returned to Marjorie, who was resting her head on her arm on the mantelpiece and was staring into the dying fire.

Bill had busied himself with the ceremony of selecting and lighting a cigarette, a ceremony performed in swift, nervous jerks.

'Clay would call that "bouncing him",' he said eventually. He had watched Marjorie for any reactions. 'Somehow I think Clay would have completed the job with a clip on the jaw.'

She had lifted her head and a little smile had played round her lips.

'And sent him walloping down the stairs?'

'. . . to break his damned neck.'

'And her with him!'

He had taken her in his arms. 'Wipe the blood from your drooling jowls, minx, I want to kiss you.'

Later he had said, 'Have you had any trouble with those people below while I've been away?'

She had lied like a lady. 'No.'

He had accepted it for what it was, a gallant lie, and had not pursued the point. Instead, he had switched off all the lights, except a small reading lamp, and by the light of that they had sat and talked. When the war was over, they would have a house, out on the fringe of London, where the fields were not too far away, a house with a garden where The Boy could play, a house with this, a house with that. All the sentences had started with 'And we'll. . . .' Such is the texture of dreams.

Regan and he had carried on conversations like this, planning, hoping, building on a future which hung by a thin thread, which hung on the sights of some German pilot, or trailed tenuously from the rusted curve of some mine, or the squinting eye of a German sailor's eye glued to a gunsight.

And that night she had known that he lay wide-eyed in the darkness, sleep a million miles away, a circle of thoughts going round in his mind like a revolving roulette wheel. A number. Think of a number; gamble on it; change the number to "yes" or "no"; anyway, the choice lies not with you; when the wheel stops momentarily the ball will hover, then finally drop into a slot. "Yes?" "No?" For Regan it had dropped into "no". For him it might drop again into "yes", as it had done before, or it might. . . .

A soft arm had stolen across his damp chest, resting on it; a gentle hand had sought and found his face; with scarcely a perceptible motion the fingers had caressed his temple, slowly, timed to his breathing. He lay still; to move would spoil it. He had scarcely heard the faint whisper, 'Go to sleep, darling.'

A jangle of steel-framed milk bottles outside had awakened him. It was morning. Alongside him she lay, tousled head on the pillow, still asleep. In the cot near the bed The Boy lay on his back, bedclothes kicked clear. He was gravely inspecting one foot elevated to the upright.

Haley had lifted himself on one elbow.

'What yer, cock!'

Two wide eyes had scrutinized him, flickered towards her, and come back. The Boy had crowed at him.

It was daylight, and all was well—for a time.

After Marjorie had closed the door in Mrs. Madden's face, conclusively ending the brief conversation, she stood leaning against the closed door, breathing heavily and gnawing at her bottom lip. Finally she shrugged, looked down at The Boy and smiled. Soon they would be getting away from here, to start translating dreams into action and action into a home with a garden. Suddenly she swooped down and picked The Boy up in her arms.

'Gracious, my tart!'

A swift examination reassured her. She lifted it out.

'Now, little man, shall we make ourselves beautiful for Daddy? Not that there is much to do to you. How beautiful are you?'

'Two ton.'

Marjorie gurgled delightedly. It was one of the little parlour tricks he had learnt on Bill's previous leave, a supreme measurement for all that was wonderful. The yardstick for perfection was "two ton".

'Two ton it is. Let's see if Mummy can reach a few hundredweights.'

And to the bedroom they went to prepare.

As she busied herself at her dressing-table she indulged in some self-criticism. Her fingers lingered over small lines on her face, at the corners of her eyes and at each side of her mouth. As she twisted her features the blemishes either disappeared or were accentuated. She found that they disappeared entirely when she composed her face in a wide-eyed baby stare.

"But I can't go through life looking like that," she decided, and stroked the little lines at the corners of her eyes once more. Again she essayed the flashing smile, then suddenly dissolved into almost helpless laughter.

52

Standing at her side, his head barely level with the top of the dressing-table, was The Boy. Gravely he was duplicating her gestures. At the moment when she caught sight of him his eyes were open to their fullest extent, and parted lips showed a few pearly teeth framing the tip of a pink tongue. The tip wriggled momentarily, escaped beyond the tiny teeth and flopped out. She swept him into her arms and sat on the bed with him, holding him closely. Emboldened by the response to his performance, he began to give his tongue another extensive airing.

'Gracious me, if Daddy sees that he'll chop it right off. Put it back.' She gently squeezed the little tongue, which shot back behind the protection of tightly compressed lips.

'Shall we see how time is going?' In the small lounge the clock ticked away and she made an impatient noise when she looked at it.

'Somebody has hung a seven-pound lead hand on those hands,' she murmured. It was a phrase she had picked up from Bill.

There were other phrases she had found dotting her vocabulary, phrases with a tang of the sea. A tangle of any description, either mental or in knitting wool, was a "bunch of things". Any mild panic was a "state of French calm". If she was hurrying anywhere she was "going full ahead both", and to stop doing something, or going anywhere quickly, was to "bring up with a round turn". They had crept in, or had been unconsciously grafted on to her vocabulary, and she found herself using them without effort of thought.

Would the past five years have had other effects? In the odd leave periods throughout the war—never more than six or seven days at intervals of four to six months—there had been scarcely time to get their relationship on an even keel. Another phrase of his. The leave periods had followed a fairly well-defined pattern. First would come a telegram, then a time of breathless waiting, then the moment—tumultuous with a wide variety of emotions racing through her—and almost shyly he would take her in his arms.

The first two days were periods of gentle release from the

strain. There would be moments of sudden irritability for no apparent reason; there would be hours at night when she knew that despite his deep, steady breathing he was not asleep; sometimes she would catch the gleam of his eyes as he stared at the ceiling. But there were moments when she would catch him looking at her fixedly at odd times in the day. And when she caught him he would be momentarily confused, like a shy schoolboy caught unawares in a display of emotion. He would take her hand in his, his fingers would run over hers, or his arm would slide round her waist. He would look deeply into her eyes, a steady warmth would come into his gaze as his eyes travelled over her features. His voice would be scarcely above a whisper as he murmered, 'Nice.'

An unimportant little word, but it would bring a thrill.

The last day or two would race by until he would stand in the hall, suitcase at his feet, face hardening again.

No time for tears. They would come later, when she was alone.

'See you again soon. Chin up!'

'Higher than a kite. Don't fall over the doorstep.'

Inane little words—but brave ones. The click of the latch as the door closed, footsteps down the steps.

From that point she became all woman, with her own way of saying farewell.

Now he was coming "home for keeps". There would be no racing clock or a brave struggle at the door. He would be home always.

Six years geared for war, with its unnatural values, would be bound to have altered him. But in what way? Let time tell, and produce the answers to the problems that time itself would produce. Of one thing she was certain, and this sent a gentle, warm smile to her face. He WANTED to come home. Let tomorrow take care of itself.

"Boom-diddy-bomp-bomp"—pause—"bomp-bomp."

And her heart took up the theme. She knew the trick. He had been doing it from the first days of their marriage.

It was a trick of the fingers and heel of the hand on the panels of the door. What he called his "up portcullis, down drawbridge—or else" knock.

The Boy stumbled along after her as she flew to the door. Her fingers fumbled with the catch, then she succeeded and the door was open.

Such a familiar picture. He stood slightly in the shadow, the light shining from his brass buttons and from the badge on his cap. One step inwards and they were together, she tightly in his arms, breathless. The world was complete.

'Good God!'

She felt him relax and put her head backwards to see his face, a sudden anxiety tingling through her. He was staring downwards at a spot behind her. She turned, and a gale of laughter engulfed her. She put her head on his shoulder. Behind her stood The Boy, a gigantic, wide-mouth smile on his face. His tongue was out as far as it could possibly be and, having caught sight of it, he added a violent squint to the spectacle. His world, too, was complete.

'Good God!' Haley said again.

4

LIEUTENANT-COMMANDER OWEN MEREDITH woke up.
It was a gradual process, a sudden consciousness that he was
awake, then a surge, rather like the sensation of a forward
movement on a high swing. It was a feeling of climbing to the
surface, of being poised. It was at that moment of poise that he
started co-ordinating his reflexes. Something was missing. He
missed the almost imperceptible vibration of the engines, the slight
roll of the ship, the conglomeration of faint sounds which,
welded into a whole, were ship's noises. Yet he could hear the sea,
could hear its regular swish.

Meredith opened his eyes—and closed them again swiftly.
The light stung, making him squeeze up his eyelids to prevent
entry. That was something odd. He had always kept his room
in a sort of half twilight except when reading. This light was
blinding. Carefully he opened his eyes again, and kept them open.
This was not his orderly berth on his ship; it was a strange room,
of uniform cream walls with a tall, oblong window facing him.

The first thing he realized was that it was not the sea he could
hear. It was the wind in the trees, which, stark limbed and empty,
waved outside the window like beckoning black arms.

Between slitted eyelids he saw a figure standing outlined
against the window.

'So you are awake? Good! Now we can have a talk.'

The outlined figure approached the bed, and to follow it
Meredith had to squint his eyes far over to the corners.

'Turn on your side. You look like a puzzled Chinaman.
Perhaps a little less light from outside will help.'

The figure reached above Meredith's head and pressed a bell
push. In the meantime Meredith studied the man. He was short,
almost squat; his shoulders were raised up towards his ears as if
he was ready at all times to ward off a blow.

'Come on, turn on your side.'

Meredith did as he was told and watched the man. On his sleeves were the three rings of a commander with the red piping of a surgeon between them.

A sick-berth attendant came in silently.

'Pull the curtains, switch on the lights and tell sister that I would like some coffee—for two.'

The curtains rasped faintly as the rings ran over the runners. A soft light took possession of the room.

'Sir, I don't know about the coffee. It——'

'Tell sister I want coffee for two.'

'Yessir.'

Down in the inner recesses of his mind Meredith knew this man had the power of command. No argument, no back-chat.

The surgeon-commander reached into his pocket and extracted a cigarette case. He lit a cigarette and let the smoke escape slowly from his lips.

'You can't have one,' he said. 'Sister would crucify me on the bed post. Quite a dragon, sister. Eats men. Sometimes she dips them in salt, but mostly it's just "snap-snap".'

Meredith noticed that the surgeon's voice stayed on a constant level, as if he were mouthing a set piece, as if speaking with his mind on a totally different plane.

The surgeon rubbed his hands together firmly while the cigarette remained hanging from the corner of his mouth. Meredith could hear the faint rasp of the skin as the palms rubbed over each other.

'Such an interesting case you are, my boy. Almost the perfect case. I would say you have been belting yourself quite a lot. Such a tangle, such a tangle! But between us we'll unravel it. Yes, between us we'll undo all the knots.'

Meredith stirred slightly.

'You go to hell.'

The surgeon-commander wriggled the cigarette from one corner of his mouth to the other, then brushed the disturbed ash from his coat.

'Splendid! Just what I wanted. Overcoming initial inertia is always the hardest job. What did you say?'

'Go to hell.'

'Splendid!'

The surgeon pulled a straight-backed chair towards him, swung it round so that the back faced him, sat down cross-legged over it and rested his arms on the back.

'Splendid! We're making progress already. But we must make some more.' He reached out and took from the foot of the bed a short, square board clipped to which was a sheet of paper. 'This, of course, tells me nothing. Temperature—um—pulse—um—yes. Lieutenant-Commander Owen Meredith, R.N.V.R., D.S.C. twice—um—less than nothing.' He tossed the board on to a bedside bureau, crossed his arms on the back of the chair and rested his chin on his arms. To Meredith it seemed that he was lowering his head in preparation for charging like a bull.

'Less than nothing. And the bright boys in the Big House in London contributed less than that. "This gink Meredith you've wished on to me. What's he been doing?" I asked. "Dunno. In command most of the war, minesweeping and escort. Got a couple of gongs. Good record. Has been out East." Beyond that they were as useless as— What have you been doing to get to this state?' He barked the last sentence and Meredith felt himself give a mental jerk.

'You go to hell.' It was little more than a whisper, each word said slowly and distinctly.

'Wrong course. It should be "You come to hell", because you're waiting there for me. Come now, let's start at the beginning. Always a good place to start.'

Before Meredith could reply there was a tap at the door and a young nurse rustled in carrying a tray. Following her came a woman not much older, dressed in the blue, red piped, naval nursing sister's uniform.

The girl put the tray down with a slight clatter and stepped back. She looked at the sister, intercepted a slight signal, took the board from the bureau and hung it at the foot of the bed.

'Must have everything orderly, you see, Meredith. Nothing

58

out of place. Everything "just so". Good idea, too. Get out, girl, get out. Stop barging about like a female elephant.'

The young nurse smiled sweetly, as if she had received a glowing compliment, included Meredith in the smile and disappeared through the door.

The surgeon-commander leaned over the tray, inspected it and looked up at the sister.

'Sugary biscuits, too. And three cups. We're going to have a party, Meredith, quite a party.' He waved a hand at the tray. 'You play "heavy mother", Sister, and pour out. I hope Meredith doesn't take sugar, then I can have his whack.'

The sister poured neatly as the surgeon-commander returned his chin to his crossed arms. She looked once at Meredith, got no reaction and put one spoonful of sugar in his cup.

'Well, we've got him awake and taking notice, Sister. As you see. He was in quite a state when he arrived, wasn't he?'

The sister leaned over Meredith and before he realized what was happening, lifted him swiftly to a sitting position, propping him with a pillow. She handed him the cup of coffee and suddenly he was aware that the cool, impersonal look on her face had disappeared. She gave him a swift smile, a smile which wrinkled the corners of her eyes and puckered up the ends of her mouth.

'That comfortable?' she said softly.

Meredith found that he had difficulty in holding the cup and saucer steady; it shook slightly and persistently so that little rings wavered in from the edge of the cup to the centre.

And without warning his eyes began to burn, a tightness came in his throat; for no reason that he could determine tears started rolling down his cheeks.

'You go to hell,' he said thickly and tried to put the cup and saucer on the bureau. Swiftly she took them from him and laid them down.

'That's a repeat performance for your benefit, Sister,' the surgeon said calmly.

She picked up the square board and moved under a light to

study it. The surgeon-commander remained on his chair, never taking his eyes from Meredith.

The sister took up her coffee, sipped it and stood in front of the surgeon.

'There are two things I would like,' she said in a low voice. 'One is an intimation when you propose to visit patients in my corridor and the other is that you realize that my nurses cannot go making coffee every time you want it. Will you remember, Commander Maldon?'

'I heartily concur, Sister. Couldn't agree more. Don't let it happen again.' He answered as if the words meant nothing to him. As he spoke he maintained his steady scrutiny of Meredith.

When the man on the bed breathed in with a long, tremulous sigh, the surgeon sat up.

'That's better. Now get on with that coffee while I rapidly recapitulate what we know. Always tackle the known first, Sister. Then explore for the hidden. Good axiom that. Any grains of sugar left over?' He craned over the tray, scraped in the small basin and salvaged a quarter of a spoonful which he stirred into his coffee, still keeping his eyes on Meredith.

'If you promise to say something else besides "Go to hell" I'll let you have a handkerchief. It will relieve that distressing sniff.'

Meredith held his hand out and the surgeon nodded approvingly.

'Good! "England expects that every man this day will give his nose a good blow." Better? Now for the recapitulation.'

'Where am I? And why am I here?' Meredith managed the two queries in a husky voice.

'All part of the recapitulation. You needn't wait, Sister, if you've something else to do. If he gets tough I'll ask for Big Bertha. You must meet Big Bertha, Meredith. In fact, you will. She stands about six feet, weighs—what? Fourteen stone, Sister? About that. We keep her around for our tough cases. She simply LOVES tough, obstinate men. Right, don't wait, Sister. I'm likely to be some time.'

He watched the sister slide through the door and close it.

'Bet you five bob there is a notice on the door, "Do not disturb". Take me on? No?' The surgeon touched the tip of his little finger with a thumb. 'We have your name and rank.' The thumb moved to another finger tip. 'We know you arrived from London—and in a shocking state—and'—he waved a hand—'that is all we know, barring a few incidentals.'

'Where am I? And why?'

'Those are easy answers. You are in a naval hospital in the West Country and you are here because you are a sick man, a very sick man, Meredith. What we have to find out is why.'

Meredith felt a faint return of the pugnacity which had always been a part of him, but which seemed to have disappeared in the past few months. He struggled to sit up in bed.

'Sick be damned! Four days ago I was in command of a ship—brought her home from the Far East. I'm deadly tired— or I was. All I want is to get out of here and—and——'

'And what?' It came softly with the last word on a dropping note.

'Oh, anything. I've to be at some place in London on the 28th where I'll be dished out with a bowler hat and civvy suit. Then I'll fight my own battles.'

The surgeon-commander stood up slowly, reached for the square board from the foot of the bed, glanced at it and turned it round so that Meredith could see it. Over its squared pattern Meredith could see two lines, one red, one blue, leading from two words "Temp" and "Pulse". In a margin for notes he saw "Restless". "Restless" and a meaningless phrase—to him.

'Well?'

'Look at the date.'

Meredith dropped his eyes to the last entry. It read "Decr. 29".

'Good God! Have I been here——?'

Surgeon-Commander Maldon nodded and retrieved the board. 'You have, and you might as well know it now. You can forget all about your bowler hat for a while. Your demobilization has been suspended indefinitely.' He sat on the foot of the bed. 'We—that is, the Navy—took you in as a fit man, and we must turn you out as one.'

'How long?'

'How long is a piece of string? Depends on you—and one or two other factors. Look, Meredith, all we know at present is that some bright lad had the sense to whip you into hospital in London where you were found—in shall we say a state of acute tension?—at Paddington, and that was four or five days ago. Since then we've kept you in suspended animation. I'm going to leave you now, but after you've had some sleep I shall want to talk to you. My lad,' he leaned forward and prodded Meredith in the chest, 'you are most interesting. You hold a lot of promise for me. Quite my most interesting case, that's what you'll be. Off to sleep!'

Surgeon-Commander Maldon, R.N.V.R., stood up, flexed his arms and smiled. 'Into battle, eh, Meredith? Into battle.'

He clicked his fingers as he seemed to remember something.

'You have a family? Married or something? Somebody you would like us to inform? You can have visitors in a week or so.'

It hit Meredith like an icy douche. It came sweeping back like a deeply laden cloud. Relatives, family—for a few moments he had forgotten. For just a short and merciful interval he had laid aside the dreadful loneliness which was his.

Maldon watched him keenly, a rapidly tapping finger on his knee. He saw Meredith's face square in tension, saw the chin jut out, the mouth writhe and the lips tighten. He listened as Meredith breathed heavily through his nose, in short, deep breaths.

Without a word Maldon stood up and moved towards the door. As he reached it he delved into his pocket, pulled out his cigarette case, extracted a cigarette and put it between Meredith's lips. Silently he applied the light from a lighter and watched Meredith draw deeply two or three times.

'If Sister finds out she'll strangle both of us. I'll be seeing you again soon, Meredith.'

And Meredith was alone.

A few yards along the corridor Surgeon-Commander Maldon tapped on a door and entered. The sister was sitting at a table writing.

'Sister Sugar Plum Fairy,' he said sitting on the corner of the table, 'I've got something to work on.'

She laid down her pen and looked at him with the beginning of a smile on her face.

'Yes?'

'Women, or a woman. Not surprising. They provide the key to most problems. Only they have a habit of hiding the keys, the—the—lady dogs.'

The smile on her face widened, then disappeared.

'Has it occurred to you that you MIGHT be wrong? I've got his naval record here.' She tapped a file of papers. 'He's had a long, long war. It might have been just too long for him.'

Slowly he shook his head.

'Welshman, isn't he? One of the small dark people. Half a chance and they live in the shadows, thriving on their own fears because they are only a cat-jump away from the primitive. And when their fears become too big they either sing or fight their way out. And when fighting or singing fails them——'

'Well?'

'That's where we step in, Sugar Plum Fairy.'

'Quite how?'

'Between us we provide the fight, or the song. At the moment I think I am scheduled for the fighting bit.'

'And the song?'

'Sugar Plum Fairy!' There was reproach in the words.

I would point out, Surgeon-Commander Maldon, that I am Ward Sister Payne with upwards of forty patients to look after——'

'And to thirty-five of them you can give a dose of castor oil, a soulful kick on the bottom and toss 'em out tomorrow, with an easy conscience.'

He stood up. 'Same drill. Keep him asleep except for a light meal, mashed potatoes and egg. Not more than one waking hour in the next twenty-four. Right?'

'You teach your grandmother to suck eggs,' she replied inelegantly.

'Delighted! Oh, by the way, I left him smoking a cigarette.

Go in just in time to find him finishing it, and play hell. We must make these concessions hard to get. See you anon, Sugar Plum Fairy. And find out about that woman—or women.'

'Yes, sir,' she said primly. 'And if there is no woman—or women?'

He leaned forward. 'Sugar Plum Fairy, you're trying to revise life as it has been since your forbear deluded her spouse into a fruit diet.' He became serious. 'Find out, will you?'

After he had gone the sister sat tapping her teeth with a thumbnail. Then she rustled out and after knocking at Meredith's door she entered. She sniffed, and looked at the cigarette now burning low between his fingers.

'Who said you could smoke, Commander Meredith?'

Meredith took no notice. His face was set in tight lines; his eyes were staring into space; desperately he was trying to drag his mind away from one thought which had been his for every waking hour since the stumbling padre had broken the news to him.

The sister took the cigarette from him and stubbed it out in an ashtray.

'It's bad for you on an empty stomach.' She took his wrist in her hand, glanced at her watch and checked his pulse. 'Um, um. Well, let's get you comfortable.' She busied herself straightening his bedclothes, beat up his pillow and settled him down with the bedclothes tightly round his chest. 'Now you must get some sleep.'

She watched him for a while, slipped through the door with scarcely a rustle and returned with a small tumbler in her hands.

'Drink this.'

It was bitter, and somehow familiar. Meredith chased the fugitive taste round his mouth with the tip of his tongue and remembered. The drink he had been given in the hospital in London had been bitter. . . . Then he remembered how he had slipped off to sleep, starting from his toes.

'When you wake up you can write a letter. Only a short one. Are you married? There must be somebody you want to tell you are in hospital. We can, of course, send a formal notice,

64

with permission to visit, but they are rather frightening. Is there anybody? Next-of-kin?'

Meredith shook his head. 'Nobody.'

Meredith never quite remembered how it started, but he found himself with his head against her bosom. The starched front was cool, stiff; her soft hand gently stroked his forehead as he poured it all out. In a flood of words he told her of the padre's visit, of the waking nights, of the feeling of emptiness. Then relaxation started creeping over him. He breathed in with a shuddering sigh.

'So I meant to go back to where we met. Somehow I felt that—that——' He lost the thread of his story; the words began to blurr. 'I was going back to look at the sea——' He snuggled down on to the pillow, the tension surrendering to the merciful drug. The sister lowered him down beneath the bedclothes and tucked him in. From a long, long way off he heard her voice, so faintly.

'. . . much too much of a load. . . . We'll help . . . we're here to help. . . .'

Somehow the voice, and the hand, brought him comfort and he slept, without dreams.

Back in her room the sister picked up a house phone, pressed one of its many buttons.

'Surgeon-Commander Maldon? If you please . . . oh, Sister Payne here, Commander. That officer in twenty-seven—Meredith. I've found out quite a lot.'

'Good, Sister!' She guessed from his formal reply that he was not alone. 'I'll be right along. Is he asleep now? Good!'

In a few minutes he was sitting on the edge of her table again. 'Tell me, Sugar Plum Fairy, what did you find out?'

She related what Meredith had told her, putting the story in more orderly array.

'Poor man! What a blow, and what a load to carry. Wife and family wiped out like that and he thousands of miles away. No wonder he broke down.'

Surgeon-Commander Maldon chewed his lip, gazing out of the window.

'And you think that was the straw which broke the back and so on?'

'Don't you?'

'No, not by a long chalk. Didn't he tell you to go to hell when you caught him smoking? Um, strange. Still, it's a start, Sugar Plum Fairy Sister Payne. A start, a fingerhold—not even that, just a finger-tip hold—but something. We'll bring him back gently and I'll start work on him in a couple of days. I'll have to put him through the wringer, of course. Active dislike, that's the thing, Sister. I must make him hate my—my intestinal economy. Mental inertia, that's the thing to avoid. I would say three months, maybe more. And occasionally a little softness, not much, but a fragrant moment now and then, a moment to be earned.'

'Softness? From you.'

'Sister Sugar Plum Fairy! From you. Who else?'

A week later Surgeon-Commander Maldon tapped at Sister Payne's door, moved in and took his favourite perch on the edge of her table. Abstractedly he pulled his cigarette case out, offered her one and lit both cigarettes. He rubbed his chin and screwed up his eyes.

'Somewhere along the line somebody is laughing at me. Couldn't be you, could it?'

'Not me.'

'You know what is happening, of course?'

'Yes.'

'Why?'

'You are the doctor. You decide; I merely give the pills.'

'Lady dog!'

'As you say.'

He pulled on his cigarette for a while.

'You know he is going to die on me, don't you? You know he is trying to die, and is succeeding with damnable efficiency.'

'That is obvious.'

'But why? Why, Sister Payne?' She realized that he was acutely concerned, because always in the privacy of her room he never called her anything but a variation of Sugar Plum Fairy.

66

'Can you tell me why?' He stood up and started to pace the room, screwing a clenched fist into a cupped palm.

'I'll run through the facts as we know them——'

'Like they do half-way through a mystery novel. Go on.' She sketched a meaningless design on her pad, scribbled over it and looked up with impassive face.

'Here we have a man who throughout the war fought with a degree of dedication which should place him among the crusaders. I've been digging into his record, so I know. Then his family is wiped out. A terrific blow, enough to knock a man off his point of balance—for a time. Losing somebody one loves is——' He stopped and looked at her. 'Well, you of all people would know that.'

She twisted a thin gold band on the third finger of her left hand.

'Yes.'

'We'll accept all that. He could, probably did, hit the bottle. Went into action not caring a damn for the result. But'—he emphasized his point with a driving fist—'all that, painful as it was, should have built up into a resistance. That flagrant disregard for life, that hitting the bottle, all of it should have had a blunting effect. From that he should have progressed to a point where the jagged mental wound started leaving a healing wound—painful, perhaps, but none the less healing—which in time would have become no more than a tender scar.'

She nodded.

'But the damned man doesn't do anything like that. He just lies there and decides to die. We hear of natives doing it, just sitting down in the sun with a blanket round their shoulders and dying by numbers, but they are primitives. He can't do that to me. I won't let him.'

A new design was started on her pad.

'Has it occurred to you that he may want to do it?'

'It has. And I am damned well going to stop him. See?'

'Hooray! Big medico decides to become God.'

'Blasphemous lady dog.'

'Surgeon-Commander Maldon, might I point out that you

have under your care a number of men who have been through quite a lot?'

'You mean my ex-prisoners from the Jap camps? In three months I'll have the lot of them ramping-stamping full of beans, going home and leaping on their women with a wild animal cry, the memories of the prison camps nothing but a blurred picture behind them. Why?' He spun round and slapped the table with a flat palm. 'Because they never lost the will to live. Through it all, the beatings, the starvation, the incredible animal treatment they had the will to live. All I have to do is to fan that spark until it grows, expands into a flame, build them up physically until they can stand the heat of it, and toss 'em out into the world, nearly as good as new. Oh, I know they'll have scars which will stay on their minds until they die. But so have I, so have you.'

Another design suffered obliteration.

'Has it struck you that he may not fit into any plan you may have in mind?'

'All men—ALL men—are of a pattern. It may be complicated by a few meaningless shapes, but in the main the pattern does not vary a lot.'

'Famous psychiatrist speaks—hang on his golden words. "Here is the pattern, now conform and be damned." If one doesn't?'

He ran his fingers through his hair. 'Don't rub it in. I was generalizing. Dangerous, but permissible.' He resumed his seat on the edge of her table. 'Seriously, Sister, I'm baffled. You know my methods, my dear female Watson. Usually I can arrive at a basic formula in a week, and work patiently on that. But——' He shrugged and spread his hands palm upwards. 'What can I do with a man who won't conform to a formula? He just lies there and decides to die.'

She leaned back with the pencil held between two hands, rolling it gently with her thumbs.

'I've found out something.'

'Yes?'

'He's afraid of the dark.'

68

'Help yourself to a medal. So am I, so are you. So is every policeman on a night beat, after a fashion. Ask them and see. It's an instinct older than reason.'

'Not the darkness he is afraid of.'

'Wait while I grope after that one. What darkness can there be other than the black of night? He's not going blind?'

'No.'

He plucked at his bottom lip. 'You might be starting me off after a hare which will turn out to be a rustle of the wind in the undergrowth. But it's worth while chasing. He rested a hand on her white-cuffed wrist. 'Anything you say will help. Any other ideas?'

'Look, look, I'm only a poor hard-working ward sister here. You are the big——'

'Trick cyclist. Go ahead—say it!'

' "Big cheese" I was going to say.' She leaned forward and added a couple of half circles to the complicated design on her pad. 'I have a half-formed idea. Can I stew it over for a while? It might be the answer.'

'It might be. And if you find a key which fits the lock——'

'I might throw it away, being a woman.'

'You—you——'

'I know—"lady dog".'

'No, just plain bitch.'

'Commander Maldon!'

'You go to hell.'

'That's plagiarism.'

'It helps.'

A half smile illuminated his face.

'I begin to see what you are getting at. Or do I?'

'I wouldn't know.'

He moved towards the door. 'Go to it, woman. And God have mercy on you if you throw away the key.'

A few minutes later she stood in the window of Meredith's room. Behind her he lay a still, straight figure in bed, just his face resting on the pillow above the bedclothes. His tan had paled until he looked almost yellow against the whiteness. When she entered he had not moved at all. Not even a flicker from the eyes. She gave him one look, then leaned against the window.

'Nice view from here,' she said, folding her arms. 'You can't see it, but there is a ploughed field, a rich, warm red. The furrows run over the hill. Beside the field is a path; that goes over the hill, too. I know what is over the other side of the hill. Life. Everything looks dead now. But soon there will be a tiny bud of green on the trees, and a touch of green on the field. That's life. I was country-born—lived on a farm, I've seen it happen every year.'

She turned from the window and walked over to him. Not by a half a gesture did he show that he saw her. His eyes barely showed through half-closed lids. She laid a hand on his forehead, felt his pulse.

'Odd thing, life,' she said. 'It comes—and goes—no matter what we say or do. It just comes.'

She stepped back so that she was in line with his eyes, then shook her head.

'Men—men.'

Then he heard the door click.

Gently at first, then increasing in volume, a glistening started in his eyes, rolled down his cheeks until the tears reached the white bedsheet, which absorbed them and left only a slighter darker stain.

Sister Payne stalked into the lounge which adjoined the large ward. A nurse stiffened; some junior officers waited for the storm.

'The ashtrays are for use, gentlemen. And, Nurse, I would like to see you in my room.' Later. 'You must stop that familiarity with the officers, Nurse, and your finger nails could do with a clean. That is all.'

'Bitch!' the nurse murmured outside the door.

'Fancy waking up and finding that alongside you every morning,' an ulcerated sub-lieutenant said.

'Death, where would be thy sting?' another laughed.

Sister Payne sat fingering her bottom lip. 'Men—men,' she murmured.

5

SURGEON-COMMANDER MALDON sat in state behind his large, orderly desk. Slightly to his rear and to the left stood a surgeon-lieutenant, R.N.V.R. Flanking the other shoulder stood Sister Payne nursing a large blue folder and a board to which were clipped some papers. Sitting facing Maldon was a young sub-lieutenant, R.N.V.R.

Maldon rustled documents on his desk, leaned back and looked up with a smile.

'There you are, as good as new—better, in fact, because you have had the benefit of experience.'

The youngster facing him smiled uncertainly.

'Sleeping all right these days?'

It was a question to which Maldon knew the answer.

'Good! Well, there is no reason why we shouldn't toss you out into the waiting and bewildering world. I think a spot of leave, say fourteen days, then you come back and we sign on the dotted line. And you'll be on your own. How does that strike you?'

The uncertain smile became a broad and certain one.

'Suit me fine, sir. When can I go?'

'From a.m. tomorrow. I'll arrange it with the wardmaster. On your way, and stick to beer, Wisbeck, when you celebrate. That's harmless enough. It's damned nearly water, anyway. Remember, no spirits.'

'Yes, sir.'

When the door closed behind the sub-lieutenant Maldon turned to the surgeon-lieutenant.

'You've done a nice job of re-conditioning there, helped I've no doubt by some advice from—from the silent Second Citizen.' A sidelong glance included Sister Payne.

71

'Thank you, sir. Really all he wanted was a little confidence and—and——'

'No gin.'

'As you say, sir. No gin, and the rest was easy.'

'Playing about with the human mind is never easy,' Maldon said with a touch of severity. 'At least, not the male mind. There are booby traps galore.'

'And the female mind, sir?' the young doctor asked bravely.

'There are limits to my courage. Ask me tonight when we have a couple of brandies inside us and I'll dilate at length for you.'

'I'll remind you.'

'By the way, where is that lad going for his leave? Any idea?'

'To his parents—at least, to his mother.'

Maldon poised a pencil on its point, caught it as it swayed and poised it again. As it fell he allowed it to spin in a complete circle.

'A nice little watertight case. Here we have a youngster who three years ago was probably grieving because he didn't get his House colours with no second chance to come. He gets into the Navy, progresses from the lowest form of marine life—midshipman—and when his one little ring is still newly glistening on his arm he gets married to—to a Wren, wasn't it? She looks upon a wedding ring as a licence to bat around. As soon as his back is turned she starts broadening her scope and writes to tell him, the silly ass. Instead of going home on leave and beating the bejazzus out of her, dragging her to the bedroom and emerging the next morning pale but victorious he surrenders the victor's palm to—a fighter pilot, wasn't it? After that, the familiar storm. He drinks far too much—imagine an adolescent tummy on a steady diet of gin! Now,' he spread his arms, 'back to Mum.'

Sister Payne shifted her weight from one hip to the other and momentarily distracted the attention of the lieutenant, who wondered what she would look like in full war paint and whether that shift of weight could be developed into a steady, rhythmic movement. Maldon's voice brought him back.

'. . . I have long held that if the Admiralty could be persuaded to staff this hospital with mums two-thirds of our job would be done.'

'Or wives,' Surgeon-Lieutenant Clark murmured blandly.

'No, definitely not. With wives men always want to appear the strong, husky hero. When they fail they have a sneaking fear that some lusty oaf will sneak in and occupy their territory. And it happens, too, sometimes.' He waved a hand towards the closed door. 'As you have seen.'

'I gather she was a wrong 'un from the word "go", anyway, and his mum has convinced him that it is better to write her off.' The surgeon-lieutenant grinned.

'Exactly. And Mum is going to build up his ego by letting him weep on her bosom and kid him that he is far, far too good a man to waste on trash. Why weren't you a mum?'

'Who? Me, sir?' The lieutenant's eyes widened. 'To the best of my knowledge, a biological impossibility.'

Maldon pressed a button and when a sick-berth attendant answered he said, 'Sister Payne would like some coffee, so you might as well make it a pot for three.'

The S.B.A. looked across at Sister Payne.

'C'mon, man, you're wasting time.'

'Commander Maldon, I——'

'You see? Jump to it!'

The S.B.A. jumped and disappeared.

'I really must protest——'

'Protest heard and acknowledged. Sit down, Sister, and you, Clark. This is going to be a long session. Who has all the cigarettes?'

Surgeon-Lieutenant Clark took the other easy chair in the room and Sister Payne sat primly on a straight-backed one.

Sister Payne knew definitely, and Clark had a hazy idea, that behind all Maldon's talk he had a problem. It was his habit, when faced with such a situation, to indulge in long and rather rambling elaborations with the main problem embedded somewhere in the talking.

73

The S.B.A. entered with a tray.

'Why is it that if I want coffee, which stimulates the thought, I have great difficulty in obtaining it? Yet Sister Payne gets it at the drop of a hat,' Maldon said shamelessly. 'No, no—put the sugar where I can control its fair distribution. You don't take any, Clark, do you? Good!'

The S.B.A. wiped a faint grin from his face and silently left the room.

When the cups were distributed Maldon leaned back with his cup and saucer poised precariously on one knee-cap, helped by just a touch from two fingers.

'If we had to produce a balance sheet, which, thank God, we don't have to do, I would be in danger of being complacent,' Maldon went on. 'We have had some sticky ones here, real beauties, especially among those ex-prisoners, but up to now not one out-and-out complete failure.' Carefully he stirred his coffee. 'No comment?' He raided the small sugar basin near his elbow. 'Not yet, anyway.'

Sister Payne received one swift look but refused to be drawn.

'Clark, what are your views on Lieutenant-Commander Meredith?'

Clark shrugged.

'Exactly! And he looks like spoiling my nice balance sheet. I wish you were a mum, Clark. I would have him weep on your bosom twice a day for a week and have him fit in a month.'

Surgeon-Lieutenant Clark chuckled and looked over towards Sister Payne. Maldon followed his glance and shook his head.

'You would, would you? Well, you would be wrong.'

Sister Payne's eyes dilated momentarily, then she sat upright and rustled the papers in her hands.

'You see, Clark,' Maldon went on, 'men are afraid of nurses. Oh, yes they are. When they are very sick they resent the inevitable trespass into their intimacy, and when they are half fit they spend their time patting nurses' bottoms or trying to catch them in a quiet spot. Don't they, Sister?' he asked blandly. 'And it's all part of the assertive male. One of the perks of nursing, in fact. Watch a nurse walk down a ward full of

74

really sick, strict-bed men. Then watch that same nurse sway past men who are getting better.'

'I've never heard such arrant nonsense in my life.'

'I thank you for the corroboration. Coming from an expert like you it is a bright green garland.'

Sister Payne achieved a redoubtable snort.

'So you see, Clark, your superficial theories about mums and wives, while holding a glimmering of value, would have certain drawbacks.'

Clark accepted the authorship in surprise.

'Meredith is a real—real stinker. Every time I think I have him beginning to fit into a pattern he destroys that idea—without batting an eye. At first I thought he was just going to die on us by not eating.' He clicked a thumb and finger. 'That would have been easy. But physically, all things considered, he's not in bad shape.' He leaned back until his head rested on the back of the chair with his gaze on the ceiling. 'It's mentally he has frozen up on me. And I can't get through it. At first I thought I had activated a nice line in hatred. But all he hates is my intrusion into that aura he has created round himself. It's a cold resentment, and nothing to work on.'

Maldon disposed of the remainder of his coffee before he spoke again. He placed the empty cup on the table, abstractedly. There followed a trick familiar to the other two. With thumb touching finger tip to enumerate his points he went on, 'A long war, with far too many adjacent bangs, losing a ship, a few men—— Well, all could add up to quite a strain on such a mercurial Celtic mind. Even losing a wife and family could be enough to knock a man off balance to conform to a pattern, a well-defined one at that. But he doesn't. And the damnable part is I can't discover why. He just lies there completely aware of what is going on and. . . .'

An expressive shrug completed the sentence.

Maldon stood up and moved towards the window. He stood there jingling some small money in his pocket. Then he spun round.

'I'm going to take a chance. This is not a case for shock

treatment. I'm going to mix 'em. I'm going to send him to sleep for a week, and try a little hypnosis. I know—I know!' He saw Sister Payne stir and anticipated her protest. 'I am quite aware that there is the risk that if it doesn't come off he'll be a— a. . . .' He used the expressive shrug and a spreading of the palms. 'For years, maybe for the rest of his life. But if I don't he'll be that, anyway. If he doesn't shut his eyes one night and omit to open them again—ever.'

Briskly he stepped towards the table.

'Right, Clark, we'll give the injection tomorrow morning. Eleven o'clock.' He raised a hand in facetious benediction, 'Peace be unto you. Don't worry. I have a hunch it will work out.'

As Clark and Sister Payne moved towards the door he allowed a hand to rest on her shoulder.

'Thanks for the coffee—Mum.' A boyish grin illuminated his face.

Owen Meredith's world was very small. Visually, it consisted of the foot of his bed, impeccably tidy, without a crease or fold in the neatly tucked-in bedclothes, the tall oblong of the window, against which fluttered the dead-black branches of a tree. And his thoughts. It was a world far too big for him. If he closed his eyes to shut out the window and the dead branches which seemed to wave to him, seemed to call him on towards what lay beyond, the world expanded in his mind. He had reached a point at which he had detached himself from everything, even from himself. It was a curious disembodiment. It was only with an effort that he could remember that he was Owen Meredith, Lieutenant-Commander, R.N.V.R. All that went with it, all that was attached to it, was a long way off, a misty picture in which details appeared for a moment, then disappeared into tenuous, vague outlines, like a scene watched through the smoke of a garden fire.

It was a detachment which brought relief, but at the same time imposed an almost unbearable strain. To relax meant remembering, sharply, acutely, painfully. With his eyes closed, the wind in the tree became the sound of the sea, and the sound of the sea brought him closely to ships. And from ships his mind would wander into worn and jagged tracks along which he had travelled so often, so often that he knew each step which would cause him agony.

From ships he would remember—the padre—the growing realization, enveloping him like the noise of a train rushing through a tunnel, that they were gone. With the difference that the rushing noise of pain did not diminish, but kept on and on. It must have sounded like that to them when they crouched beneath the futile little tiled roof, hearing the buzz-bomb come overhead, cut out and descend.

"It was all over immediately; they could not have felt anything. . . ." He knew it like a well-worn lesson, had muttered it a thousand times to himself until it had ceased to bring any comfort, any ease.

So remembering brought a dull ache. He would open his eyes to mere slits and concentrate on the window. He knew every branch and twig, every movement they would make at the buffet of the wind. There was the crooked branch, shaped like an elbow, which bobbed slightly then swooped down like an arm stretching towards the window. There was the thin, spread-fingered branch with long, twisted ends which swayed at the least touch. There was the stubby, imperative twig which tapped imperiously and almost continuously on the pane— maybe it was worn stubby because it so constantly and so vainly tapped. Twigs and branches . . . lofty trees. . . . "Us old country-men say when the rooks build high in the branches 'tis going to be a fine summer." The Boss, the farmer, revelling in the tumultuous wave of constantly inquiring, perpetually curious childhood round him had said that. It was Yvonne. . . . Meredith retreated from memory, drawing back within the almost empty shell he had created protectively. The effort shaped his mouth, brought deep breaths hissing through his nose. The branch, the twig which still held in a cleft a dead and dried leaf, held it firmly as if reluctant to release evidence that it had once lived, had been a warm glowing green. The wind spun the leaf, which fluttered vainly like a trapped moth, then lay passive.

There were unguarded moments when sleep captured him, when dreams took possession, vivid dreams when they were all together again, together with childish laughter, when an all-embracing look would pass between himself and Her, a look which always ended in a smile of complete understanding. But always in the dreams there was some unseen but tangible barrier preventing him from getting closer, from enjoying to the full any intimacy. It was as if he was just permitted to see them from a foreshortened distance, but was not allowed to join in. In the dream the tap of childish feet dancing, tapping out a childish but formed rhythm, would be with him when he woke, sweating and trembling, too close to the life he was rejecting, the life he was afraid to meet. And at the window a branch would tap . . . tip . . . tap.

There was one retreat from which Meredith shrank without conscious effort. It was a curious retreat into which he had several times travelled a short distance, a restful, almost blissful, retreat nearly physical in its form. It was like looking down a misty tunnel, a long, colourless tunnel, the sides of which were indeterminate. All he could realize was that they were curved, smooth, revolving gently and restfully. In the distance, at the end of the tunnel, was a glow, a faint, attractive rosy glow which pulsated gently to something. Was it to the tune of soft laughter?

Once he had allowed himself to slip down that tunnel. It was so easy; merely lie still and let progress take care of itself. But as he progressed, leaving behind the complicated pattern of life, the rosy glow became a sharp, garish glare. With difficulty he had wriggled and squirmed, stopped his progress down the tunnel, halted and laboriously struggled back. Clutching something which he vaguely recognized as a lifeline, he had hung on to it until the tunnel was merely a nebulous gap behind him. For a time he had remained on its brink, gasping like a stranded fish, torn between no desire to stay on, and an almost equally insistent desire to go back into the grey tunnel with its promise at the end. But the lifeline remained; slowly he had identified it.

A voice, almost beyond the scope of his ears, a feminine

voice. . . . 'A rich, warm red . . . there is a path that goes over the hill. . . . the other side of the hill is life . . . everything looks dead now, but . . . that's life. . . .'

Meredith had hung on to that lifeline, that gentle voice, a voice coming from a long way off.

It came to him this morning.

Nurses had been in and had fussed over all the intimacies which are nursing; the duty surgeon-lieutenant with his attendant accolytes had grouped round his bed in a meaningless, murmuring tableau, then he had been left alone, except for an indistinct figure framed against the window. From a long way off Meredith heard the soft voice. 'The rain has left everything fresh and clean. The sky is a pale blue, with only a few clouds. The path across the field and over the hill looks a new red. Sometimes I wonder. . . .' Then the voice had taken on a new note, a brisk, impersonal tone which Meredith found mildly distressing.

'This sleep will relax you, help you to get a grip on yourself, and on life.'

The dim figure disappeared and reappeared standing beside his bed. 'Do you know that all life wants is a little effort by you? It has a lot to offer yet.' The cool hand rested on his forehead. 'I'll see you later.'

Meredith shrank away from coherent thought, fixing his lame and limping brain on the tapping twig which seemed more insistent this morning. Tap . . . tap . . . tip . . . tap . . . come outside . . . come . . . see what there is beyond that retreat into which you have gone . . . tip . . . tap . . . come outside. He slipped off into a dream which followed the pattern . . . his resistance was down . . . there was laughter . . . and childish voices . . . something horrible and grotesque held him back . . . stopped him from joining in the laughter, seemed to be tearing him away . . . farther away from them. He heard a voice groaning, and awoke to realize that it was his own.

Surgeon-Commander Maldon stood a little way from the bed. Near him was Sister Payne and bending over Meredith was

Surgeon-Lieutenant Clark. A sick-bay attendant stood with a shining tray at Clark's elbow.

Meredith felt a slight pressure, sustained for not more than a few seconds.

'Good!' Maldon moved in nearer. 'Pull the curtains. I'll have perhaps three or four minutes before he goes off.'

The curtains rasped sharply.

'Right, Clark! Thank you. You and the S.B.A. can leave us now. I'll want two men in here in twenty minutes to stay with him constantly. Right?'

Maldon looked at Sister Payne. 'Three minutes, and they can be so important. If he is tough and it runs to four, so much the better—or so much the worse.' Maldon blew slightly and moved nearer to the man on the bed.

Meredith felt a soft, velvety feeling stealing over him. It had been something like that when they had given him the first drug in London, a curious, relaxing feeling. But there was a difference. This feeling was smoother. It seemed to take charge of the tension which had been part of him for so long—too long—and seemed to be letting it down gently, like somebody taking the tension off a powerful spring, gently but firmly.

Maldon listened to Meredith's breathing for a few moments then signalled to Sister Payne. She leaned against the side of the bed and took his wrist in her fingers.

'You are going to sleep, a nice, long, restful sleep with no dreams. It is the dreams which have been bothering you. Now we are going to help, but first. . . .'

She nodded silently to Maldon, laid the hand down outside the coverlet and moved away.

Meredith found the voice was deeper, more insistent, but was still soft and restful.

Maldon leaned over him, talking quietly.

'Get it all straight in your mind, then tell me all about it. Tell me everything. I want to know so that I can help you. We do want to help you, you know, and you want that help. It will be hard, but until we know we cannot do much. Now start thinking from the beginning. Don't hurry. Get it all straight in your mind. Get it straight—every fact—I want it all.'

Slowly Meredith dragged himself from his retreat.

Like an itemized schedule things began to appear in tabulated form, then became jumbled. In an effort to find the beginning he rolled his head from side to side and moaned. He knew that finding the beginning would hurt; he didn't want to be hurt again. Again he moaned.

'Not that.' The voice became sharp. 'Take your time.' It softened until it became almost a caress. 'Don't hurry. Get it all straight in your mind, and when you are ready I'll listen . . . listen . . . listen. . . .'

Meredith sighed deeply once and started to talk slowly. It was such a long while back. They used to laugh often, and when he was afraid She would laugh with him. She was always there when he wanted her. She. . . . Then the padre said. . . . Keep thinking of the branches . . . don't let the wind remind me of the sea. So it began when. . . .

Meredith slipped off into a deep sleep.

Maldon stood up and braced his shoulders. He watched the hand outside the coverlet pluck at the bedclothes a couple of times, tweak once more, then slowly relax until it lay limp.

'Right, Sister! We'll pick this up again in a week. I could be wrong. I could be doing——'

'You are not.'

It was dogmatic, firm, accepting no alternative.

'Thank you, Sister.'

Meredith slept, and remained asleep for eight whole days except for a few minutes in each twenty-four.

The world swooped and dived. The upward swoop went swiftly, slowed down and stopped at the top for a breath-taking moment, hovered there, then surrendered to a dive which increased in momentum until all semblance to an arc was lost. It became an endless dive, which went on and on, which seemed to be pointed towards a vague, luminous light which never became formed, definite. Behind the luminous light there was a focal point on which Meredith strove to fasten. It was a voice.

'Don't hurry; just lie back. Sister will give you a cup of coffee in a moment. She is a sort of conjuror—brings coffee out of the blue. Just take it easy.'

The swooping dives decreased and the voice grew nearer.

'We've all the time in the world. Just hold the cup for him. Don't pour it over his blasted chest—hold it to his lips. For God's sake give it to me.'

'Tip me up and pour it into the other end.' Meredith heard himself say it with a strange intonation, a leavening of laughter. 'I've tasted better coffee made with an old sock.'

He heard a jumble of voices; they seemed to be threaded on one which was more insistent than the others.

'. . . half-an-hour . . . I'll want you to walk him up and down the room . . . only a few minutes . . . pull the curtains apart . . . nobody is to come into this room until I ring . . . nobody . . . don't argue . . . now, outside.'

'Bloody bully,' Meredith said succinctly, without opening his eyes.

A chuckle of laughter was the only answer he got.

'If the light is too bright say so, and we'll pull the curtains again.'

Meredith opened his eyes and the vaporous light began to take shape, resolving itself into an oblong frame, the window. From an indeterminate shape it took sharp edges. Soon he could see the branches and the twigs. The stubby one was tapping imperatively. He squinted at it; it wasn't moving. From whence came the tap? Meredith slid his eyes over to the corners. Near his head a hand tapped with a pencil, a long, bright yellow pencil which tapped steadily, incessantly. It fascinated him. A voice kept time with the tapping.

'We were talking about the padre—when he came and told you. . . .'

Meredith tried to freeze. The pencil tapped, the voice went on inexorably.

'You were telling me. . . .'

Meredith heard another voice from a long way off, an analytical voice which seemed to know all about him, all about his fears, seemed to be able to describe his innermost thoughts, the terror of his waking moments, the dreadful moments of his dreams.

'I didn't want to go on without Her,' the voice went on, 'and yet I didn't know how to stop.'

The voice seemed to rest and Meredith struggled to prevent it revealing any more of the secrets he had kept to himself. But the voice was insistent.

'When I heard they were gone . . . all of them . . . something went from me . . . left me empty . . . there was nothing to go on for . . . all my life I've been afraid of . . . of the darkness . . . of something beyond the dark . . . when She was there . . . or when I knew She would be waiting for me . . . I could face it . . . She was a sort of audience . . . all of them were . . . I could . . . sort of put on a face . . . be brave because they would want me to be. . . And when they went . . . there was nothing for me to go on for . . . when we were hit the steam screamed . . . it sounded like the men screaming . . . I wanted to leave it all . . . there was something beyond the . . . then the engine screamed . . . on the station. . . .'

The tapping stopped. Meredith felt himself slip back in a gentle movement, like the sway of a ship at the beginning of a gale.

'Enough! Just let him walk up and down the room for a few minutes. No more.'

Meredith opened his eyes and found himself looking into a dark, saturnine face creased in a smile which furrowed it in a multitude of creases.

'Somehow I hate your guts,' Meredith said slurringly. 'I don't know why, but I do.'

'Thank God for small mercies. It was more than I hoped for. You'll hate them all before we finish. Now a walk up and down to begin with.'

And the face was gone.

Meredith felt hands under his armpits, arms round his waist as he was helped from the bed. With assistance he struggled into a dressing-gown. When he was more or less upright the

83

room swam. He tried to focus his eyes and failed. The oblong of the window came into sharp definition for a fraction of a second, then receded. A faint feeling of nausea took possession of him.

'Breathe deeply and slowly. Don't hurry, just take a few steps.'

Meredith knew the voice.

'Phew! This feels like a morning after a classic night before. Who was flying the gin pennant?'

'Don't talk so much; just breathe and try to walk.'

Between the two S.B.A.'s Meredith took a few staggering steps towards the window. His legs felt rubbery, quite unable to take his weight, and the three of them did a brief sideways stagger which rocked the dressing-table.

'Ooops! Hold her up—we're sagging away to leeward.'

'Stop talking.' The voice held a tang of authority. 'Bring him to the window.'

A cold draught played over Meredith's face and his partly bared chest.

'Breathe deeply. You'll be shaky for a while. It's the drug. When that passes you'll feel better.'

Meredith breathed deeply half a dozen times and it made his head swim again.

'Now up and down a couple of times more and that will be plenty.'

The staggering course was traversed again and Meredith found himself sitting on the edge of the bed. He shook his head.

'Right! Where's my clothes? Let's get out into the open and——'

'You've walked enough for one day. Back into bed.'

'Give me my clothes. I'll——'

'Into bed, at once.'

Before Meredith could orient the rebellious phrases which bubbled inside him he found himself in bed with the clothes fitting tightly over him.

'That will be all. Tell Surgeon-Commander Maldon what we have done, and tell him, also, that I will be along in a few minutes.'

'Yes, Sister.'

The door lock clicked. Meredith opened his eyes. She was standing framed in the window.

'Tomorrow I'll let you sit by this window for a bit. Say, ten minutes. Then ten minutes walking up and down the room and——'

Meredith frowned.

'Look, Sister. I'm not a cripple. I've been in bed a couple of days—a bit off the wicket—and now you want to——'

'You've been in bed twenty-one days in all,' she said, calmly moving from the window to the side of the bed. 'For the last eight you have been asleep. We put you to sleep. You couldn't, or wouldn't, help yourself. We had to help you.'

'Eight days?' His voice climbed in a note of incredulity. 'Eight days?'

'Eight days,' she repeated. Her cool hand travelled to his forehead and rested there. 'You are only about twelve ounces to the pound now. You'll have to take it easy.'

'Twelve ounces? What was I when I came in? What——?'

'You're talking too much, and at the wrong time. I would say about four ounces, not more.' She turned to the table and picked up a small glass of milky liquid. 'Drink this.'

It was bitter and stung the back of his throat.

'Brrr! I seem to remember the taste of that Micky Finn before from somewhere.'

'You had a steady diet of it for the first few days. Now settle down. Off to sleep.'

'Sleep? After eight days of it?'

'Sleep.' She nodded. 'Only a few hours this time. Then Commander Maldon will want to talk to you.'

'Maldon?' Meredith groped back into the shadows. 'Is that the man with the yellow pencil?'

'Yes.'

'I hate his guts.'

'So you said before, and it pleased him immensely. I want you to relax. You are talking a lot.'

Meredith wanted to talk. He wanted to tell her now he

85

remembered her standing by the window, how he came back from the tunnel to hear her talking, but he began to sway slightly. He started to relax from the feet upwards; before he could stop it long enough to tell her it swept over his head like a wave and he was asleep.

Sister Payne tapped on Surgeon-Commander Maldon's door. He was sitting back from his table, knees crossed. Round the tips of his fingers he had a rubber band.

'Take a pew, Sugar Plum Fairy. Oh, all right, stay formal. What do you think?'

'It's going to work.' She folded her arms so that each elbow was cupped in a palm. 'He's talking—or was—nineteen to the dozen. I gave it to him and he's off for three or four hours. What time do you intend to see him?'

'It's a movable feast—late afternoon—then we'll reduce the dosage and bring him back slowly.'

The rubber band on his finger was stretched from thumb tip to the tip of the index finger.

'There he is, Sister. Stretched to the uttermost. Now, will he come back when. . . .' He closed his hand and the band shrank. 'Or will he stay stretched, brittle, always near snapping point?'

She shrugged. 'That's your job.'

'And yours.'

'If it is any help, before the—what did he call it?—the Micky Finn bowled him over he informed me that he hated your guts. Inelegant, but forceful.'

'Splendid!' Maldon sat up. 'Sugar Plum Sister, we're on the home-stretch—a long stretch, I grant you, but on it we are. Anything else?'

'He remembers you by that yellow pencil.' She lifted her chin towards his desk.

Maldon picked it up and toyed with it.

'Did he indeed? That is useful. That the lot?'

'He wanted his clothes and played the devil with the poor S.B.A.s because they staggered all over the room with him.'

Maldon threw back his head and laughed. 'These Celts!'

86

These small, dark, mystic people! Scratch them emotionally and they want to lie down with death. Saw them in half with a blunt knife and they think you are joking with them. Complex, knowing no logical balance. Poised on a needle point so that a zephyr will sway them wildly, yet so firmly set that a hurricane will recoil from them.'

'You are talking in riddles.'

'Not really. From either they recover, full of beans and full of fight, but when the two combine it is too much.'

Sister Payne sniffed.

'Quite how you can have a zephyr and a hurricane together I fail to see.'

'Do you? Metaphors are a bit mixed, I agree, but one could be mental and the other physical.' He ran his hands through his hair. 'It's going to be a long home-stretch, Sugar Plum, because the short and easy way would leave him brittle. That I don't want. Now, which would you rather do? Stay here and interfere with my constructive thought, and order some coffee, or leave me alone with my problem?'

She moved towards the door.

'You order coffee.' As she closed the door she said, 'And see if you get it!'

He chuckled. 'Be generous with the sugar.'

6

MARJORIE HALEY heard the click of the lock in the door followed a moment later by animated conversation, partly in a deep voice, partly in a very childish treble.

This flowing dialogue always made her smile.

'Half the time he doesn't know what you are talking about, and the other half leaves you in complete ignorance,' she had once explained.

'And two-thirds of the time we arrive at complete agreement,' Bill had answered her argument. 'If the rest of the world were like it, life would be so much better.'

At times she felt that Bill was merely thinking aloud, using the boy as an instrument for the orientation of his thoughts. Once she had advanced that theory to him. For a short time Bill was quiet.

'I think you are right,' he had ultimately agreed. 'Perhaps I am using him as a sort of mental whipping boy.' He stopped her half-voiced protest with an upraised hand. 'Don't take that too literally,' he added with a degree of irritation. 'I talk my way out of a mental tangle—a jumble. Inside me things are all tied up in a bunch. If I can flake it out, by talking out loud, so much the better. See?'

Marjorie had nodded. 'I think I understand. But would it help if sometimes you talked to—or at—me?'

'Most assuredly. In fact, I was beginning to wonder if you were not getting just a teeny-weeny bit tired of hearing my voice.'

His gaze had softened as he looked at her and the tight lines round his mouth had slackened. She had learnt to accept that as a smile, to watch for its fleeting passing.

It was a fragment of knowledge that had come slowly. As days followed it had dawned on her that for much of the time he was mentally a long way from her. He would answer a question in a detached, almost off-hand manner and with a far-away look in his eyes. Sometimes, when they sat in the evening, with the boy safely in bed, he would sit sprawled in a deep easy chair, apparently at complete ease, but a sudden convulsive movement of his hands would attract her attention. She would see his face set in hard lines, his eyes half closed, and she would realize that what she had taken for relaxation was in reality a sustained tension.

Once or twice she had attempted to break the tension, hoping that she would bring about ease.

'Penny-and-a-half for them, darling.'

The lines would tighten round his mouth, his fingers would clench convulsively and a look of intense irritation would flood over his features.

'Does it matter?' The tones would be deep and tinged with hoarseness. A few nervous movements would follow, a cigarette would glow in short, vigorous puffs, and soon he would be back behind the barricade of his thoughts.

She soon learnt that if she did not interrupt he would ultimately emerge and look at her with a flicker of warmth in his eyes, and the lines would relax slightly.

'How about some tea? Sit still, I'll make it.' And as he passed a finger would travel softly down the curve of her neck from her ear to her shoulder. Scarcely above a whisper, she would hear 'Nice.'

But it was at night time she realized that he was living under some strain she could not define. Often she would hear him breathing deeply and steadily as they lay together in the dark and she would imagine he was deeply asleep. Then the breathing would stop; the steady inhalation would be replaced by shuddering gasps. Once she raised herself on an elbow and caught the reflection of light in his wide, staring eyes. She placed her hand on his chest and found it wet with sweat.

'Dreaming, darling?'

The bedclothes were flung violently aside. He jumped from the bed and strode over to the window.

'For God's sake let me alone. I was wide awake.' For some moments he had thumped the window frame with a clenched fist. She had heard him fumbling, heard the scrape of a match, seen his face glow in the flame and had watched the violent, short puffs at the cigarette gradually decrease until they were measured, long and steady. With her head bent on her arm she had lain in silence until the cigarette end suddenly described an arc through the open window.

He had crossed to the bed and sat on it. His hand had stolen across the pillow, searched uncertainly until he found her head. Gently his fingers followed the curve of her neck from her ear to her shoulder.

'Sorry, darling.' It was scarcely above a breathed whisper. 'I can't quite explain. I was dozing off quite nicely then a damned car went whining past in second gear. It sounded like—— Well, I started thinking of E-boats, and planes. . . .'

Vaguely she had understood although he had left untold the feeling of terror, the feeling that the noise would rise in a crescendo, that there would be the whistle of a bomb, the grim rat-tat-tat of a gun, that sometime sooner or later the thin half-inch steel plate would not be enough to stop the splinter, or the mine, or the bullet, or the bomb. Regan had been good; his ship, *Solan*, had been top line—but the bomb had come. She had failed to emerge from the tree-shaped column of spray and smoke; that one rosy flash was *Solan*, with Regan on board. And *Sheila*—she, too, had gone the same way.

Gently she would arrange the bedclothes over him, she would slip her arm round his shoulder and draw him to her. When his head was safely pillowed on her arm she would tighten her hold. Her whisper would be scarcely above a breath.

'But it's all over now, darling. You are home and safe. Tomorrow, you and The Boy—and perhaps we'll go. . . .' Fragments, part thoughts, part breathed, but all soft and soothing.

Then would come a long, shuddering breath; she would feel his legs reaching down to their full extremity; she would feel relaxation creep over him. One more deep breath, followed by others, measured, slow and even.

The damp spot on the pillow, from his sweat-drenched head, would expand slightly, but not only from sweat, because her cheeks, too, would be wet.

So, understandingly, she did not inquire too deeply into the one-sided conversations which so often took place between Bill and his small son.

One day they arrived home from a morning promenade and Bill said, 'I was afraid we wouldn't make it in time. I thought we would have had to duck round some corner and start "Operation Spend-a-penny", and it would have been three-halfpence at that. The boy is nothing but a tosspot, an embryo wine bibber of note.'

She looked at him inquiringly. The flickering warmth in his eyes reassured her.

'We went round the park and down to that pond behind it —any trout in that pond, by the way?—and his lordship demanded a "glink". I bought him one. A fearful pink thing with a long straw. He shifted that. A few minutes afterwards he demanded another. "Two-bottle man," thinks I, and I stood him another round. But half an hour afterwards he wanted a third. I got it, but it beat him. He wound up blowing bubbles in it.'

Marjorie sat down on a chair and hooted with laughter.

'Oh, you man! "Glink" to him means anything wet. He didn't want a drink, when he asked for a "glink"—which does mean drink sometimes, he wanted you to take him back to the pond to throw stones or sticks.'

Bill stood with a faint, almost indiscernible, crinkle at the corners of his eyes.

'I see. He had me worried for a moment. Could you rough out a sort of bi-lingual dictionary so that I can understand the essentials? A kind of "*pardonnez moi, voulez vous promenade avec moi*" sort of stuff in baby talk. I would hate him to go short of anything he wanted.'

She gurgled at him. 'Make up your own as you go along. I have to.'

Bill looked at her fixedly for a moment.

'In three seconds flat, from now, there's going to be lots of "glink".' His eyes shifted to The Boy and Marjorie's eyes followed his.

The Boy was standing with a reflective look on his face, his legs were crossed and he was rocking to and fro slightly.

Hurriedly she swept the child up in her arms and retreated towards the bathroom.

'While father has a "glink", the sun being well over the yard-arm,' Bill concluded, moving towards the sideboard.

Six weeks of his three months' demobilization leave had slipped by in almost a flash. Without fully acknowledging it, he appreciated the shrewd reasoning of the individual responsible for initiating it. More and more every day he found himself retreating from the mental routine of naval thinking and was absorbing a civilian outlook despite the fact that he was still in uniform.

It had come to him with a sudden jerk a night or two previously when he had found that the buttonholes on his monkey jacket were becoming a bit frayed. Unthinkingly, his mind had turned towards a new uniform, and he had been brought up with a jolt when he realized that he would not have to order another.

'A grey, I think. A lightish grey with a check,' he had said unexpectedly, leaning back in the chair with a column of faint blue smoke rising from his cigarette.

She had looked up from some child's clothing on which she had been working and smiled.

'Not too much like a bookmaker's, darling. I'd hate to hear people shout "Twenty-to-one the field" when you passed.'

Haley had sat up abruptly. 'How the devil did you guess what I was thinking?'

'Deduction. You finger the buttonholes of your uniform, pull the elbow round to see if it is shining, search the bottom of your trousers for whiskers. The rest was easy.'

Haley had shaken his head.

'Right! Now, witch, tell me what else I have been churning over in my mind.'

She had nimbly bitten off a thread and folded the article of clothing on her lap.

'How many guesses?'

'Just one. All or nothing.'

Solemnly she had cupped her hands as if holding a crystal ball and stared down into the palms. Then in a deep, assumed voice she had gone on.

'The ball is cloudy . . . it clears now . . . I see a man . . . he is dressed in uniform . . . might be a bus conductor . . . no, a railway guard. . . .' She had looked up with an air of triumph, her eyes twinkling. 'He's a naval officer.'

'Cut the clowning, Gipsy Lee.'

Again she had pretended to study the crystal ball.

'He stops outside a house; it has a garden; he opens the gate . . . enters . . . he reads a sign . . . it says "House for Sale". . . . He leaves——'

'Hey, hey!' Haley had sat bolt upright. 'Easy, girl! They used to burn people for that at one time.'

She had moved over to her favourite spot, on the edge of his armchair; her fingers had stroked his temple.

'No good, darling. I wouldn't burn. I'm too green.'

'But tell me seriously—how did you guess that I had that in mind?'

'Well, if I leave you outside a shop for a few minutes when I come out you are studying the window in the estate agent's place. Not the window with expensive furnished flats, but the half with "Houses for Sale". When we go for a walk your eyes always stray to notice boards. And I watched you study the adverts in the paper. You make little marks in pencil against some.'

'Easy, just like that. But why didn't you say something?'

'I guessed you would open up in good time.'

'Quite frankly, darling, I don't know how you stuck it so long here with those people below. Besides, we must have a garden for The Bloke.' A hand ruffled his hair. 'But I've seen some shocking bits of work described as a "mature semi-detached house, all conveniences". I consider it very remiss of the Luftwaffe to have missed them.'

'This hasn't been too bad.' The fingers went on ruffling. 'It was somewhere for you to come when on leave.'

'Of course I've only made tentative stabs, looking at a few obvious places; some of them have been in the market for a long time, which damns them in my eyes, anyway. And there is the question of finance. We'll have to borrow, of course.'

And the rest had been "Then we'll . . ." and "If we can . . ." and "I would like. . . ." The stuff of which dreams are made.

Haley had gone to the office to which he would return when he finally picked up the threads of civilian life and had discussed it with his immediate chief.

'I don't want to rush you, or try to influence you, Haley,' his chief had said, 'but—we are rather proud of you, my boy, and if you decide, I am certain the company would arrange a loan. An investment, my boy; just as well to let you have it as to pay it in surtax. We've done well during the war—couldn't help it. It just poured in. So when you've made up your mind let me know.'

His chief had leaned back. 'Different from when I came back to "the land fit for heroes to live in". That was in 1919. We had to run riot at Boulogne before we got any action. After the war —that was the other war, Haley—things were chaotic.'

'I didn't know you were in that, sir.'

'Indeed I was. P.B.I. That was me. I spent two years in the trenches in France and Flanders. Two long years.'

'I never heard you mention it.'

'By the time you came to me I had learnt that the last thing people wanted to hear was the story of the returned warrior. You'll find that out, Haley. You'll find it so. There is no greater drug on the conversational market than a warrior home from the wars. The fighting is over, people feel safe . . . and. . . .' An expressive shrug completed it. 'Men who talk about their wars have been bores since the Roman legionaries went home.'

'I'll remember that, sir.'

'You'll be the only one who ever did.'

Much of that came back to Haley as he leaned against the mantelpiece. He felt oddly excited and waited with impatience for his wife to return. When she did he slipped an arm round her waist.

'I don't want you to think that I've jumped in without consulting you. But there were so many stumers coming along. Houses which looked wonderful on paper but turned out to be wrecks. So I waited until I had something really lashed up and stowed.'

'Yes, sir,' she replied primly, with a twinkle giving the lie to the primness.

'Good lord! Was I sounding so much like a commanding officer?'

'Yes, sir.'

He grinned. 'All right, Number One. I'll try hard to be human.'

'Do! Make a real effort.'

He leaned his shoulders against the mantelpiece.

'Do you know that road which runs round the back of the park? The one with the old red brick houses set well back from the road.'

She thought for a moment.

'I know. Where the landmine fell. Several of the houses were hit. There are two or three boarded up. Real ruins they look from the road.'

He felt a momentary irritation. Was everything to be dated from the time the landmine fell, or the day the bomb dropped? Was the war to be the milestone from which all future measurements of time were to be dated? Rather coldly he continued.

'I've seen one or two apparent wrecks in the past couple of years which were nothing of the sort. But if——'

Swiftly and diplomatically she interjected, 'Of course, dear. But you were talking about the house.'

'I was talking about a road which runs behind the park. I was going to say——' A smile lit his face. 'Sorry, dear. I'll start at the beginning. When I went scouting today with The Bloke looking for a possible place for "Operation Spend-a-penny" I went into the garden of one of those houses. It is up for sale. It is one of the houses which were damaged; it is boarded up, windows gone, garden is a jungle. The damage seems to be mainly blast. I moved a board and had a quick look inside. Strange to say, it is as dry as a bone. So. . . .'

He stopped and produced his cigarette case. With elaborate care he took one out, offered her one, which she refused, and spent some time lighting it to his satisfaction.

'If you don't go on, I shall scream.'

'Scream away. Mrs. Madden will be able to tell all her friends that now I am home I wallop you.'

'Blow Mrs. Madden! WILL YOU GO ON?'

'So I spent twopence——'

'What?'

Haley threw back his head and laughed. 'On the telephone, idiot. I phoned the agent and asked the price, about war damage allowance, when the work could be done—I asked as many questions as I could with His Nibs hanging on to my leg wanting to try the phone.'

'Well?'

'The price is considerably lower than some of the mansion prices I have been asked for glorified Council houses.'

He examined his glowing cigarette, but failed to get a rise. She stood before him, lips slightly compressed, waiting. Finally he went on.

'I have arranged with the agent for him to have a man there to open the door for me so that I can see the inside.'

'For US to see inside.'

'For US to see the inside,' he amended.

'When?'

'When you feel like it.'

'Today?'

'Scarcely.' He looked at his wrist watch. 'I could ring and arrange for tomorrow.'

'Do that. Or somebody else will get in first.'

'I hardly think so. It has been empty since 1941. It was that which impressed me.'

'Yes, yes, darling. But there have not been so many people looking for houses as there are now.'

In a few minutes he was speaking again to the agent. At the end of the conversation the agent, a smooth-faced, blond young man with wide blue eyes, but with a certain underlying shrewdness, turned to his typist.

'Tell Parker to be at that shambles in Brisbane Road to-morrow afternoon at half past two. I have a couple of suckers who are interested.' He rubbed his hands as the girl made a note on the pad. 'Never were such times, my dear. Never were such times. Anything with a roof on it will sell for thousands. Anything. Never were such times. What's the upset price of that lot?'

She ran a finger down a list and told him.

'Hm, hm. We must whip it up a bit, say five hundred, so that we can be generous to the brave hero and come down two-fifty.'

'You won't,' the girl said flatly. 'If that is a lieutenant-commander man, he phoned earlier and I told him the price.'

'Foolish girl. Don't ever do that. Why, we'll have returned heroes coming in here by the dozen all wanting houses. Let me do the quoting. Those heroes will be bursting the doors in. Never were such times, never.'

She pecked away at her typewriter, then looked up.

'That's something you'll never be.'

'What's that?'

'A returned hero.'

His face flushed. 'Look, I've told you a dozens times. I tried, but I had a murmuring heart.'

'Yeah? I can hear it murmuring from here.'

'I did my best. I did what I could for the war effort.'

'I know. She still phones you. Landgirl, wasn't she? Some-where in Hertfordshire. The place where one bomb fell. An R.A.F. sand-filled practice bomb.'

'You seem to know a hell of a lot about——'

She renewed her pecking attack on the typewriter.

'She's called in here, as well as phoned.'

His face was red with anger as he ruffled papers on his desk. 'I can see you and me parting company.'

'So can I when my husband gets home.' She fingered a Winged Horse Airborne Regiment brooch in her lapel. 'He is longing to meet you.'

'You didn't tell him? I was only joking with you.'

'My husband enjoys a joke; he likes a laugh—all six feet, fourteen stone of him.'

She pecked again.

'Parker will like to meet the lieutenant-commander man.

Parker was in the Navy until he was invalided out. He should be able to tell him a lot.'

The agent clicked his fingers.

'P'raps I'd better go myself. Never mind——'

'You pull nails and lift heavy boards? Think of your murmuring heart. Think of the strain.'

He thumped a file on the desk and stood up. With a venomous look on his face he strode towards the door.

'Parker to be there at half past two, to pull nails and lift boards with his one arm,' she intoned in a flat voice. 'The returned hero officer knows the price. Any message if anybody rings, say from Hertfordshire?'

The door slammed.

She pecked away at her typewriter, repeating the same word along the line in capitals. "RAT" "RAT" "RAT". She tore the sheet from the machine, inserted a clean one and her fingers started racing.

My Darling, I can't sleep thinking that now the war is over, even out East, that you will be coming home for always. It's been a long time, but it doesn't matter now you are safely through it all. I am keeping my eye on all the ads. which come in. At this job I see the "Flats to Let" first. There are not many, but that is the only thing which makes this job worth-while. . . .

Her fingers flew on in a ceaseless tattoo.

Ex-Able Seaman Parker was waiting outside the forlorn-looking house the following afternoon when Haley and his wife turned up. From his coat pocket protruded the handle of a claw hammer.

'Good afternoon, sir.' With unconscious ease he pulled himself to attention and there was an involuntary movement of the one arm he had which suggested the beginning of a salute.

'Good afternoon. I don't want to take up too much of your time. If you can open up the house for us we would like to spend some time looking at it. Then perhaps you could come back later and close it.'

'No trouble, sir. I'll pull the board holding the front door—

somebody has pinched the lock—open a few windows and be back in an hour. Will that do?'

'Splendid!' Haley looked briefly at the empty sleeve, recalled the easy, almost graceful, momentary springing to attention, far removed from the military jerky movement.

'Navy?' he smiled.

'Yes, sir. Destroyers. Got this lot at Crete.' The empty sleeve moved slightly. 'Few months hospital in Alex, wound up at Capetown, then home for my ticket.'

'Bad luck.'

'Could have been worse. The others on my gun bought the lot.' He hesitated as he looked at the ribbons on Haley's chest. 'Small ships, sir?'

'Minesweeping.'

'That was a whale of a game. I remember the sweepers which used to——'

Haley's wife coughed. 'Hm—hr—m—m.'

He laughed. 'Sorry, my dear. But you know what it is. When two old sailors get together they start to——'

'I can guess.'

Parker chuckled. 'My wife says the only time I talk is when I'm talking about ships. So I go down to the local, when it's open, and I usually find somebody who was in the war.' He turned to the door and with his heavy claw hammer pulled some nails, lifted down a stout board and swung the door back.

The hall was wide, lofty, half-panelled and in the dim light they could see a broad stairway leading up from it. It was a double-fronted house of the late Victorian period, built at a time when people had sickened of ornate and lavish decoration, meaningless and formless, and it leaned almost towards the severity of a later date.

Haley, Marjorie and The Bloke stepped inside the hall, little squitters of dust rising protestingly about their feet and settling down again as if they realized that the invasion was likely to be only a short one.

'I'll open a couple of windows for you. The back door works on an inside bolt if you want to go into the garden.'

They heard his feet clump hollowly from room to room and then upstairs as they stood in the hall.

The Bloke, unusually subdued, clung to her skirt.

Haley led the way and they progressed from room to room. Parts of ceilings were down, floors were covered with plaster debris, windows were out with boards substituting for glass, and their feet rang hollowly as they went.

Almost as if holding a conversation with somebody, or something, Haley began a pro and con debate in his mind. Predominating was cost. The price was right, was extremely low in fact. It all depended on how much of the repair and decoration would be done by the War Damage Commission. And as he pondered it seemed that the house developed an eager personality, a personality anxious to persuade him into buying it. Fancifully, it seemed that the house argued and eventually became appealing. Look, it seemed to say, I am a fine old house, well built, solidly built in the days when men knew how to build things to last. I was built in the days when men were craftsmen. I know I look a wreck, but that is not fair wear and tear. Nobody knew anything about bombs and landmines when I was built. I was designed and erected to meet a square battle with the elements. Be fair to me. Even when the bombs fell and blasted me they could not do more than knock down plaster, blow out windows. I'm solid, firm as the day the builder left me and handed over to the new owner. I've met my natural enemies, the elements, alone, alone for the last five years, and I've defied them. Search me, find a place where there is rot, find a place where there is damp, I defy you. I was built for laughter, to hold a family, to hear the patter of feet, to feel the busy turmoil of life in and around me. I'm not a wreck.

Haley stood by a window frame looking out over a tangle of greenery, a jungle which had been a garden. I'm not a wreck. It's not a wreck. She's not a wreck—his mind slipped back to the last moment he saw his ship, the ship he had commanded for long, long years. She lay against the quay wall, her bow twisted and torn, red, her hull streaked. She had looked forlorn, deserted.

'What do you think, darling?'

He came back to reality with a surge, to find his wife standing at his side. Without looking at her he slipped an arm round her waist.

'This is not the moment to ask me to be practical. I would like to think over it for a while,' he said. 'If I said "yes" now I would be saying "yes" to a—a——' He waved an arm.

She moved closer up to him.

'A dream, darling?'

'A dream, if you like. It's as good a description as any.'

'Dreams—that is, day-dreams, which one can control to a certain extent—are the foundations of reality.'

'Full astern! Gipsy Lee is going to jangle her ear-rings and take a look into the future.'

'It's the first time I've dared to do it.'

She moved out of his grasp and stood in the gap which had been a window. She stared out, then she turned to him swiftly and said, 'Don't laugh, but—there is something which says—something I can't describe about this house which seems to be saying to me——'

' "Buy me. I'm alive. I'm not a wreck." '

A smile crept over her face.

'You feel it, too?'

'That was why I said it was not the moment to ask me to be practical.'

She spun away from the window.

'This could be William Terence's room. It must have been a dressing-room from the main bedroom. He would get the morning sun——'

'Which would wake him up about five o'clock on a summer morning so that he would rouse us——'

'And the main bedroom looks out over the trees——'

'Dead leaves in the winter, darling.'

'And live ones beginning in the spring.'

A hand flew to her lips.

'Where is he?'

'He was in the other bedroom.'

They rushed from room to room without finding him. Then out on to a small wooden veranda which overlooked the garden. She called, her voice shrilling a little as it joined her husband's deeper tones.

The jungle of brambles and weeds which was the garden rustled. Ex-Able Seaman Parker stood up, just his head and shoulders showing above the tangle.

'He's with me, ma'am. I'm showing him where the goldfish ponds used to be.'

The tangle agitated violently and The Bloke burst from cover. Parker followed more slowly.

'I know this house very well, sir. My mother used to do some work here years ago. It was a good house, with good, warm people in it. We always started our Christmas carols outside here. Mr. Martynside—he owned it—had two sons and a daughter. I remember being called in to help with the big tables when she got married.' He waved his hand at the tangle. 'This was a lovely lawn. Held the reception on it. The sun was shining. Lovely. Nice people, they were. Mrs. Martynside died just before the war. The two boys went into the Forces——'

'Yes?' Haley's query was gentle.

Parker shrugged. 'Both R.A.F. After they'd been reported dead Mr. Martynside stayed on alone until the landmine fell, so I've heard. Now he's dead and the daughter has put the house on the market.' He brushed some debris and leaves from his coat. 'It's a nice house, a warm house. It's always had children. A friendly house.'

Haley looked at his wife. She gazed back with wide eyes. Parker diplomatically moved away.

Haley spread the view before him. The trees wore their late autumn tints, from gold through red to deep purple.

'Dreams are the foundation for reality.'

'With dead leaves, darling.'

'And new ones growing in the spring.'

' "A warm house," ' he said. ' "A house for children. A friendly house." '

The Bloke suddenly said 'Glink.'

'He wants to stir the water in the pond with a stick,' Parker said, moving closer.

'How the devil did you find that out?' Haley asked.

Parker chuckled. 'Got a couple of my own. They've a language of their own, too.' He moved the plaster debris with his toe. 'Excuse me, sir, but has there been any mention of price? Not that it's my business, but——'

'There has,' Haley said, rather coldly.

'Because I was in the office when she came in and put it on the market.'

Haley told him the figure.

'That's it, sir. The guv'nor wanted to hoist it up, but she said, "That's the figure, and perhaps some family will buy it and make it happy again."'

Haley took his wife's arm in his. As they watched Parker nail up the front door again he felt her hand close tightly on his arm. 'Those nails won't be in for long, will they?' she whispered.

They waited for Parker at the gate.

'Used to feed the goldfish with ants' eggs, I did as a kid.' He turned to the house. 'A nice friendly house it was.' He smiled at them and amended, 'It is, I mean.'

As they lay side by side in bed that night she heard him breathing steadily, and knew he was awake.

'What are you thinking about, darling?' she whispered.

He turned towards her so that in the faint, diffused light he could see her face on the pillow.

'Same as you, sweetheart. A nice, friendly house.'

'It was friendly, wasn't it? I felt it as soon as I went inside the door.'

'Me, too.'

'It's wrong to think of it as a wreck just because it has been knocked about by the war.'

'It's not a wreck,' she said stoutly. 'It's a house.'

'A friendly house.'

'Hm, hm.'

She felt his arm steal round her.

'A friendly house made for children.'

7

FROM THE WINDOW of the wardroom Meredith could see nearly all the hospital buildings. It was constructed in the form of a letter "T", with the officers' section one part of the cross-bar, staff the other half, and the wards were taken up by the long leg. Where the cross-bar and long leg joined, a squat tower was the administrative section. It was, in fact, a modern mental hospital built by a progressive West Country city and had been requisitioned by the Admiralty.

After he emerged from the long, drug-imposed sleep he was allowed out of bed for an hour or so each day, to stagger up and down the room with two sick-bay attendants propping him up. The first few minutes of the earlier perambulations were torture. All he wanted to do was to lie down again and let the room swim in dizzy circles, taking it with him. Then came a period of resolute pugnacity. He would walk. He WOULD walk by himself.

With Sister Payne watching with barely concealed admiration, he climbed from the bed, struggled into a dressing-gown and thrust the attendants from him, steadied himself against the bed, then plunged across the room in a devastating fall which ended in his forehead hitting the corner of a dressing-table.

An hour later Surgeon-Commander Maldon looked critically, and rather admiringly, at some extensive bruising which included an embryo black eye of no mean dimensions.

'Oh, oh!' Maldon chuckled. 'Great strength returns the penny. Nothing broken. How did this happen?'

Meredith's eyes swivelled under Maldon's probing fingers until he could see Sister Payne standing near, a prim, disapproving look showing faintly on her face.

'She did it. Bashed me because I wouldn't get out of bed,' Meredith said shamelessly, and was rewarded by an audible gasp from her and complete disruption of her hitherto apparently impregnable calm.

'I—he——'

Maldon's laugh ended the attempted explanation.

But Meredith persisted in his efforts to walk alone, and it was during one such excursion that he found the barred window. He staggered to it and attempted to open it. It moved upwards only six or eight inches. Beyond the opening were steel bars set closely together. In a burst of futile rage he grasped the bars and shook them. They were immovable. In a flash came to him another significant fact. At all his meals, which had been of a light character—mashed potato, egg and milk puddings—he could not recall a knife, only spoon and fork. Things hitherto of no importance slipped into the picture. His pyjamas and dressing gown had no cord; there was that small inspection peep hole in the door, the door which could not be fastened from the inside except with a key carried by a nurse or Sister Payne.

The result had been an upheaval in his little world.

A young nurse walking along the corridor found herself confronted by a raging man who clutched the front of his pyjamas with one hand and steadied himself against the pale green wall with the other. His eyes were vivid with flashing rage. After one futile attempt to restrain him, she flew along the corridor to Sister Payne.

Meredith recalled afterwards, with a pronounced feeling of shame, his stormy greeting when she met him in the corridor. By this time two sick-berth attendants were trying to get behind him, and when she had arrived they had completed their sparring for an opening and were closing in.

'Walters! Carpenter! That will be all. Commander Meredith, back to your room at once.' It was like the crack of a whip.

The attendants retreated cautiously. Sister Payne concentrated on Meredith.

'At once. And into bed.'

With almost incongruous meekness Meredith obeyed. When he had climbed into bed and lay there breathing heavily and not before, she listened to his explanation, which to him had sounded lame then.

Meredith also had revealed to him another aspect of Surgeon-Commander Maldon, a stern, inflexible side, and heard his normally cheerful voice drop a few tones and develop a steely edge.

'This place was designed and built for the treatment of people mentally sick,' Maldon told him, 'and as such the Admiralty have taken it over. When we get a man in here, whether he be sub-lieutenant, ordinary seaman, admiral or . . . lieutenant-commander recently in command, to us he is a patient, mentally bruised—or broken—just as there are hospitals full of men physically broken. Our job is to get them fit again. We do not know what a man's attitude towards life will be when he arrives, so we have to start from scratch. Some get here in a state of acute anxiety—with suicidal tendencies. Have you ever thought of suicide, Meredith?' His eyes bored into those of the man on the bed.

'Good God! Me? No.'

Maldon turned and looked out of the window.

'I've still to learn where you were going, and what you were going to do, when you arrived at Paddington—before you came to us.'

'I—I—somewhere—maybe——'

Maldon turned again to face him, this time with the beginning of a smile a long way back in his eyes.

'We'll get to that by and by. In the meantime, I see no reason why you shouldn't be moved to the convalescent block, once you can walk, and'—this time he smiled outright—'once you have got rid of that testimonial under your eye to Sugar—Sister Payne's efficient right arm. What is it today? Wednesday—well, we'll say Saturday, with luck.'

And on Saturday a clothed, pale-faced, shaky-kneed Meredith moved over to the block wherein was the big wardroom. It was a larger world, broader in scope, with greater freedom, and with more people in it.

It was not until he started walking in the spacious grounds that he struck the next evidence of the nature of the hospital. He walked along a path through some trees until brought up short by a tall barbed-wire fence topped by triple strands on an angled arm. He tested the strength of the wire with his hand and foot and turned away to see a sick-berth attendant standing a few yards from him.

Meredith breathed deeply once, gained control of his surging temper, then said coolly, 'Seem determined to keep people in, don't they?'

The attendant's face remained impassive.

'Or keep 'em out, sir.'

'Could be.'

As he regained the main path Meredith saw from the corner of his eyes the attendant wave, and from the top of the administrative tower came an answering signal.

But gradually he found the minor restrictions disappearing. At one of his interviews with Maldon the surgeon-commander asked, apparently inconsequently, 'Do you play darts, Meredith?'

'After a fashion.'

'We are sending a team up to the local, The Falcon, to play the village team. They're a hot lot. Care to go?'

Meredith hesitated. 'I think not, sir.'

'As you wish. It would be a change. Some of the fellows take a walk up there lunch time for a noggin or two. You are quite welcome to go if you feel like it. Think it over.'

He watched the assembling of the darts team that night. They acted as if they were to be presented at Court, were almost vividly excited. One spoke to him, 'Coming, Meredith?'

'Don't know; can't make up my mind.'

When they had gone he felt that the wardroom was strangely empty. On an impulse he went to his room, donned his bridge coat and hat, and strolled down the long drive to the gate, walking under the hooded flood-lights which created alternate pools of light and shadow. At the gate a petty officer stepped from the small gatehouse with studied casualness, as if he wanted merely to view the night.

'Going far, sir?'

'To this—this Falcon pub. I want to see the slaughter of the innocents.'

107

'Slaughter is right, sir. Those village boys are mustard.' The petty officer fumbled with the gate and covertly looked at a list of names on a framed notice board.

'What name, sir? For the log, you see.'

'Meredith—Lieutenant-Commander.'

'Aye, aye, sir.' The gate swung open. 'Best drop of bitter for miles around at The Falcon. We use that pub a lot.' He said it as if awarding an honour. 'But lay off their cider, sir. It's rough—and tough. You'll be flaked down in left-handed coils before you can breathe. Have a good time, sir.'

The long, dark lane faced Meredith as he heard the gate go clunk behind him.

Back in the gatehouse, the petty officer studied a list of internal phone numbers, brooded over his instrument and finally pressed a button.

'Gate here, sir. Yes, sir. He's gone out. After the others, by himself. Gone up the road towards the pub. Yes, sir, dressed for the beach; bridge coat and hat. Smoking, too, sir. Aye, aye, sir.'

Maldon leaned back from his desk until his face was out of the circle of light cast by his reading lamp. He sat with finger tips touching. 'Now we shall see what we shall see,' he murmured profoundly.

Meredith felt curiously elated as he walked along the dark lane. In an undefined way he felt a sense of freedom. He was away from restrictions. His stride lengthened.

The Falcon, a reproduction coaching inn, loomed before him, its array of lighted windows exciting. A wave of sound, a conglomeration of voices with a background of music, met him as somebody opened a door, throwing a wedge of bright light along the ground. He reached the door, and excitement drained from him. His heart started to pound, and weakness attacked his knees. These would be strange people he would meet, not the people of the hospital who would understand. He did not want to meet strangers.

He caught a glimpse of the room through a window. A group of men stood watching a dartboard, waiting for an unseen player to throw. A woman laughed, a high but musical laugh; heads turned to her in irritation, then back to the dart-board. She shouldn't have laughed; darts is a serious game—his mind slipped back to another country pub, visited during one of his short leaves. The farmer, The Boss, had agreed to keep an eye on the kids, and with Her he had gone to the local. There they had become involved in a light-hearted game of darts with an Air Force officer and his wife. That she had known less than nothing of the finer arts of the game had instantly become obvious; her first dart had gone completely off the board. 'Keep 'em in the perishin' diocese,' the flying man had commented and She had laughed.

And now She. . . . It came flooding back, like a sudden tidal wave demolishing all before it, and Meredith swung away from the inn with a semi-articulate sound which ended in almost a groan.

With purposeful strides he hurried back to the gate. The petty officer studied him keenly as he opened the gates. Without speaking, Meredith strode past him, towards the place where people understood, where they knew how to take the load off when it became too heavy.

The petty officer pressed the button again.

'Coming in now, sir. Didn't say anything. Just went straight through. I believe he broke into a run when he got up to the drive.'

Maldon frowned as he replaced the instrument and looked at his watch. "I'll give him ten minutes." Later he knocked on Meredith's bedroom door, after a swift scrutiny of the ward-room. The room was in darkness except for the reflection from the floodlights outside.

Meredith was lying on the bed, face down.

Maldon stood by the window, a black shape against the diffused light, listening before turning to say, 'Hard sledding, eh, Meredith? Maybe we hurried things too much.'

Meredith just rolled his head on the pillow, trying to get deeper down into it.

'By and by you can tell me whether it was you, or something outside. But not now, not now.' He moved over from the window and let his hand rest lightly on Meredith's shoulder. 'You'll have to face up to it, you know.' It was so soft that Meredith scarcely heard it. 'We'll try again, later. In the meantime, in ten minutes you will get up and go to the wardroom. THAT IS AN ORDER.' The last words came with a jarring rasp totally different from the earlier almost caressing tone. 'TEN MINUTES. IS THAT CLEAR?'

'You go to hell! Go to hell! Do you hear?'

But Meredith was speaking to an empty room. A few minutes later he climbed wearily to his feet, switched on the light and straightened his hair.

The three or four occupants of the wardroom did not look up when he entered and picked up a magazine, aimlessly turned over the leaves for some time, then found a sick-berth attendant at his elbow.

'Commander Maldon's compliments, sir, and could he see you for a few minutes?'

Meredith's lips twisted into a snarl but he followed the youngster. As they reached the corridor turning into the administrative block the sick-berth attendant checked him. 'Not there, sir. In the ante-room.'

Maldon met him as he entered.

The ante-room, strangely, startlingly different from the remainder of the coldly efficient wards and rooms, seemed to have a warmness. It glowed softly with indirect lighting and was splendidly furnished with a wealth of easy chairs. A round dozen people, men and women, were there. 'Meredith, you are a small-ship man and we want your help. Langley has just been appointed to a destroyer and wants to know what it will be like.'

Meredith found himself facing a fresh-faced youngster wearing the two rings, red-piped, of a surgeon-lieutenant.

'Langley, Lieutenant-Commander Meredith.' As they shook hands Meredith saw the youngster eyeing the array of ribbons on his chest and somehow it had given him a feeling of superiority. His resentment shrank.

A small glass was thrust into his hands—a whisky.

'Good for the hair on the chest, old man.'

'Now, about doctors on small ships. Tell him the worst.'

'We never had doctors on minesweepers and corvettes. We used to——'

'What happened if a man fell ill?'

The voice startled Meredith. It came from a woman who, he could see vaguely, was wearing something fluffy which nestled close to the gentle curve of her neck. He sensed that she was softly feminine. It was Sister Payne.

Meredith managed a grin. 'When a man fell sick we stood him up. If he stayed up he was all right. If he fell down we gave him a pill—and hoped.'

'Fundamentally sound, too,' Maldon chuckled. 'But Langley is alleged to be a doctor. What will his job be?'

'Wine accounts, a bit of decoding and re-coding, making a four at bridge, and when in harbour arranging for a supply of lady visitors.'

'He'll be good at that!'

Langley protested but Maldon met him with the retort, 'It will be an order. How can you expect men to trust you with their appendix if you can't do a simple thing like find the lady?'

Meredith looked into the young man's slightly troubled eyes. He realized that the surgeon-lieutenant was finding it difficult to separate leg-pulling from the serious matters which worried him.

'I shall be horribly sea-sick, and completely useless,' the youngster said.

'You should have joined the Air Force, or the Army.' Maldon pursued him mercilessly. 'What made you pick on the dark blue uniform, anyway? Some idea of it suiting your particular brand of beauty?'

The surgeon-lieutenant drew on his cigarette before replying. 'Maybe it was because I had an elder brother in the Service. I don't know exactly. Maybe it was because somebody told me that the Navy was short of doctors.'

'What is your brother?' Meredith asked.

'He was in the submarines.'

'And now?'

The young surgeon-lieutenant studied the glowing end of his cigarette.

'He commanded a submarine trying to get to Malta in 1942. That's all we know.'

It was Meredith who broke the silence which followed.

'If ever you are given the choice, pick a small ship. That is where you will find the real companionship, where you will feel close to your fellow-men. Big ships are too detached, too many people, but in a small wardroom you soon know everything about the other fellow.'

'And knowing all about him will be a great help.' Maldon was leaning against the table with his legs crossed and a quizzical look on his face. 'A great help indeed.'

Sister Payne crossed to Meredith and took his empty glass. 'I am only a guest here, like you,' she said, 'but I think getting another drink will be in order.'

Meredith accepted the charged glass from her and allowed himself a long, appraising look as she crossed the room. She no longer carried the air of cool authority. He saw that her hair was tawny, with gold highlights; a long, slender neck held her head superbly poised so that her chin was just slightly tilted. Her eyes were blue, a deep blue, and when her face was in shadow they seemed almost violet. The fluffy lamb's-wool jumper she wore seemed to emphasize the ivory tinge of her skin and clung closely to her figure. To Meredith she seemed unexpectedly warm and human. Was this the woman who could give orders like cracking a whip, who could be so cold and impersonal?

'This is a bit of a birthday party. It is Surgeon-Commander Maldon's birthday and we are letting our back hair down.'

'I didn't know his type were born—I thought they were—were——' He waved his hand as he sought for the right word.

'Rough-hewn? Will that help?'

' "Quarried" is the word I was struggling for, but "rough-hewn" does very well.'

'He has his softer moments, his gentler side.'

'So I see.'

'We all have, I think.'

'Have you?'

'What do you think?'

'Probably in spots, little spots far apart.'

She let her head go back in a laugh which stayed in the contralto range, and the curve of her throat made Meredith catch his breath.

'I must remember that one. I know somebody who will appreciate that.'

'Your husband?' Meredith looked at the thin, plain gold band on her finger.

'No.' She clipped it.

Maldon crossed the room in easy strides. 'I'm going back to the patients' wardroom for a few minutes. Care to come with me, Meredith?'

Meredith recognized that for him the party was over. He tossed back the remains of his drink, squared his shoulders and inclined his head.

'After you, sir. And thanks for the party.'

He turned to Sister Payne. 'Maybe the spots are closer together than I thought.'

She pouted out her bottom lip and her mouth twitched.

'I'll have to look, won't I?'

Maldon looked from one to the other interestedly.

'If you two have started a preliminary anatomical discussion, a preliminary to Topic A, I'll wait.'

'It was nothing of the sort. And your patients wait,' she said primly. 'So do your guests.'

'Let 'em all wait. Good for their souls, and yours.'

Meredith followed him from the room, stalking along the corridor, Maldon silent until they reached the wardroom door. Before Maldon could open it Meredith stopped.

'Was that invitation part of the order, too?'

Maldon halted with his hand on the door. 'Sometimes it's a good thing to see people other than doctors and nurses and patients.'

'Weren't they doctors and nurses?'

113

'No. Just people.'

'And I wasn't a patient?'

'No. Just a man. Just a naval officer.'

Meredith put his hand on the door.

'How did you start in this game? As a small boy with flies on the end of a pin?'

He pushed the door violently and went in past Maldon, holding the door for the other to follow. Maldon stood in the doorway, looking round the room in which half a dozen men were lounging in chairs, a couple engaged in a game of chess, two or three dozing.

'Aren't you coming in?'

Maldon shook his head.

Meredith stepped back into the corridor and allowed the door to close behind him.

'I'd give a lot to know how in hell you knew I had come back to the hospital, or, for that matter, how you knew I had gone out.'

He stood in front of Maldon with his legs apart, shoulders hunched, hands hanging loosely, the epitome of pugnacity.

'I knew. It's part of my job to know. I can hazard a guess what made you decide to go. I'll hazard another guess what made you come back.' He tapped Meredith on the chest. 'People, just ordinary people. The world is full of them, Meredith, and you'll meet them.'

They heard footsteps coming along the corridor and neither spoke as a lieutenant hove into view, paused when he saw Maldon, then walked on more carefully. But his care was not sufficient to prevent a musical clink coming from the beer bottles he had in his raincoat pocket.

'Good evening, sir. The locals caned the pants off us. But the boys are having a good time.'

'Glad to hear it. Why are you back so early?'

The lieutenant licked his lips.

'Oh, a—a—couple of letters to write and things like that.

'Give her my love. And tell her you'll be out of here in a week or so.'

'I will, sir. But she'll have her time full coping with my love.'

'Good!'

The lieutenant passed them, carefully keeping his sagging raincoat from touching the doorway.

'Good night, sir.'

'Good night.'

The door closed and Maldon looked airily up at the ceiling.

'I would say a round half-dozen bottles. All against the rules, of course.'

'And you live by rules.'

'I must have them—to break them.'

Meredith bumped the door open with his back.

'Good night.'

'Good night, Meredith. I'll see you at twelve o'clock to-morrow.'

'Yes, sir.'

The door closed behind Meredith as he stepped into the room.

'Clever bastard,' he said.

The lieutenant grinned. 'Accepted. I don't think he spotted them. Works out about six bottles between ten of us. Who's got the bottle opener?'

Before anybody could answer the door opened again and Maldon looked round it.

The lieutenant swiftly stepped in front of the table to hide the illicit bottles.

'One thing, chaps,' Maldon said. 'Don't dump the bottles outside the window in the bushes. It gives the ward a bad name, and makes Sister Payne furious. Be decent people.' He laid slight emphasis on the last word, a significance which did not escape Meredith.

When the door closed again the lieutenant blew sharply.

'I see what you mean. But they weren't showing, were they?'

'Things don't have to be showing for him to see them. Count me out. I've had a couple of hefty whiskies.'

'Whiskies? Where did you get Scotch? Only beer and cider at The Falcon. And I didn't see you there. Where have you been boozing?'

'With some people.' And he, too, emphasized the last word.

Maldon re-entered the ante-room with a thoughtful look on his face. Sister Payne turned to him.

'This is your birthday party, you know.'

'Yes, isn't it lovely? A Scotch, I think.'

'Patients all right?'

'Tell you tomorrow. And stop talking shop.'

' "Tomorrow, and tomorrow, and tomorrow," ' she quoted.

'Shakespeare was a darned good psychologist.'

She accepted a light for her cigarette.

'There are times when my feelings towards you undergo a remarkable change. It's a purely temporary change at this moment.'

'Good heavens, you are not starting to flirt with me?'

'I wouldn't dare. You would break it down to a cold analysis, and would give me a written report, in triplicate, by mid-day tomorrow.'

'And I would be dead right.'

'You are always so darned right.'

'I wonder, sometimes.'

'Hullo, a crack in the fabric! Don't tell me the Great One has made a mistake.'

'Mistake being failure?'

'Almost inevitably.'

He tossed back his drink. 'I'll tell you something after mid-day tomorrow.'

'So soon?'

'So soon. And WILL you stop talking shop?'

'Happy birthday to you——' she sang softly.

'It would make it a happy birthday, I assure you.'

'Who's talking shop now? Get your guest a drink.'

'Certainly.'

With a warm light in her eyes she watched him walk to the table.

Meredith looked at his watch, checked it by the electric clock on the wall behind him, and wondered if he had time for a cigarette before Maldon sent for him. He heard a faint buzz from the house phone outside the wardroom door and a little later a nurse poked her head round the door, saw him and smiled.

Meredith met her. 'I know—I've been waiting for it. Thank you. Surgeon-Commander Maldon, isn't it?'

'Yes.'

'Right! I know my way to the torture chamber.' He raised his hand in gladiatorial salute. 'Hail, and farewell. We who are about to die, salute.'

'Go on, you're not going to die,' the literal-minded young miss replied. 'You'd better hurry. He sounded a bit uppish.'

Meredith tapped on the door and entered.

'Sit down, Meredith; this is going to be a long session.'

Maldon was wearing the white coat he always donned for his morning tour of the wards. From that Meredith deduced that it was to be a formal inquisition.

Maldon studied a blue folder holding a file of papers, then closed it, threw it to the side of his table and leaned back.

'That's you,' he said crisply. 'And on all there is in that,' he tapped the folder, 'I could quite confidently say to higher authority, "This man is now fit to be discharged", and with equal confidence they could reply, "Discharge him". And you would go out into the world with a bowler hat, a gent's natty suiting and—what?'

Meredith stared steadily at him without replying.

Maldon picked up his house phone from the hook, laid it on the desk and walked over to the door to click the lock.

'That disposes of any interruptions,' he said as he resumed his seat. 'I asked you "and what"?'

Meredith found himself breathing heavily through his nose, felt his lips purse tightly. He wanted to take the folder and throw it in Maldon's face, tell him to go to the devil; felt he wanted to stand up and shout, "I'll fight my own battles. Send me out of here. I'll get by. I always have."

'Somewhere in that,' he nodded at the folder, 'there is a dotted line. Sign on it. I can be out of here by this afternoon.'

'Out to where? To what?'

'What in hell has that to do with you? Sign it, and be damned. I'm not a child, a baby. I've bucked this world for nearly thirty years, and on my own. I'll do it again.'

'You've been afraid of this world for twenty of those thirty years, and you've been putting on an act for the other ten.'

Maldon said it evenly, without emphasis, so smoothly that Meredith missed its impact.

Maldon continued. 'And now you haven't any audience. Look, Meredith, I don't want to confuse the issue. I am not suggesting that you are, or have been, a coward. In fact, you have suffered from a surfeit of courage. You have done things, and driven yourself beyond the reasonable demands of duty— that's more-or-less the official phrasing, isn't it?—to convince yourself that you are not lacking in guts. That's the physical side of it. Were it that, and that alone, I would sign on the dotted line, as you call it, let you get out of here this afternoon and dislocate my arm patting myself on the back saying, "Well done, thou good and faithful chump". No, no! It's more complicated than that.'

'Stop talking in riddles. What are you getting at?'

'I'll abridge. When you were found at Paddington you were going somewhere. Where were you going?'

Meredith rested his elbows on the arms of the chair, joined his hands and allowed his chin to prop on them. Where had he been going? The room, Maldon, and all that had immediately gone before slipped away. He felt the overwhelming loneliness, the almost physical pain, that came with the knowledge that there was nowhere for him to go, nobody to whom he could go.

They were not there, would never be there unless he met them in some mysterious hereafter.

His head dropped until his hands supported his forehead.

'Exactly! You see, Meredith, I know a whole lot more than you think I know. When I started you off on that long sleep I got beyond that barrier you had erected—trespassed, if you like —and we talked. In fact, I know a lot about you that you don't really know yourself. At least, I think I do. And I know where you were going. Again, at least I think I do.'

Maldon sat with his finger tips together, watching Meredith over them as if he had him in the sights of a rifle. He paused and waited until Meredith lifted his head, and their eyes met.

'But for that engine at Paddington you would have journeyed through the night, you would have gone down to the sea, or to the cliff tops, and——' Maldon paused with his finger-tips itemizing his points as he made them. 'And what?'

Meredith looked past Maldon's shoulder and waited so long before replying that Maldon was about to repeat his question when he saw the beginning of a smile appear on Meredith's lips.

'I would have found them. I would have found Her.' It came in a whisper. 'I could always find Her in the dark of the night at sea. We met on the cliff tops. We did our courting there; she used to sit on them and watch for my ship to go past before the war, when I was on a regular coasting run. Before the kids were born we used to go out there and sit. "Letting them know about the *out*" is what we used to call it.'

Maldon watched him through narrowed eyes, still sighting him over his finger tips.

'She would have made a good sailor; She knew and under-stood the sea. A long way down I was afraid of it. I still am. There is something dark and mysterious about it that——'

'I understand.'

'Then, when I heard that they were—were—that She was—a part of me seemed to go away. I felt empty, hollow. When people left me alone I could get them back. Could talk to them, hear them laugh. On the bridge at night was the best time, unless somebody wanted something, or something happened. It got harder and harder to get them back because there was always something interrupting. Then a Jap sub hit us. Maybe if I hadn't been trying to get them—I don't know—but men died because my mind wasn't on the job. I wasn't keeping the ship right up to scratch. From then onwards there were so many things. I couldn't reach them. She never came close. I could never get any time alone. There were always people—people around me talking—always talking—interrupting.'

Meredith's head went down again between his hands.

'Go on.' Maldon's voice was sharp.

Meredith shrugged.

'I hadn't been afraid, not really, since I was a youngster. I had more-or-less got it under. I used to put on a tough act, chin out, bring-on-the-world-and-I'll-lick-it, and all the time I was scared to be in a bedroom by myself. I don't know what I was scared of, because I could—and have—got up and gone all round the house in the dark, looking in every room. Sometimes I would get the feeling on a ship; there would be something, and I would search the ship from one end to the other, or climb to the top bridge and battle it out—with Her.'

Maldon stirred. 'And where were you going when the engine stopped your journey?'

Meredith shook his head wearily. He wanted no more of this. He wanted to answer no further questions from the man opposite. He wanted to get out, to be alone.

'Does it matter?' Meredith stood up.

'Sit down. I'll decide when this interview is to end. Not you.'

The sheer command in the voice made Meredith seat himself again and, strangely, from it he felt comfort; somewhere there was something to lean upon for a while.

'And where were you going?'

'I've told you.' The feeling of comfort evaporated and resentment took its place.

'And what were you going to do when you got there? You would have found yourself on some gale-swept cliff tops, at night, in a remote part of Wales, in mid-winter, Christmas Day, to be exact. And then?'

Meredith shook his head like an animal pestered by flies. 'I somehow felt that I would find Her again. Together we would——'

Maldon stood up and walked over to the window. 'And a jury would have decided that you had done it while of unsound mind.'

The other man sat upright with a jerk. 'Then the members of that jury would have qualified for a punch on the nose,' he snapped, his chin sticking out.

Maldon appeared to be interested in something outside and craned his neck.

'Coroners' juries don't sit on people who can punch noses.'

Meredith's eyes opened wide as the import of this struck him.

'You mean?'

'What any normal man would think. That you had committed suicide.'

Meredith held his breath for a time. 'Unsound mind. Is that what you think? Is that why I am here? Is that why there are bars on the windows? Is that why there were no cords to my pyjamas or dressing-gown? No knife with my meals? Is that why the S.B.A. followed me? Is that why?'

'No.' It clipped across Meredith's vehemence.

Maldon turned his head until he was looking at Meredith over his shoulder.

'The brain is a funny thing, Meredith. People abuse it, strain it beyond all normal reason, and it comes back for more, given a chance. Just as there are people born with twisted limbs, or have them broken and twisted permanently by accident —or design—so there are people with permanently warped brains, warped by disease, and there is nothing we can do for them except see that they do no harm to themselves, and get the best out of what little life has left for them.' The finger tips again started itemizing. 'Just as there are men—and women— who have been physically wounded in this war who with treatment get well and fit, so there are people whose brains have been wounded, strained beyond their capacity. And it is those people we have here. You are one of them.'

Maldon swung away from the window.

'If I had my way, Meredith, I would make it a penal offence for anybody to use the expressions "round the bend", "in the nut-house", "batchy", "crackers". People who use them would not contemplate for a moment saying "game-leg" or "one-arm" or "scar-face" to people wounded physically. Would you?'

Meredith shook his head.

'Of course you wouldn't. And if you had been wounded

physically you would have looked upon it as an extra decoration. But because. . . .'

Maldon crossed to his table, sat down, pulled the folder towards him, selected a buff form and after scrutinizing it he signed at the bottom. As he blotted it he smiled at Meredith.

'I get a bit hot under the collar on that topic. Understandable, of course. But I have sent men from here as mentally fit as they ever were. Yet when they came here they were in the state that, for want of a better term, years ago they used to call "shell shock", and give them a pension and turn 'em loose. I'm going to add to that list, too,' he wound up significantly. As he closed the folder Meredith looked at it.

'That my death warrant?'

Maldon raised his eyebrows.

'You know—my discharge?'

'Professional secrets remain secrets.' Maldon replaced the telephone on the hook, walked to the door and slipped back the catch.

'Confessional is over.'

'Don't you mean "inquisition"?'

'Please yourself. It's your standpoint. I'm satisfied.'

'Meaning that I'm cured?'

' "Cured" pre-supposes a sickness, and that was never there. It would have been easier had it been.'

'Well, what?'

'Let us say an excellent example of "prevention".'

Maldon leaned back. 'I shall want to see you again in a day or so, Lieutenant-Commander Meredith. Say Friday.'

Meredith paused, started to speak but accepted the formal dismissal.

When the door had closed behind Meredith Maldon sat staring at it.

"Well, I've got you to the end of the plank. Now I've got to get you off and into the sea where you'll sink or swim. It can be a head-first, clean dive, or a God awful belly flopper. But you'll go."

8

HALEY LEANED AGAINST the window with his forehead just touching the wooden sash. Outside the rain lashed the glass and ran down it in quivering sheets, turning it into a multi-coloured screen as it twisted the reflections of the lights. Although he could not see them, the trees threshed in agony as the wind tore through their bare branches. His fingers beat a ceaseless tattoo on the window, a soft, rhythmic tattoo which Marjorie, sitting in a chair near the fire, could scarcely hear. In her lap lay some fine sewing, but her fingers were idle. Although her head was inclined downwards her eyes were on him. She recognized the signs of suppressed irritation and, wise in her ways, waited for him to provide an opening.

Haley swung away from the window, put a cigarette in his mouth and tapped his pockets.

'My lighter is on the sideboard,' she said.

Haley clicked it, applied the thin plume of flame and blew the first contribution of smoke towards the ceiling in a strong column.

'Sometimes, when we were at sea, I used to get a—a—sort of instinctive feeling—a sort of hunch, if you like, that something was wrong. Young Booth used to call it my third eye beginning to blink.' He studied the lengthening stalk of grey ash on his cigarette and silently she pushed an ashtray towards him.

'Thanks, dear.' He rested against the mantelpiece. 'For no reason at all I would alter course, or slow down, or do something, and as sure as the Lord made little apples something would come along which would justify my action.'

'Where was this third eye situated?'

He shrugged. 'It varied. Mostly it—it resided between the shoulder blades. Quite often, of course, it was shut when something was due to happen, but as sure as it was open and blinked —there would be a scuffle of some sort.'

'And is it blinking now?'

Haley moved away from the mantelpiece and sat down in the deep easy chair opposite her.

'It's wide open and staring.'

She waited.

Haley screwed one clenched fist in the other palm. 'A number of little things are splicing up into something big.'

'In relation to what?'

'The house.' He smacked his knee. 'Damn it all, it is six months since we bought it. Allowing for all the delays and frustration which seem to be part of life these days, there should be enough work done on it for us to move into part of it, at least.'

'Have you seen the surveyor or builder today?'

'Both of them, and they are both slick talkers. They deal excuses from the top and bottom of the pack as quickly as a cardsharper. They——'

'But isn't that cheating, dear?'

'Isn't what cheating?'

'Dealing from the bottom of the pack.'

Haley laughed, leaned forward and patted her knee.

'There are times when I am grateful for your literal mind. It is cheating, but the thing is to catch them at it.'

'Do you think the builder and the surveyor are cheating?'

Haley pursed his lips in a soundless whistle.

'The estate agent, the surveyor and the builder are a trio of perishing liars, by implication, at least. Do you remember when we paid the deposit and started making inquiries about builders and things? If you remember, we were assured that there were war damage licences and Council permits for enough work to restore the house to its pre-war condition. In fact, the War Damage Commission surveyor told me that the previous owner had been very smart and had obtained the maximum. He seemed to think that we had made an extremely smart buy. Then the snags started. Remember?'

She nodded.

'I didn't know any builders or surveyors. So when that

smooth merchant in the estate agent's said they had a surveyor attached to the company I took the suggestion at face value and engaged him.'

Marjorie closed her eyes in retrospection. A tongue tip moistened her top lip.

'I've often wondered why the one-armed man who showed us round—what was his name?—Parker—why he screwed up his face when he heard that we had put the house in the hands of that man and the builder.'

'Did he? I didn't notice.' He studied the thin, climbing line of smoke from his cigarette. 'Probably he knew things then which I am just finding out.'

'Such as?'

'Well, at our first get together, we, the builder, surveyor and estate agent, there were introductions all round. The builder and surveyor shook hands and acted as if they had never met before. The surveyor told me afterwards that he would make a few inquiries about the builder and if all was well he would give him the job. I got tired of telephoning today and went to see the builder personally. His office and yard are right alongside the estate agent's, and the surveyor has a room immediately above. Nothing wrong in that, of course, but why pretend to be strangers? I got very little joy out of the builder. The same story. He has the permits for this and the permits for that, but there is no material. As an afterthought he thinks he can get some second-hand stuff, implying that it will be from the Black Market and that he will have to pay heavily for it. Then he hints that the surveyor will have to do some wangling to meet the extra cost—or I could meet it personally.'

She sat upright. 'But we've seen all the permits and licences for new stuff.'

'And he blandly says it is not available. And I can't prove otherwise.'

'So he could make the job run on for a year or more by that method.'

'He could try.' Haley's mouth set into a grim line. 'But he is going to have a shock. I have sent him a formal letter saying that as his promised date of completion is now well past I want one part of the house ready for occupation in three weeks—and no alibis. So now, my dear, we move in, whatever the state, in three weeks.'

'Will any part of it be ready then?'

'The surveyor confidently said so today, so I nailed him down to that date and made it an ultimatum.'

'But, dear, there's gas, and light and——'

'I've arranged all that. The gas, light and all that, as you call it, is being put on this week. You see, dear, I saw the house a few days ago, dropped in without warning, and there is only plastering and painting to be done on the first floor. The men working there said they could finish it in a week. One of them said an odd thing. He said they could finish the house in a fortnight from their point of view, if they were allowed to. When I pressed him one of his mates stuck an oar in and said, "Keep your trap shut, chum", and keep it shut from then he did. But, basing it on their estimate, I bearded the surveyor and nailed him down to a date. So in we move.'

Marjorie carefully put down her sewing, stood up, struck a dramatic attitude and thrust out her hand.

'Into battle. I'm with you.'

He ruffled her hair then allowed his hand to run down over her shoulder and round her waist.

'That's what I thought. They don't know what they are tackling when they tackle us Fighting Haleys, do they?'

'Up the Fighting Haleys! One for all and all for one.'

'Including His Nibs.' He jerked a head towards the bedroom where the boy was sleeping.

She moved closer into his arm round her. 'I think it is all for him, don't you, darling?'

'Nearly all.' The other arm went round her to complete the circle. His lips were close to her hair as he whispered, 'There are odd bits for somebody else.' His clasp tightened. 'This was the sort of thing we used to think about, quite a lot.'

'What, darling?'

'Coming home, for keeps, for always.'

'Me, too,' came from the region of his shoulder. 'Me, too, all the time.'

Then started a period in their lives which at one point came near to turning him into a stark, elemental being with homicidal intentions, and turned her into a wasp-tongued virago from which her only refuge was tears behind a locked door.

It was a period about which, after time had mellowed the sharp, jagged edges, and healed the wounds, Haley would refer to as the period of man's inhumanity to man. Yet through it there came occasional flashes of kindness and helpfulness from most unexpected quarters, fragments of light in an almost overwhelming darkness, glimpses of warm humanity when they were on the point of admitting defeat and going away from it all.

A week before they were scheduled to move into part of the house Marjorie went along to it to measure up some windows for curtain material. The rooms they intended to occupy immediately were bare, but were clean. They smelled of new plaster, fresh paint, and the floors were swept clean, if not scrubbed.

As she measured and jotted down figures she hummed quietly to herself and occasionally broke into the verses of a song.

'Two-and-a-half yards down . . . bit more to be on the safe side . . . "Sally, Sally, pride of our alley" . . . hm . . . hm . . . hm . . . hm . . . hm . . . that's six yards altogether . . . ". . . more than the whole world to me". . . . I'll want all of twelve yards . . . glory be, I'll have to scrounge some coupons . . . musn't tell Bill. . . . "Sally . . . Sally . . . hm . . . hm . . . our alley". Now that will do for that window.'

She heard footsteps on the bare stairs. She took little notice because she knew that men were working in the lower part of the house.

A knuckle rapped the door.

'Are you there, missus? There's some blokes down below with a gas cooker. Want to know where to put it.'

'Oh, I'll come down. It had better go in the kitchen, hadn't it?'

The man, a painter, pushed his cap to the back of his head with a thumb.

'Up to you, missus. The kitchen's still bein' done. Still a bit of plasterin' and paintin' to be done there.'

Their feet clattered on the bare stairs.

Two men, in washed-out, faded dungarees stood in the hall with a gas cooker between them.

'This way, please.' She led the way over a tangle of planks and step-ladders to the small, compact kitchen. 'In here. How long will it take to fit it in?'

The older of the two men smiled. 'Half an hour. Then we'll test it, and after that shut the gas off again at the meter until you are ready. It's quite easy, just a turn of a key on the meter.'

The painter, who had followed them in, leaned against the door.

'If it gets splashed with paint don't blame me,' he said morosely. 'We'll be working in here.'

The gasfitter smiled, pulled a few tools from his bag and knelt down. 'You can cover it up, can't you? Or you can wipe the spots off when they are still wet.'

'It ought to wait a week or so until we are through.' The painter sounded dogmatic. 'It wouldn't hurt to wait a week or a couple of weeks for that matter. You ain't moving in right away.'

'We are moving in next week, in five days' time, to be exact,' Marjorie interjected.

'And if you don't have it now it might be a couple or three weeks before we can get round to it. My orders were for today,' the gasfitter said.

'Moving in when?' asked the painter. 'Did you say next week?'

'I did. We are taking the upper part of the house, which seems to be nearly ready, while you get on with the lower part. We arranged that with——'

'Have you seen the guv'nor lately?'

'Do you mean the builder?'

'Yes, or his side-kick, the fella lookin' after things.'

128

'The surveyor?'

'Yes, that's him.'

'I haven't, but my husband has. And it is all arranged. We move in next week.'

Because they appeared to be in the gasfitter's way Marjorie and the painter moved out into the back hall and into the front hall.

'There's no watchman, or anybody looking after this house when we finish at night, missus.'

'I didn't imagine there was. But you lock it up, don't you?'

'Somebody does; depends who's working here. We move around to different jobs. We have a key to the back door.'

'Who has the key to the front door?'

'Don't ask me, missus.'

'But it is kept locked, surely?'

'I suppose so.'

'So getting in wouldn't be easy, would it?'

'Not all that easy.'

'Well, why shouldn't the gas cooker be safe? Nobody could take it out under his coat.'

'Why don't you keep your trap shut and get on with some painting?'

The voice came from a room off the hall and Marjorie and the painter stepped inside the room. A younger man, hat well to the back of his head, wearing a painter's white apron, stood on a plank set between two step-ladders.

'If you slapped on paint half as much as you yap, we'd have finished this job by now.'

'I was telling the lady that——'

'I heard you, and it's none of your business. We've got a price for the job and the sooner we finish it the sooner we can start on another. Now, lash up and stow on the yap and lay on to a brush.'

A twinkle stole into Marjorie's eyes. She had heard phrases like that before.

' "Lash up and stow" and "lay on" sounds like Navy to me,' she said. 'My husband was in the Navy.'

The young man on the ladder carefully laid his brush down on the plank, looked at her thoughtfully and pulled a cigarette from behind his ear. When it was glowing he said. 'Was he? What was he in, ma'am?'

'Minesweepers, all through the war.'

'Sticky job, too. I saw a lot of 'em catch it on the Italian job and off Normandy. I was landing-craft mainly. Destroyers before that. What was he, ma'am?'

'Lieutenant-commander.'

The cigarette glowed two or three times.

'Some officers was all right.' It was a flat statement which seemed to demand no comment.

She harked back to a fragment of the conversation. 'I heard you say you had been given a price for the job. Don't you work for the builder?'

'We're on our own, lady. Me and him,' with a jerk of the head towards the other man who was climbing up to the plank, 'have set up on our own. We want a little business of our own, see? We are both tired of being ordered about. We contract with the big builders for a painting job, we get a price and get cracking.'

'I see.'

'The plasterers, they're on the same lark. You don't get much change out of this builder. He'd skin a flea for its hide. But we got the price.'

Marjorie nodded, wondering where all this was leading her.

'It was better on small ships. Officers and men were sort of closer together. Not like big ships, where you was just a number.'

It was so completely unrelated to the immediate topic that she was left groping.

'I—I—suppose so.' She smiled at the man. 'Some of the men from my husband's ship still write to him with their problems. Some are finding it difficult back in civilian life.'

'A lot of us do, lady. When we was in we wanted to get out. "Roll on, my twelve," we'd say. Now we're out we——'

'Miss the friendship?'

'Something like that. Not many of the blokes were on the

make in the Service. A man had a pal or two and they stuck by him. Ships was chummy ships and would go out of their way to be chummy.'

'My husband's ship had a—a—"chummy ship". They were all very upset when it was blown up.'

'I know. I've seen it happen.'

Marjorie still wondered where this tangent was leading her but she decided to let the painter provide the leads and she would follow.

The older man dipped a brush into a paint pot, then carefully covered a length of the window work on which they were engaged.

'Your husband the dark fella who has bin here with the surveyor, missus?' he asked.

'Could be.'

'Runs his hand through his hair and taps his leg with his fingers like he's playing a piano?'

Marjorie chuckled. 'Practically a portrait. When that happens it means there is a storm in the offing. That's right, isn't it? Offing, I mean.'

The younger man smiled. 'Fair enough, lady.' He climbed down from the plank and stood with one elbow on it. 'Did you see this house six months ago, ma'am, when the work first started?'

'I saw it before the work started. Why?'

'Have you been round all the rooms since, ma'am?'

'Now who should keep his yap shut?' came from the older man on the plank.

'I know what I'm doing. He isn't the only fish in the sea. There are other builders.'

'And they stick together like—like——' He gagged on the simile which instinctively came to him and finished up lamely, '—like glue. Quarrel with one and they pass the word "no jobs for that bloke".'

'And I've got the answer to that. I know enough. . . .' He turned to Marjorie. 'Look, ma'am, take a look at the rooms and see if they are any different to when you first saw them.'

'I—I have.' She thought he was seeking a compliment on their handiwork. 'And they look very nice. At least, the rooms upstairs do.'

He shook his head impatiently. 'I don't mean the painting, ma'am. I KNOW that's good. But look around.'

'He means look at the fittings, missus,' the man on the ladder blurted. 'That is, if they are still there. When we started on this room there was some good electric wall and ceiling fittings. We didn't have to take 'em down to paint and distemper.'

Marjorie breathed in deeply. 'Do you mean . . . ?'

The young man turned to the step-ladder near him and started to climb it.

'My advice, ma'am, is to get your husband and have a good look through the rooms. You'll have an eye-opener. Look at that door for a start.'

She looked blankly at the newly painted door, then back to the painter.

'These old houses had good solid locks on 'em missus. Can't be got now,' the older man said. 'You'll have to fit tin things.'

'But don't you have to take locks and—and things off to paint?'

'Sometimes, ma'am. And when it's necessary we take 'em off, put 'em where we can find 'em and when we've finished we put 'em back.'

'So?'

'They wasn't on when we started. That's what I'm trying to tell you. I don't want anybody asking where they are when we finish the job.' He searched for another cigarette, found one half-smoked in his cap and lit it. 'No more than we want somebody laying the blame on us when we've gone, and us not here to stick up for ourselves.'

'Well, where have they gone? I remember now there were beautiful wall lights and a chandelier in this room, and—I WILL have a look round. Thank you.'

'What I always says is "nothing like leading with your chin". It shows which way a fight is going,' the older man said.

132

'And you got the bleeding nerve to tell ME to keep my yap shut.'

The younger one looked thoughtfully at the doorway through which she had gone.

'It was all right if you had a decent officer to talk to when things was tough. I met one or two.'

'What the hell are you talking about?'

'His blokes write to him now when he's out of the lark. He must have been all right.' He picked up a paint brush and studied it intently.

'This bloody thing is coming apart. Look at it.' He plucked two or three paint-laden hairs from it. 'Now, in the Navy a paint brush was a brush and no arguments. It lasted years, properly used. Only the best was good enough for the Navy.'

'Stone the crows! You spend five years in the Navy, you moan for five years waiting for the time when you could get out, and now you're out they was the best years of your life. For Pete's sake slap some paint on.'

A brush dipped into the paint and covered a few careful strokes.

'And if he's all right, then she's all right and I don't stand to see 'em gipped.'

'Here we go! What are you on about now?'

'You wouldn't understand, cock. You didn't have chummy ships in the Home Guard.'

The reply was advice to attempt a biological and physical impossibility, but provided a terse and satisfactory feeling in the giving thereof.

They worked in silence for a while, then heard the hollow clatter of her feet coming down the stairs. The footsteps paused outside the door of the room in which they were working. They both turned to the almost closed door.

After a while she said flatly, 'I've looked. I see what you mean.' A few more seconds passed, then, 'Thanks—sailor.'

They heard her clatter to the front door, heard it shut with a hollow thud.

The younger man loaded his brush thoughtfully, selected a

target and started working on it with long, carefully made strokes. Gradually the pace of his strokes quickened. He broke into a quiet whistle.

> We've got a Navy, a fighting Navy.
> Our foes all know that's true . . .

He continued his whistling until he reached the last few bars; then he broke into the words:

> '. . . When they know they've got to face
> The lively lot of lads in navy blue.'

The older man studied him covertly from the corners of his eyes.

The other dipped his brush into the paint once more, pursed his lips for a whistle but changed his mind.

'P'raps he'll come down here to talk it over. If he's tapping his legs with his fingers and runs his hands through his hair it ought to be good.'

'How do you know?'

'How do I know? Listen, cock, there's a lot of things naval officers can't do but, believe me, when they wants to they know how to use cuss words. And this one's been in command. She said so.'

He executed a little jig.

'Hey! Whadyer think you're doing? You'll have us off the bleeding plank.'

'If you was in the Navy, cock, and you was painting over the side you'd have a rope and a petty officer watching.'

'What for?'

'Ask yourself.'

'Where would the rope be? And why the petty officer?'

'Round your perishing neck so that if you slip the P.O. could pull it tight and hang you. P.O.s like hanging matloes.'

He broke into an almost soundless whistle again.

The older man shrugged and concentrated on a delicate bit of work on a sash. At last he spoke.

'I been thinking.'

'Did it hurt?'

'Chuck the jokes. Maybe the fittings was pinched a long time ago. Remember, this house has been empty for four or five years.'

The younger painter finished a long hair stroke and surveyed it in silence.

'And the holes where the screws were are fresh. Same as upstairs. No dirt or dust in 'em. Clean, new holes. So is the paint and plaster round 'em.'

After some cogitation the other spoke. 'Well, what do y'know?'

'That's something you learn in the Navy—to keep your bleeding eyes peeled all the time. Gimme a hand to shift this plank.'

Haley's key clicked in the lock. He opened the door, pocketed his key and bumped the panel with his hand.

Bomptiddy bomp bomp—bomp bomp.

'Hey, lady! There's a man in the house.'

Then the ritual departed from custom. A tight-lipped, blazing-eyed face met him.

'We've been robbed.'

Haley stared at her.

'When? What?'

'All the things have been stolen from the house. I went there today and the painter told me to look. So I looked and all the things have been taken——'

'Now, now, easy a moment, old girl. Let me get in and you can tell me all about it.'

She followed him, her head close to his shoulder, a disjointed protest bubbling from her lips.

'. . . then I saw all the locks were gone—and the wash basin from the bedroom—and. . . .'

He stood with his back to the fire and put his hands on her shoulders.

'Now let's have the full story.'

Marjorie took a deep breath.

'I went to the house today to measure some windows for curtains. Sheila looked after Boy for me. I was measuring a window—where I'm going to get the material, I don't know. One window takes six yards. Well, as I was working, the men came with the gas cooker. Then a painter told me to look round the rooms. He was in the Navy. So I looked round the rooms. And everything was gone.'

She stopped and breathed heavily. Before she could go on Haley checked her with an upraised hand.

'Now, easy, old girl. Let's get things in some sort of order.'

'Well, that's what I found. The locks were gone, and all those lovely long shelves from the wardrobe, and the electric fittings and a fireplace——'

He held his hands to his head so that the palms were close against his forehead.

'Pipe down, dear. You race ahead like—like a——'

One hand, palm downwards, checked her. 'I've got it that when you went to the house today, and after information received, as they say, you had a look round. Now, now, steadily, just tell me what you found or what you didn't find.'

Once again she breathed heavily.

'After the painter told me to look round I went in all the rooms. You remember that there were nice wall fittings in some of them? There was a large fitted wardrobe in the biggest bedroom, there were lovely large shelves in that airing cupboard, there was a nice large firegrate in the lounge—or what I was going to make into a lounge—there was a pedestal wash-basin, a beautiful pale green one, in the main bedroom, and there was another in the bathroom.'

'Well?' He rapped it out.

'Now they are all gone. The rooms are bare—nothing in them. They are as bare as—as. . . .'

For a few moments he stared over her shoulder as he visualized all the features she had recalled. He allowed himself a quick survey of the rooms as he had first seen them in the half-light coming through the rents in the torn blackout

136

material and the first-aid boarding the windows. Then a possible explanation came to him and he smiled.

'Has it occurred to you that some of these things would have to be taken down for plastering and painting work to be done?'

'The painter—the young one, the nice one—said "No". He said they were gone before they started work. He was in the Navy. Now he wants to be his own boss, so he and the other one have started up on their own. He said——'

'Slow ahead. Let's have the facts about the house first. I'll hear about the painter and his navy life afterwards. Now, what is missing, and why do you think so?'

'Well, those electric fittings from the lounge are gone. So are the locks from the doors. And after the painter suggested I look round, I found the wash-basins were gone, and the wardrobe, and the shelves.'

Haley listened to the detailed story, his face growing grimmer each minute. Finally, with his bent fingers running through his hair, he exploded.

'I knew it. At least I knew something was off course somewhere. The old third eye. Remember?'

She nodded. 'But what can we do? They'll have to put them back.'

'Who took them?'

A pensive finger reached her lips. 'Of course, we don't really know. I mean, we know, but——'

'We can suspect, but can we prove it?'

'Well, the painter said——'

'All the painter said was that they were missing, and to clear his own yardarm pointed out that they had not moved them. That's only his word, for what it's worth.'

'But he looked so nice and honest.'

Haley's mouth twisted up into something that was nearly a snarl.

'I'm rapidly learning that a lot of things which LOOK honest are nothing of the sort in this brave new world. Well, there's nothing I can do tonight, but tomorrow I'll have a lot to say.'

The next day Haley incautiously committed a cardinal error; a major error, he realized, as he was doing so.

In the morning he telephoned the surveyor and gave him a rough list of things which Marjorie had found missing in the house. When he had completed his list there was silence from the other end of the telephone.

'Are you there?' Haley asked.

'Yes, yes. This is discomfiting news, Mr. Haley. But I must point out that there is an enormous amount of thieving going on from bombed property. After all, we can't keep an eye on all the houses we have in hand all the time. We do our best.'

'Doesn't it strike you as odd that the house was empty for a couple of years or more, yet nothing was taken until the last few months?'

'Well, as you know, Mr. Haley, we have had to remove some of the boarding from the windows, and it is also my experience that activity around a house draws attention to it. And, as the good book says, "thieves break in and steal!"'

'There's a lot of other things in the good book, as you call it.'

'No doubt, no doubt, Mr. Haley.'

'I want you to meet me, with the builder, at the house this afternoon. Possibly he has removed the things I have mentioned to a safe place. Would that be possible?'

'Could be, but—perhaps we had better leave it until this afternoon. I would point out that none of them are irreplaceable. Until this afternoon, then, Mr. Haley.'

Immediately Haley had rung off, the surveyor telephoned the builder.

'This man Haley, the one who has the house in Brisbane Road, has been on the telephone. He has found a number of things missing, wash-basins, electric light fittings, and so on.'

'You don't say?' The builder's voice was vibrant with laughter. 'Maybe it was the rats.'

'Anyway, he wants to see you and me at the house this afternoon.'

'Hm. I was figuring on going to the dogs this after-

138

noon I've had a hot tip about a skin running in the third race at——'

'I think you had better be there. He is one of the quiet type liable to explode. He struck me that way. Possibly a little talk and we could explain that, as I told him, "thieves break in and steal". See what I mean?'

'I see. I'll be there. But they're going to be a bit of a nuisance. He tells me they are going to move in next week. To hell with that for a lark! I've got a client who wants an oak floor. Willing to pay the earth, and he wants a large square bath, with——'

'No, no, it's too late to do anything about the bath. She was there yesterday, and saw it.'

'I could nip along now, find it was leaking and whip it out.'

'We'll get one somewhere else.'

'That's not all that easy. Things are tight, old boy. I'll tell you one thing: you'd better find dry rot or something in that lounge floor, so that we can whip it out smartish—like before they move in. Those are lovely nine-inch oak flooring boards. Take a polish beautifully.'

'God, you're asking something, aren't you? We've got painters in that room today.'

'Now, listen. I've got a suggestion which will meet the case in several ways. They figure on moving in next week. We can delay that for a fortnight, if you listen to me, then I'll be happy. Get there early today. Find things wrong with the plastering and painting in the rooms on the first floor. We can put on a bit of a show and I'll agree in the end that we'll have to do it again. They can't move in if we have the rooms full of paint. That will give me all the time I want. Got it?'

'It won't be easy. I'll——'

'Like falling off a log. You play angry, looking after your client, I'll play sorry and string along, and Bob's your uncle.'

'About the wash-basins and things?'

'Well, we could find something, substitute stuff if they want it—at a price, of course. It's not in the specifications.'

'Rightho! That's the way it will be. I'll meet you at the house about half past two.'

139

'Half past two it is. By the way, my client is very well pleased with the built-in wardrobe and the electric fittings we managed to get for him after a lot of trouble.'

The surveyor listened to the chuckle at the other end.

'He was, eh? Well?'

'There's a fiver for you. It would have been double had we been able to find him an oak floor. Maybe more.'

'I'm inclined to think we have hidden dry rot in that house, you know.'

The chuckle rumbled again.

'I think so, too. Pity if it was overlooked. I've got some old deals we could put there. At a price, of course. Not in the specifications. It would have to be done under the hat. No permit or licence, you see.'

'Yes. Well, half past two.'

'See you then. And don't forget—that's bloody awful plastering and painting on those first-floor rooms. You must look after your client's interests, old man.'

'Never seen worse. It'll have to be done again.'

'Easy now, not all of it. Just enough to mean taking the plant up there again.'

'Leave it to me.'

To Marjorie and Haley came the bitterness of defeat after more than an hour of listening to the suave, slick cross-talk between the builder and the surveyor.

They were waiting for Haley and with almost boisterous goodwill the builder extended his hand.

'This is sad news I hear, Mr. Haley. Tck-tck. The amount of dishonesty about today is shocking. Really shocking.'

The surveyor dutifully fed him lines in the approved cross-talk manner.

'Really is shocking. We try our best, of course, but. . . .'
A shrug and expressive gesture with hands completed his brief survey of the decline and fall of morals.

'Of course,' the builder went on briskly, 'we'll try to do what we can. We'll find some shelves and a cupboard, or something.

And I have my foreman searching the yard for a wash-basin. What it will be like, I don't know.'

Marjorie interjected tersely, 'It will have to be pale green and have a pedestal, because that is what was there.'

The builder's eyebrows arched as he shook his head.

'Couldn't get one like that for a king's ransom, Mrs. Haley. Not for a king's ransom. I doubt if——'

'Somebody has one, now. Did that cost a king's ransom?'

His eyes narrowed and his lower lip came out. 'You are not suggesting, Mrs. Haley, that I have had anything to do with——'

The surveyor cut in. 'I explained to Mr. Haley that it is our experience that when work starts on a house it seems to attract attention to it. It is our experience, also, that thieving starts then.'

Before Haley could reply she said swiftly, 'That is a glimpse of the obvious.'

The builder felt that the dialogue was deviating from its established course.

'Well, I'll tell you what I'll do. I'll get one of my men to keep an eye on the property during the evenings. And I'll promise that where it is humanly possible we will put in some fittings of some sort. I can't say fairer than that. Of course, they are not in the specifications. They were drawn up some months ago. But we can get together on that, can't we, mister?'

'I think so,' the surveyor replied briskly. 'I'll discuss it with Mr. Haley and let you know.'

He smoothed his chin thoughtfully, took a deep breath and said sternly, 'I'm not entirely satisfied with the work done in the upstairs rooms. Some of the plastering and painting is rather rough, you know, even by modern standards. I. . . .'

The builder registered the right amount of concern and professional indignation.

'It seems all right to me. You know we have a devil of a job to get material.'

'Agreed. But in the interests of my client I must point out these things. After all, we don't want to have to complain to you in a couple of months that the work is falling down, or that the paint is flaking off.'

141

The dialogue went smoothly, with the builder pointing out that he was working for next to nothing and the surveyor becoming more insistent that it would have to be touched up, and in parts re-done.

Haley cut in at last. 'These are the rooms we intend to move into in a few days. How long will this—this—extra work take?'

The builder and surveyor exchanged swift glances.

'I estimate five or six days. It must be allowed time to dry, you see, Mr. Haley.'

'I see nothing wrong there. It seems satisfactory to me. And we intend to move in in four days.' Marjorie said stoutly.

The surveyor looked down benignly at her and continued as if there had been no interruption. 'Once you are in and accept the work we cannot in all conscience complain later. For the sake of a few days' delay it would be folly to——'

'There is no question of folly. Our tenancy of the flat finishes in three days. A new tenant moves in when we go out, so we should be left in mid-air.'

The surveyor shook his head sorrowfully and the builder dutifully followed suit.

'I don't see any way round it. You have complained, through your surveyor, of the quality of the work and—under protest, mind—I have accepted the complaint and will do some of the work again. But with you in the rooms. . . .' He shook his head again at contemplation of the magnitude of the problem.

'Well, we'll have to try to solve it somehow. I'll talk it over with Mr. and Mrs. Haley,' the surveyor said briskly. 'There is another thing I want to raise. We might have to stop work in the lounge. I'm inclined to suspect dry rot under that floor. Terrible thing, dry rot, Mrs. Haley. It will go through a house from top to bottom unless it is tackled thoroughly. The brickwork might even be affected.'

The builder contributed his lines.

'Dreadful thing. There's only one thing to do if you find it. Be ruthless, Whip it away. But mind, if you find it, let me know, and I'll treat the brickwork for you. As far as the floors are concerned——' He shrugged. 'Rip it out and burn it. That's the only answer.'

Haley looked from one to the other. Suddenly, out of the blue, he had an idea.

'I quite agree that dry rot is a terrible thing. I've seen it run through a ship. I have a naval friend who is an expert at coping with it. He spent half the war treating wooden ships. I'll get him to come along and——'

The surveyor climbed up on his dignity. 'I think, Mr. Haley, that with my qualifications I can deal with the problem.'

'If it arises,' Haley said blandly.

The other nodded. 'If it arises. I will have a board lifted here and there and——'

'And two experts will be better than one. So when you do it let me know and I'll invite my friend along. He is quite an expert, so don't worry.'

Haley and his wife walked home in thoughtful silence and it was not until they were seated at the fireside that he spoke of what they were both thinking.

'Somewhere along the line we are being sold a nice, large, fat pup, my dear.'

She put it more frankly. 'We are dealing with a couple of smooth sharks, if you ask me. You know, and I know, that they have taken out the fittings, all of them. They intend to get in on the swings and the roundabouts.'

He looked up.

'Quite how?'

'They will put us in a bill for substitute fittings, at black market prices because they are not in our what d'you call 'ems——'

'Specifications.'

'Yes, those things. We buy new fittings. The beautiful ones from our house go to somebody else, also at black market prices.'

Haley breathed deeply.

'And where in the world have you been getting such deplorable ideas? After all——'

She went off at an angle.

'Do you know who is getting this flat when we get out?'

He shook his head.

'The girl from the estate agent's office. She nipped in smartly and got it when we bought the house. Her husband was a commando. She had a cup of tea with me a few weeks ago. From odd hints she dropped I have my doubts.'

'We can't go about making accusations based on hints. I'd be in court and hit for a packet.'

She ignored the warning.

'Then the painters, especially the one who was in the Navy. They said so much, and hinted at more.'

'And some of their work has been condemned and will have to be done again, so that places a low value on their words.'

'Is it so bad? You saw it. So did I.'

He rested his head on his hands. 'I don't know whom to start to believe. I've been used to men who would go out of their way to help, whom one could trust in any way. Any trouble, and they were ready to help. If this is the brave new world——'

'It can be the world we want if we make it the world we want. And we will. You'll see.'

And ultimate victory was hers, but only at the price of tears shed in private.

Four days later, warm with expectation, she arrived at the house to find the furniture van, which was delivering some of their goods which had been in store for years, waiting at the gate.

'Good morning, ma'am.' A grizzled-haired man greeted her.

''Morning. All this is to go up on to the first floor. Then you will pick up the rest at our flat. That right?'

The man leaned against the side of the van.

'Upstairs, you say, ma'am? Have you been up there?'

'Yes, yesterday. It's all ready.'

'Well, we'll have a look again, shall we?'

Marjorie felt every muscle in her body stiffen in blazing rage when she reached the rooms.

Instead of the bare boards which she had swept and cleaned the previous day there were ladders and planks. In the middle

144

of the floor of one room a paper bag of cement had been dumped, had burst open and its contents spread over the boards.

In another room buckets of paint, brushes and planks filled the empty space. On the floor was one window taken out of its frame.

'See what I mean?' the removal man said. 'Can't put stuff in here, ma'am.'

She stormed downstairs, into the lounge in search of the painters and found them in the kitchen standing over the stove making tea.

They listened to her tirade, then the younger one held up a hand.

'It's no use you squawking at us, ma'am. You've complained about the plastering and painting and the gaffer says some of it must be done again. So——'

'Who complained?'

'Well, your bloke did—the surveyor.'

Marjorie came to a sudden decision. 'My husband and I are satisfied with the work as it is. Could you shift that stuff out for me? If not, I'll throw it out myself.'

The younger painter chuckled. 'I'd love to, ma'am. Tell you what,' he picked up a cracked and handleless cup, swilled it under the tap and filled it with tea, 'you have a cup of char and me and my mate will soon clear up that mess for you.'

In an hour's time the expert removal men were juggling with furniture and soon the van was empty. She gave them the keys of the flat for them to collect the remainder of the stuff and while they were gone she shared her precious cigarettes with the painters. After a while she mentioned that the surveyor intended lifting the floor boards of the lounge to search for dry rot.

The younger painter shook his head, but said nothing until she left the room. Outside, she paused in thought and heard him say, 'If there's dry rot here, chum, I'm in the family way.'

The answer made her giggle.

'Could be, but I think it's the way your coat is fastened.'

The surveyor and builder fought a strenuous rearguard action, but so far as they were concerned Haley had the last word.

At a club for ex-officers he met a wartime acquaintance, a surveyor who pulled a lot of scales from his eyes.

'You could go to the War Damage Commission and lay all before them, but in actual fact you have nothing hard. My advice is to fire the builder and surveyor. You'll have to start from scratch again.'

'Can I do that? I thought——'

'Of course you can. You employ them, you can fire them. You will run into snags, you'll have to fight for permits and licences again. But, from what you've told me, in the long run you'll be better off.'

Haley drew thoughtfully on a cigarette.

'Would you take it on?'

'I wasn't working up to that, but I'd be glad to. And if you like, I know a couple of blokes, in a small way of business (one is an ex-serviceman), and they have one quality you want. They are honest.'

And so it was. An enraged builder and ruffled surveyor departed from the scene in a blaze of indignation, leaving Haley and his wife to face-up to months of frustration.

It was Marjorie who had the last word as the builder indignantly walked away.

'What's wrong with us? That's what I'd like to know,' he almost snarled.

'Dry rot,' she said sweetly.

Haley looked peculiarly at her a few moments when they were alone. 'What did that last crack mean?' he asked.

'I'm not sure I know. But it got home. That's enough.'

With the help of his acquaintance and the men he found, one by one the affairs of the house were gradually straightened out.

The day the last brush stroke was made, and the last nail hammered home, Haley asked his surveyor friend to call.

In a little group they stood in the lounge, Marjorie, Haley, the surveyor and the workmen with glasses in their hands.

'This reminds me of a commissioning party,' the surveyor said. Lifting his glass towards her, he added, 'And then all the hard work starts for Number One—that being you, Mrs. Haley.'

146

'Thank you. I'm looking forward to it,' she responded.

One of the workmen, twisting his hat in one hand and firmly holding his glass in the other, cleared his throat.

'My old man was in this building game,' he said, his voice holding a surprisingly broad West Country burr. 'He used to say that if a roof wasna put on with a drink the house wouldna be happy. They always used to tie a branch to the chimney and all hands would have a drink. People don' do that now.'

'We do,' Marjorie said stoutly. 'Here, catch!'

She held out another bottle of beer to the workman.

'I wasna hinting at that, ma'am. I was jus' saying——'

'I know that,' she told him, handing another bottle to the other man. 'But I'm not going to spoil the ship for a ha'porth of tar.'

'Nor the house-warming for a bottle of beer,' the surveyor chuckled. 'I said Number One always got busy from the start, didn't I?'

When the men had gone and they were seated the surveyor said to Haley, 'Taking it all in all, Haley, you have a nice property here. It will not go down in value for a number of years like some of the jerry-built stuff getting sky-high prices at the moment. Any time I can help let me know; I'll be glad to.'

And that was how Haley and his wife felt towards their home. There were snags, heartbreaking setbacks at times, but they gradually began to get the feel of the house.

It was a carol party on Christmas Eve which set out for them, crisply and clearly, what they felt. They were toasting their toes before a roaring fire when they heard the carollers outside. Haley climbed wearily from his chair and put his hand in his pocket. In the past fortnight there had been a dozen or more small groups, sometimes only two or three children, who after half-a-dozen bars of indifferent singing completely out of tune thumped the knocker and kept insistent fingers on the bell push.

'Wait, wait! These are different. Listen—they are really singing.'

147

After two or three carols she moved towards the front door and opened it. The volume of singing increased in power and Marjorie signalled to them to come inside the hall.

'God rest ye merry, gentlemen,
Let nothing you dismay. . . .'

When they had finished she took them inside, eight or nine strong, and gave them lemonade and cakes while Haley dropped some coins in the box held by a sturdy boy well wrapped up in a coat and thick woollen scarf, and who nursed a lantern.

'You've got settled in all right, sir,' a voice said close to Haley's ear.

'Of course it's Parker. You brought us here the first time. I remember.'

'That's right. That was me singing in a death-croak bass at the back. That 'un with the light is my second oldest. This is like old times. We always ended here and sung the last carol in the hall, like we did tonight. Then there was drinks and cakes, like there is tonight. And——'

'I didn't know that,' Marjorie said delightedly, 'but somehow I felt it was the thing to do. It looked like—like—well, like an old Christmas card with you all there singing, and the lantern—and everything.'

'That's the house, ma'am. I told you it was always a warm and friendly house.'

Later they stood together watching the dying embers of the fire.

'I feel it is a warm and friendly house, too, don't you?' She whispered it close to his ear.

'Something like that. Maybe one has to get friends the hard way. . . .' His eyes bored into the dull glow of the fire. 'And lose them, too, sometimes.'

She recognized the moment.

'No, you don't. Not this night,' she thought. 'If I leave you to it you'll sit staring into that fire until it's black, then lie awake half the night.'

She linked her arm in his.

'You look a bit clean-shaven for the job but you've a stocking to fill. Come on, Santa Claus—lash up and stow.'

He grinned.

'You talk like a "hostility only" seaman. One with the Seven Seas creases in his pants and——'

'Impossible in my case, at any rate. Now, you hold the pillow slip and I'll put them in——'

'Pillow slip? I thought we used a stocking.'

She held aloft a large cardboard box.

'Could you get this into a stocking?'

'N-n-no. Not one of yours, anyway. Pop it in. I'll bet you ten bob that he wakes up around four o'clock and we get no sleep afterwards.'

'No takers. Hold it open.'

And it came to pass that at four o'clock in the morning they were awakened, and it was a friendly house, a warm house, a house full of the sound of laughter.

9

MEREDITH RETURNED to his room one morning after his constitutional walk in the grounds to find a large canvas hold-all grip on the floor near his bed. It came as a mild shock. He knew it was his (he had bought it from an American officer out East), but he had not seen it since he had been in hospital. Slowly he lifted it to the bed and opened it. Underclothes, a couple of books, half a carton of cigarettes, a couple of suits of pyjamas and a large, worn leather folding photograph frame were spread out on the bed.

His fingers gripped hard on the photograph frame and he opened it. On one side was a half-length photo of his wife, three-quarter face. She was not smiling when she had had it taken, yet there was a suspicion of a quirk at the corners of her mouth. Many times he had looked at it and wondered if there really was the beginning of a smile in the photograph or whether it was because he knew the way she smiled. It always started with a momentary twitch of her mouth, which disappeared to reappear again and spread up to her eyes.

Meredith gulped hard against the lump in his throat.

In the other half of the leather frame his daughters smiled out at him. One of them was holding a puppy in a most inelegant position and it seemed as if they were peering out, faces wreathed in radiant smiles, just waiting for a word from him to turn the smiles into trilling laughter.

He shut the folding frame with a snap, then dropped it into the hold-all.

He turned at a light but brisk double tattoo on the door.

'I brought your case up from store,' the sick-berth attendant said. 'Nurse says you have some laundry to come this afternoon. Are you going out, sir?'

'Thanks. I expect so.'

'You're looking fit now, sir. Full of beans.'

Meredith frowned at the chatter.

'Oh, and Sister Payne says that Commander Maldon would like to see you at twelve hundred in his cabin.'

'Thanks. I'll see him.'

'Anything else you want, sir?'

'No. And now I want to write some letters.'

'Very good, sir.'

Meredith sat at his table with a writing pad before him and the pen rolling idly in his fingers.

Who was there to write to? His officers? An enforced intimacy inevitable on a small ship, and a basic liking, had given the companionship the appearance of a profound friendship with some of them, but parting and absence had allowed them to evaporate until nothing remained but a pleasant recollection. Haley? They had exchanged occasional letters when something of mutual interest had happened, but the letters had been few and far between. There had been others, too, but not one of them expected a letter, or would have felt a sense of neglect or resentment if they never received one.

Meredith dropped the pen on the pad and leaned back to look out of the window. Gradually he became aware of the view outside. He had seen it many times without accepting it consciously. It had been there as part of the surroundings. He followed the contour of the fields and the hedges, and a fragment of something came back to him.

' "A rich, warm red . . . there is a path that goes over the hill . . . everything looks dead now, but. . . ." '

It had been several weeks before he had seen the view from the window as Sister Payne had described it to him, and when he saw it now everything still looked brown, dead, withered, except for the furrows on the field.

He had watched the first sheen of green begin to touch the red, had watched it completely cover the ground; he had watched the first tentative buds push out timid tips on the branches, had seen them, emboldened and full of fresh young life, colour the dark edges.

And it was spring.

Meredith stood before the window absorbing it all.

What was that thing, that song the sub used to play on his gramophone until we were ready to break the record? That had something about spring in it.

His mind slipped back to an oppressively hot wardroom. Although there was no fire in the black enamelled stove the officers were grouped round it, seated either on the padded wooden rail or in chairs with their feet resting on the rail. Number One was idly flipping over the pages of a months-old illustrated paper. The warrant engineer sat bolt upright, staring into space, hands on knees, a glisten of perspiration shining on his forehead. Each held a glass in which ice fought a losing battle in an effort to cool the drink. Then the sub-lieutenant had started his portable gramophone going again.

It came back to Meredith as, in his mind, he lived again in the wardroom.

We'll gather lilac in the spring again.

He could hear the faint tinkle of the music and the light voice singing the words as it had sung them many, many times.

He remembered the argument which McIntyre, the navigating officer, had provoked.

'Lilac doesn't bloom in the spring,' he had claimed dogmatically.

'When does it bloom, then? Christmas?' Chief had chipped in aggressively.

'Spring is from the end of February to the middle of April, by my reckoning, and I've never seen lilac in February, March or April,' McIntyre argued.

'Not in Scotland, maybe. You're still under feet of ice and snow there up to August Bank Holiday,' Chief had jeered.

Meredith had smiled. He knew there was no deep-rooted antagonism between these two redoubtable debaters, they invariably took opposite sides just to keep the arguments lively. He doubted if either of them were certain of their facts half the time.

'Snow and ice be damned! Did you know that we can grow, on the west coast of Scotland, sub-tropical plants which can grow in Cornwall and nowhere else in the British Isles?'

We'll gather lilac in the spring again . . .
And walk together down an English lane

The record ground on to the end.

'Put it on again, Sub. We haven't heard that one before,' McIntyre had shouted derisively.

It was the midshipman who had brought the argument to a close, the youngster whose home-sickness was never more than skin deep, the youngster Meredith knew was the only son of a widowed mother and whose life had been filled with softness and kindness and love until he had gone away to war.

'We have a lilac tree in our garden. It's a white lilac. My mother—we always watched for the first snowdrops, then the daffodils. I used to cut a bunch of white lilac for her birthday. She liked that.'

Number One had watched the youngster from beneath lowered lids, had caught Meredith's eye and shrugged slightly.

'And what date was that?' Chief jumped in regardless.

'May—May the sixth.'

'You see?' McIntyre had started triumphantly, 'May is the beginning of——'

Meredith had glanced at the wall calendar.

'That's tomorrow, laddie.'

'Yes, sir. I've—I've fixed things.'

Number One had sat up.

'The way the Americans are belting along, slugging the Japs, you'll be home to cut a big bunch of lilac for her next year.'

'Yes, sir.'

The youngster had walked from the wardroom and soon, softened by a closed door, they had heard the record once more.

McIntyre had clicked his teeth.

'Sub in love with a Wren in England, and Snottie dreaming of cutting lilac—they'll wear that record out between them.'

To the chief engineer had gone the honours of the battle.

'I knew a Scottish C.P.O. once. He was given a gramophone and some records and used to play Harry Lauder to us until we were ready to slay him. Then we stopped it,' he said reflectively.

'How?'

'We threw his one needle overboard and he was too mean to buy another.'

McIntyre chuckled.

'You win, plumber. What'll it be?' He rested his finger on the bell push.

'As it's you, a large pink gin.'

Meredith rubbed his hand on his chin. Soon it would be May and perhaps there would be white lilac in a garden in Devon, but a lone woman would have to gather it herself, would have to walk alone down a lane, alone with her grief.

The Jap submarine had seen to that.

Meredith looked at his wrist watch. A couple of minutes to go.

From the moment he had seen Maldon sign the form in his folder he had been torn between two opposite emotions. On the one hand, he had felt a curious kind of elation because he was more or less officially considered fit and well. On the other hand, he felt a growing feeling of apprehension which he found difficult to pin down, to analyse.

'Come in, Meredith. I won't be a moment. Take a seat.'

Maldon busied himself with some papers and as he did so Meredith studied him. Suddenly he realized that Maldon was a man much older than he had at first imagined him to be. As the surgeon read the papers in the folder, and occasionally initialled them, his face was set in firm, almost hard, lines. Round the eyes were deep wrinkles which deepened, or almost disappeared, as points in the reports appealed to the surgeon-commander.

'Well, that's that. Another gin-pickled lad thrust out into a cold, hard world. Twenty-four, married, blown up twice, and tried substituting juniper juice for dwindling courage. He's going home as fit as a fiddle. Inside a year he should be inviting me to be a godfather. He won't, of course. He'll only vaguely remember me as the man who curbed his ambitious ulcers.'

Maldon closed the folder and thrust it to one side. He fumbled in his pocket and Meredith forestalled him by extending his cigarette case.

'Thanks, I will. When a patient of mine offers me a cigarette without almost shameless prompting I feel he is on the threshold of complete recovery.' The lines near his eyes deepened as he smiled. 'Now, Meredith, down to brass tacks. Will you have anything in mind when you go out?'

Meredith chuckled. 'Sounds like the classic question a prison governor asks when seeing a long-term old lag on his last day.'

'The principles are the same. The old lag has done time for busting a safe. My old lags had done time for busting themselves.' Maldon contemplated the growing ash on his cigarette. 'You know, Meredith, had you been in the R.A.F. you would have been yanked out of active service and would have been buried away in a sinecure of a job two years ago. That is one grievance I have against the Navy. The R.A.F. medical side watched their bright boys and at the first sign of a crack, even a hairline crack, they were grounded. Good business, too, because after a rest they were like giants refreshed. For the first two or three years of the war the Navy clung tenaciously to the medical set-up which hadn't progressed much from Nelson's days.'

Meredith nodded.

'I know. Set 'em on their feet and if they can open their eyes and breathe they'll do.'

'Did you carry a doctor on your battleship?'

'It wasn't a battleship. It was a frigate. I had the doctor because I was senior officer and he had to do for the whole flotilla. Some of the ships in my outfit I never saw. They were thousands of miles away. But they each had a leading S.B.A. and they were as good as the young doctors we shipped.'

'I know. Straight out of student days and quite incapable of tying a knot in a suture or of competently putting on a bandage. I was the same. But back to my opening remark. What will you do when you leave here?'

'Does that mean I am on ticket-of-leave even when I get away from you?'

155

'Master of the direct question and no refinements, I see. During the three months' demobilization leave you will have, we will want to know how you get along because if you fold up in that period you might have to come back for——'

'Another sentence. And no time off for good behaviour.'

Maldon's face creased up into a smile.

'I shall miss you, Meredith. Our little debates have brightened my drab days.'

Meredith looked straight at the surgeon.

'Damn me, I think I'm going to miss you, too, for a while, until I find somebody else getting caught up in my hair.'

'That's the nicest thing I have had said to me for a long time. And I'm still waiting to know what you will aim for when you go out.'

Meredith knew that this was no idle query; but was part of a routine.

'Will it set your mind at rest if I assure you that I do not intend to take any midnight walks along cliffs?'

'I could have told you that a week after you came here. That was a phase, and a brief phase at that. Perhaps you'll have crystallized your ideas by tomorrow forenoon.'

'Possibly.'

'I can't imagine you settling down to a shore job, Meredith. Have you any lines out at all?'

'Tentatively, several.'

'Good! In the meantime, I hope you enjoy the pictures this evening.'

'Pictures? Is there a cinema show in the hospital tonight?'

'No, but there is in town. And you are going.'

Meredith stiffened in his seat. Realization came to him that going out into the town would mean moving out from the refuge which had been his for months. It would mean meeting strangers. It would mean that he could no longer retreat into his cool, almost austere room. He would no longer have at less than arm's length the man who sat opposite him. He found that his lips were dry and ran the tip of his tongue over them.

'NO!' Meredith almost barked it.

'Yes. That is an order, Meredith. If necessary, I will detail Big Bertha to accompany you. You've heard of Big Bertha, of course. We keep her handy for our most intractable cases. Cases such as you.' Maldon sat up in his chair and with his hands described generous, voluptuous curves. 'Six feet of feminine brawn, and she'll love being taken to the pictures by you. Legend has it that before becoming a V.A.D. nurse she was a strong woman in a circus. She'll love it. So will you.'

Meredith shook his head in desperation.

'Look, I'll take it easy tonight, have a long night in, and tomorrow I'll be fit to travel.'

'You'll go out into the town this afternoon and leave will be extended for you until 20.00—and for Bertha.'

Behind the half smile Meredith detected the cold command. 'I'll go on my own. Damn you and your Big Bertha! You can take her and——'

'No thanks.'

Meredith allowed his mind to drift and started to absorb the countryside as the car sped along. It swung along a lane bordered on each side by blossom—smothered orchards with an occasional cottage nestling well back behind large front gardens. In one was a squat light green tree with a profusion of purple blossom on it.

"That could be lilac," Meredith thought. "I'm not certain." Once again he could hear the scratched record, now fathoms deep in the Pacific, grinding out—

. . . And walk together down an English lane. . . .

Suddenly Meredith realized that the leafy lane had given way to the suburbs. The car slowed down at some traffic lights, speeded up, swung round a corner and pulled in to the pavement outside a cinema.

Meredith watched the car disappear, and joined the little crowd at the ticket office. He felt a rising tide of panic sweeping over him. Perspiration broke out on his forehead; he could feel it chill beneath the band of his hat. His hands clenched at the end of his down-thrust arms; the fingers worked convulsively. Meredith wanted to force his way through the little knot of people round him, push his way through them and hurry as fast as his feet would carry him. Run anywhere away from this place. He took a step forward, then stopped. He lifted one hand and surveyed the crumpled ticket. His jaw thrust out belligerently and his shoulders lifted, he strode into the cinema and took a seat in the semi-darkness. Gradually he relaxed in his seat and a half smile crept over his face.

'No where near as bad as I thought,' he murmured.

'Pardon?' said the drab woman nursing a basket who was sitting next to him.

'Er—I said the picture was not as bad as I thought,' Meredith answered.

'No.' And the woman sat through the rest of the performance waiting tensed for the bold sailor next to her to stroke her leg, and was partly relieved, partly disappointed, when he took no further notice.

Meredith came out of the cinema into the evening, looked at his watch and saw that he had enough time for a meal before going back to the hospital. He walked along the street, past some bombed ruins, feeling full of renewed confidence. Getting out and meeting people, if only to stand near them and hear them talk, had not been anywhere as nerve-racking as he had expected. A discreetly lighted vestibule of an hotel yawned open before him and he went in. With detached calm he surrendered his coat and cap to the cloakroom attendant and stood in the vestibule looking around him.

"American Bar" said a lighted sign over a door.

Meredith sauntered in and threw one leg over a high tubular stool.

'Scotch, please.'

'Yes, sir. Large or small?'

'Large, please. You seem to have plenty in these days of shortage.'

The barman, sleek-haired, pale-faced, trim in his white coat smiled. It was almost a simper.

'There is a big American camp just outside, and an American hospital here. They are willing to pay, so the guv'nor gets it in the "black".' He glanced over Meredith's shoulder and leaned forward confidentially. 'There's stuff on the market now, sir, which I wouldn't use to paint a fence. But the guv'nor always has the best. It's expensive, but worth it. Seven and six, sir, please. Thank you. You on leave, sir?'

Meredith nodded. 'In a way. I'm going to have some dinner. Will the whisky last out until I come back?'

'Yes, there's lashings. Anyway, we have plenty of gin, sir. That's the Navy's drink, isn't it? Pinks. It's a bit early yet, but we fill up later on.'

As dinner progressed Meredith felt the first glimmerings of rebellion. "Right!" he thought. "You tossed me out to test the temperature of the world, so try it I will. I'll go back when I feel like it. In fact, I'll lay on a blind and to hell with your rules."

When he returned to the bar with his mood of rebellion still fluid it became a highly concentrated distillation. As he entered the door a wave of subdued sound met him, a familiar sound which took him only seconds to orient. It was made up largely of the broad American accents of which he had heard such a lot in the past year, punctuated by higher, softer feminine tones.

Meredith paused, took a rising feeling of mild panic by the throat, shook it resolutely and made his way to a vacant stool at the far end of the bar.

The barman remembered him.

'Seven and six, please. It was a large one you wanted?'

He sat nursing his drink and absorbing the fragments of conversation.

' "Lissen, bud", I says, "I aims jes' to hire your goddamn taxi, not to buy it. . . ." ' 'Jean is a fool. She's much much too possessive. She went overboard completely for an Australian. A pilot; he was blond and tall. Right overboard. Then she was unhappy for months.' . . .'I figure the only good fightin' man comes from south of the Mason-Dixie line. That is, for real fightin'' . . . 'And what do they do? Comb the hospitals for cripples and sign 'em up for the Dodgers. Jes' punk players. . . .'

Gradually through the subdued tumult Meredith fastened on to one sustained conversation going on between two youngsters close to him.

'Man, jes' about now the garden will be a riot of pansies and roses and the dogwood trees. I can see my ma settin' it up for us kids. She'd have a pitcher of milk and a great platter of cookies and heaps of ice cream, blueberry muffins and johnnycake. You ever ate johnnycake, Rebel? An' grape butter. An' all that to follow a pot roast, or maybe some boiled ham and salad, an' the sun glinting on the creek and trout fair rarin' to be caught.'

Meredith recognized the underlaying homesickness behind it all. He looked at the speaker, guessed his age as twenty or thereabouts. He studied the youth, looked at his heavy blue jaw, his deep, almost expressionless eyes, at his spare figure, the square shoulders accentuated by the cut of the tan blouse, and mentally summed him up.

"Slow to anger, could be mean and dangerous. I've seen his sort come back after their first fight with the Japs.' Meredith turned it over in his mind.

'New England for a bright dollar.'

'You say somethin', Cap'n?'

Meredith's eyes opened wide. 'Did I speak out loud? I was guessing you as a New England man. Sorry.'

'You don't have to be sorry, Cap'n. I'm New England all right. How did you guess?'

'Johnnycake and blueberry muffins. I've heard of them before.'

The other youngster laughed and moved in closer. He was the direct opposite to his companion. His hair was a sun-bleached blond, his face just missed being sallow by virtue of the young blood pulsing beneath the skin. His age was about the same.

'You talkin' about eatin'? Cap'n, you want to come south. That stuff we'd feed to field hands. Now I could get you——'

'Hold it!' Meredith laughed. 'Don't embroil me in any

domestic argument. I've seen too many of them on U.S. ships. Anyway, what are you doing around with a carpet-bagger? You his prisoner, and being held to ransom or something?'

Both youngsters laughed and in their laughs Meredith saw confirmation of his amusing summing-up of them. The Southerner threw back his head and boomed, showing white teeth. The New Englander just parted his lips and made it a rapid chuckle.

'After Cherbourg—an' all stations east to the Rhine—we have cancelled the debts,' the Southerner chuckled. 'Each time I pulled him outer a tangle he ups and prises me outer some ruckus. We figures we is about quits. I aim to take him south when we go back and show him something real.'

'Right now, New England is nearer than South Carolina.'

'Whereabouts is your home, Cap'n?'

Meredith opened his mouth to speak and it crashed through to him that he had no home. His lips closed and tightened.

'I'd figure you for a Welshman. We had a battalion of them little dark fighting devils alongside us after Bastoigne. Gee, they could fight at the drop of a hat. And sing. Little sawn-off red peppers, they were.' The blond boy smiled. 'Wales—from what I've heard that's the bit of Great Britain that England is stuck on to.'

'Here we go!' Meredith said, climbing ruthlessly over his hump. 'Call the Mason-Dixie line the Welsh marches and you have it all over again.'

'Then you have the Scots. They have a big beef about the English, too,' the dark New Englander said seriously.

'I figure this country would be in one hell of a spot if the Welsh and Scots decided to declare a separate peace.'

Meredith chuckled. 'To complete the picture you should have had a slice of Irish in it.'

'Them's the boyos who is friendly neutral. That right, Cap'n?'

'You're getting the hang of it.'

'More complicated than our side. We jes' got the goddam' Yankee, and the Southern patriot——'

'Dam' rebels,' the dark youth grunted.

Meredith caught the barman's eye and signalled.

'I was aimin' to do jes' that,' the blond youngster said. 'But the night—well, she's young. Don't you move no further away than I can see you,' he warned the barman. 'When I bat an eye you come a runnin', an' with your hands loaded all same as now. Right?'

'From now on out he'll do nothing but blink,' laughed the New England youth. 'It will end up him trying to fight six or four people and me taking him back to hospital.'

'Are you patients in the U.S. hospital?'

'Nothing but. They've let him out to give the nurses a rest from running away from him. And me? Well, I had to come to look after him.'

'You didn't have to end up in hospital, at all,' the Southerner jeered. 'I gets me a nice wound, he sees me being taken off and sticks his big head up. The first two bounces off'n him so he reverses and sticks his other end up. That being the spot where his brains live, he got hisself a wound and tags along to crowd my style.'

Meredith found himself enjoying the mild wrangle.

'What time are you due back?' he asked.

The Southerner looked serious for a moment, exchanged glances with his companion and they both dissolved into laughter.

'There's a lot of hours left on the clock yet. We're in the dog-house already. Tomorrow we go to the mat with Slab-Sided Sadie—she's the head nurse and hell on two feet——'

'Like the Big Bertha in our hospital.'

'You been knocked about, Cap'n?'

'Some.'

The southern lad raised his head and caught the barman's alert eye.

'That's fine. And you keep watching. My friend here has got a twitching eye too.'

Meredith felt a glow stealing through him, a glow which threatened to expand into an ambitious blaze.

'What time are you due back, Cap'n?'

Meredith looked at his watch.

'I was due back an hour ago, but there's a lot of clock left, as you say.'

'Attaboy, Cap'n. We'll all sleep in the dog-house together. You can have our Slab-Sided Sadie and we'll buck your—what d'you call her? Big Bertha.' He tipped his head back, emptying his glass, and looked pointedly at his dark friend.

'Set your eye a'twitching,' he ordered. 'Time marches on.'

Somewhere along the evening the blond southerner became attached to a thin-lipped, over-bosomed woman, leaving his companion sinking deeper into a morose depression.

'He's been doing it all along the line, Cap'n. First it was them French dames. An' he's married, too. Now, if it was me it would be all right.'

Meredith found himself hastily mixed up in a rambling argument on the ethics of adultery as opposed to plain seduction, became hopelessly entangled, ended up shaking hands fervently with the New England youth, managed one more drink before the expert barman called time and walked out dizzily into the cool night.

He stood with legs wide apart at the kerb.

"I'm supposed to be afraid of people—not afraid of the whole world. . . ." he muttered challengingly.

'Taxi!' he shouted. He almost fell into the vehicle, gave his instructions and let the universe go round in dizzy circles.

At the gates to the drive the taxi stopped.

'Can't go any farther, sir,' the driver said.

Meredith laboriously climbed out and paid the man.

As he moved towards the gate a petty officer stepped unobtrusively from the gate-house.

'I'm late, as late as hell.' He stood by the gate swaying.

'A bit late, sir.'

'S'right—late as hell.'

He started to walk up the drive with exaggerated, careful steps. After a few yards he turned back and came to the gate-house in a wide half-circle.

'Wha' do you know about lilac? You tell me that. Lilac. . . .'

The petty officer squared his shoulders, straightened his arms by his side.

'Flower class sloop, sir. Queenstown command in the last war. Good sea-boats, sir, but hard and dirty on the lower deck men.'

Meredith tried to focus him in his eyes, failed and turned away. When he had gone a few yards he broke into song.

'We'll gather lilac—in—the spring again.
Spring—April—May—who the hell cares?—an
walk together down—English lane. . . .'

"T'wasn't fair, laddie. Why didn't it take me an' leave you?" ' "An' walk together down an English lane . . . Lilac in the spring again. . . ." '

Maudlin tears coursed unheeded down his cheeks.

The petty officer watched him disappear round the bend. 'Blimey! He's been on a bend. I wouldn't give a small fortune to have his noggin in the mornin'.'

He studied the switchboard and rang a number on the house telephone.

Meredith woke up, opened his eyes, winced painfully as the light punished them, and closed them again.

'Got yourself nicely fried last night. Fried on both sides.' Maldon's voice cut through the aching throb. 'And for your information it's well after ten o'clock. I gather you didn't want any breakfast this morning. How's the head?'

Meredith groaned.

'Don't rub it in,' he moaned. 'Look, I'm sorry. I hope I wasn't a lot of trouble.'

'None at all, so I'm told. Apparently you insisted on singing. Not one of your strong suits. And being a Welshman, that leaves you only fighting.'

Meredith struggled up in bed, fought down a rising nausea and nursed his head.

'Here, drink this. It will keep that flapping lid down on the top of your head.'

Meredith drank something which was bitter and caught his breath.

'Where's your cigarette case? Ah! Got it. Want one?'

Maldon held out his lighter.

Meredith took a couple of puffs and looked up.

'I can only apologize and leave it at that——'

Maldon waved a hand airily.

'Don't, there's a good fellow. You did just what I hoped you'd do. Become human, get plastered, even get caught up in a fight. You did for yourself what I couldn't quite do. Make you human again. I'll see you in an hour, Meredith.'

'Er, do you mind if I take one to have with my coffee?'

He dipped into the open cigarette case.

Two hours later Meredith, having promised Maldon to return in three weeks for a check-up, stood in the entrance hall of the hospital, his bags at his feet, waiting for a car.

'I'll say good-bye and wish you luck, Commander Meredith.'

He spun round to see Sister Payne standing near him.

'I wasn't going without saying good-bye,' he started guiltily. 'I——'

'You meant to do no such thing. And I'll save you the trouble of saying you will write. We've had more than two thousand officers through here in the past two or three years. Half of them have been my problem and a lot of them have promised to write. They never do. Good-bye. And—good luck.'

She held out her hand, which he took.

'Good-bye.'

The wheels of the train seemed to echo it as the train sped on —"Good-bye, good-bye, good-bye, good-bye." Then suddenly it changed to "On-to-where? On-to-where? On-to-where?"

Meredith squirmed in his seat and concentrated on the outside view. Suddenly he tightened up inside, felt himself shrink into a hard-cored, quivering ball. Somebody was speaking to him. It was a woman's voice.

'Pardon me, but are there lunches served on this train now? It's so long since I travelled any distance by train.'

'I don't know.'

Meredith turned to the woman. He saw she was about middle age, and plainly but well dressed. Her face had a calm tautness about it as if she were holding something with a tight rein.

'I don't know. I think not. On these short journeys they've cut them out.'

'They offered me sandwiches at the hospital where I've been visiting, but I thought——'

'We stop at Swindon. I'll probably be able to get you a cup of tea and possibly a sandwich. It will be that spam stuff, I expect.'

He felt the hard core softening. This was meeting people, meeting and talking to strangers.

'That will be kind of you.'

'You say you've been visiting somebody at the hospital?'

'Yes. My son. He's in the Naval hospital at——' She named it. 'Oh, dear, he does look so ill. He was a prisoner of war with these terrible Japs. He—he——' Her eyes became moist.

'Was he wounded?'

'No—but he was treated terribly. He was in the Navy, like you. I suppose they have so many men to look after, but he hates the doctor who is in charge of him.'

Meredith chuckled. 'Surgeon-Commander Maldon, for a bent penny!'

Her eyebrows lifted. 'Oh, dear, you know him! Perhaps you are something at the hospital and I've said something I shouldn't have.'

Meredith's chuckle grew into a laugh.

'Don't let that worry you. I WAS something at the hospital, all right. I was a patient there for five months. And I hated Maldon—hated him to begin with.' He leaned forward and patted her hand. 'In three months he'll send your son back to you as fit as he has ever been.'

She twisted her fingers nervously. 'I do hope so. But he looks so ill now.'

'If he wasn't he wouldn't be in hospital, would he?'

She considered the logic of this in silence. 'Perhaps you're right.'

Meredith looked at his watch. 'We'll be in London in little more than an hour. I'll get you a cup of dubious tea at Swindon and I would be delighted if you would have lunch with me. Please!'

And over an indifferent lunch he heard about her son, and comforted her, and in doing so felt some comfort himself.

When finally he saw her off in a taxi to her home he was full of confidence, and ready to meet the world.

10

HALEY SORTED OUT the half-dozen letters, slid a thumb under the flaps, perused the contents briefly and tossed them on to the table.

'Three bills and two circulars,' he murmured. 'And I thought the country was short of paper! Now, what's in this one?' He smoothed out the sheet of paper and stood with his back to the fire.

'Well, I'll be jiggered!' he said after he had digested the contents.

His wife poked her head round the kitchen door.

'Your sins catching up with you, darling?'

'More-or-less. Somebody has started a reunion dinner scheme for officers who served in my command and because I was the sort of oldest inhabitant they have shoved me on the organizing committee. They can jolly well shove me off it as quickly as they like.'

She moved into the room and stood near him.

'I don't see why not. It would be rather nice to meet some of them again and talk over old times. I used to go to a school reunion before the war, before I was married. It was fun. We used to sit and talk—and talk. . . .'

His eyes took on a faraway look.

'Sometimes Regan and I would discuss what a reunion would be like when it was all over. He used to conjure up a picture of a meeting ten years after the end of the war. Regan would have all the best types turning up in shabby clothes, toes showing through shoes, and the fiddlers and shysters would drive up in spectacular cars smoking cigars. Outrageous, of course, but the way he elaborated it it sounded funny—at the time.'

'Why do you say "at the time"?'

'Because it is darn nearly true. Look at things. The war has been over for rather more than two years, yet we have a thriving black market. I've been offered petrol coupons, clothing coupons, nylons, even clothes and shoes, in the past year or so and who had them on offer—at a price? Men I knew as officers, and in most instances damned bad officers at that. Blasted chisellers.'

'Next time you have some nylons offered you, snap 'em up. I'm wearing ladders right now and I haven't a reasonable pair to my name.'

He half turned and looked at her seriously. 'Would you really like me to buy some?'

'Seriously, yes. Look, dear, there are heaps of people who do not use all their clothing coupons, or if they do they sell what they buy. Why shouldn't we have some of them?'

'It's the moral aspect which worries me. People in general put their best effort into winning the war. We are by no means out of the wood yet and this rationing is part of an effort. To buy in the black market is—is——'

She laughed lightly.

'You talk like a politically-minded clergyman. Give me a cigarette, please.' With the cigarette drawing she sat on the arm of a chair. 'As you know, The Boy gets through clothes like a house on fire. The other day I was moaning about it to Mrs. Gibbs, my char, and she said, quite brightly, "Lor, ducks, that's easy. My Emily has four kids, but she don't use up half her coupons. She'll let you have some."' The cigarette glowed briefly. 'And Emily did, and I bought him some clothes.'

'Did you, indeed!'

'Yes.' She gave him an unblinking, defiant look. 'And there were enough left over to buy you a pair of socks.' She held up a restraining hand. 'Don't take a deep breath and go in off the deep end. If I hadn't bought them she would have sold them elsewhere.'

'Somewhere there is a flaw in your logic, but my toes are twiddling in the socks, so I'll let it pass.'

'Wait until they have twiddled through holes, then I'll have another go at your conscience. But seriously, dear, I think you ought to accept that committee offer and help to have a reunion.

169

You like going to your club, and you admit that you like it because you can meet men and talk ships and war without boring anybody.'

'There's something in what you say. I'm wondering how we will get into touch with all the fellows. There were quite a number who came to us for a time, then passed on to other bases.'

'You'll find them, all right.'

He smiled at her. 'I suppose you are visualizing wives being invited?'

'God forbid! I can think of nothing worse. You might organize a wives' meeting in another room, then we could pick you out of the gutters, pour you into taxis and see you home at the end.'

'That's an idea.'

So Haley wrote accepting and for several months busied himself with the organizing of a modest reunion. To his surprise and delight, his old commanding officer, Captain Mahoney, who had commanded the Minesweeping Base for nearly five grim years, signified his intention of being present "in strength, in good health, with a thirst and a hundred and one questions to be answered, and regards to your good wife."

Marjorie watched with interest, pleasure and considerable amusement his reactions as letters came in from men who had been officers at the Base and were anxious to come to the first reunion dinner.

With The Boy safely off to bed his wife would sit in a deep easy chair while he read some of the letters.

'I'm glad he's coming,' Haley would remark. 'He was a good type. He had a Micky. An M.M.S.—a Motor Minesweeper. Had the mind of an accountant. There was a sum in sea area and mines to be solved and that was how he treated it. Oh, this should be fun! You've heard me talk about the Brains Trust. That was Bolter, our schoolmaster-fellow and Lister, the barrister. They were terrific characters. Always arguing. Apparently they have been meeting to dine together about once a month ever since the war ended. You should hear them in an argument. Lister—he's the lawyer—says, "In language that even

Bolter can understand, I bags the speech of welcome to Commander, Minesweepers. I feel I owe him one or two for the occasions when he has cut short my speech for the defence—my own defence." '

'He won't be rude to Captain Mahoney, will he?' she asked anxiously.

'Incredibly—and the Old Man will love it, and will ladle it out in kind. I am certain that at minesweeping conferences he used to let Lister and Bolter have a go at one another just for the pleasure of listening to them. Bolter always swore he would not go back to schoolmastering. He had some crazy idea of buying a boat of sorts and going out to the West Indies trading around the islands. I rather fancy that he considered the war as a god-sent form of escape for him. All the dirty side of it was incidental. He had a ship under him and that was all he cared about.'

'Anybody else you know well written to say he is coming?'

Haley stood up and leaned his forearm on the mantelshelf and stared into the low fire. At first he made no answer: Finally he turned round.

'Of the commanding officers who were there when I first arrived, there are not many left alive. I was one of the lucky ones.'

She bit a length of cotton with her teeth and glanced keenly at him under her eyebrows.

'If you look carefully in the sideboard you'll find enough for two drinks,' she said. 'One for you and one for me.'

'Tosspot! Wine-bibber!' he grinned.

'Yes, darling. And while you are on your feet put a light under the kettle.' "And that ought to take his mind off things for a few seconds," she concluded to herself.

A few days before the reunion Haley received a letter from Mahoney, his old captain.

'I will be staying at the Senior Service for a few days. As it is just round the corner from where we will be dining I thought it would be a good idea if you joined me at the club for half-an-hour for a quiet one. Just you and me. Shall we say around 1800—6 p.m. to rehabilitated civilians? Make it so.'

After a brief but extremely warm greeting Haley sat in a deep chair in the club, nursing a drink and studying Mahoney's face. Captain Mahoney was dressed in a dark grey suit and blue shirt and collar with naval tie. Haley watched his features as he talked. He formed the opinion that Mahoney looked younger. Was it the different kind of clothes? Or had peace softened the hardness of the deeply etched lines in his face? Probably a combination of both, Haley decided.

'This is the first time I've been off the leash since the smoke cleared away,' Mahoney was saying, and Haley came-to with a slight jolt. He hoped Mahoney had not said anything which had required an answer. 'My missus has given me more orders than were issued for the invasion. "See you have a well-aired bed." And me staying at the club,' he snorted. ' "See that you put your top-coat on when you leave the dinner even if there are only a few yards to walk." Well, I suppose they didn't have us for six years or so, so now they are making up for lost opportunities. By the same token, how's your wife and off-spring? Still just the one?'

Haley grinned. 'Just the one, sir. I think my wife must belong to the same lodge as Mrs. Mahoney. If I'm out in a shower of rain there's a state of French calm until I've changed my shoes and clothes, and if I sniff once or twice it is as if I've got double pneumonia. I wonder what she would have done if she had been with me sometimes a couple of years back, when I was wet for days.'

'The same as she is doing now, and it would have been good for you. Look how we revelled in the creature comforts the Wrens brought us. I always felt that a cup of tea, or a plate of soup, was the better for being served by a Wren stewardess. They used to plant it down with a sort of "now drink that while it's hot, there's a good boy" look. You've heard me say that it would have been a better war if we could have taken our wives along. We will in the next one.'

Haley carefully studied the end of his cigarette. 'Will there ever be another one, sir? Surely——'

Mahoney stirred in his chair. 'You bet your boots there will.

Some megalomaniac will spark off something. Why, it's building up now.'

Haley's eyebrows raised.

'I mean it,' Mahoney continued. 'The layout hasn't altered. We've just finished tidily hanging a few Germans, and one or two other misguided clowns, as a sop to emotionalism. In a few years' time we'll start pouring money into Germany to rebuild it for some economic reason. They'll work like niggers, recapture the world's markets, then get really ambitious for a place in the sun, or living space, or some corridor or other that another country has. And away we go!'

Haley shook his head. 'A nice prospect, that. And what would you say would be the line-up, sir?'

'Us in the front line, inevitably. America, having learnt a lesson or two, will be quicker off the mark and if we have a scrap with a combined Russian-German alliance we will have Japan on our side this time.'

'Why, that's crazy, sir, after what has just happened. People wouldn't stand for it.'

Mahoney looked steadily at him. 'People will stand for anything the damned politicians will tell them to. Look at the way this confounded Red Socialist mob are dragooning the nation. I'd ship the lot to an Hebridian island with only Karl Marx to read. That would teach 'em!'

Mahoney looked at his watch. 'Time we joined the thirsty throng, Haley.' He rested his arm on Haley's shoulder. 'I won't live to see it, thank God. You might not, but your son will. But this crowd will reduce us to a third-rate nation. Remember that speech Churchill made during the war? No, not the one about the beaches and the ditches—that was good, too—but the one in which he said, "My King did not appoint me as his Prime Minister to preside over the dissolution of the British Empire." This mob is doing just that. If they stay in for five years more the damage they will do will be immeasurable. Gloomy talk, Haley. Let's get along to the brighter things.'

The dinner started shyly, cautiously, with men looking at each other and seeing each other in a different light. When last they met they had been in uniform, all conforming to a long-cast mould. Now they were individuals. The devil-may-care lieutenant of the war years was now a sedately dressed, sober man, gently spoken. The quiet officer, sparing of words, had obviously prospered, and exuded confidence.

But the shyness departed after a few drinks and finally whirled away into nothingness when Lister made his speech. He ribbed Mahoney unmercifully in polished phrases which had not an atom of venom in them.

Mahoney replied in kind, drawing gusts of appreciative laughter until towards the end, when he dropped into a more serious note to talk about the value of perpetuating in the years of peace the comradeship they had shown in the years of the war.

Finally the dinner and speeches ended and little groups formed of men who had been contemporaries in the Command.

'Notice how the Micky officers have all gathered into one crowd? The trawler blokes are looking at you, Haley; you'd better join them. You and I make even a smaller group—the oldest inhabitants. Away you go! I know two who would have enjoyed this evening. But that was the price we had to pay. Off you go!'

'Two, sir?'

'Regan and that wild blade of a Welshman, Meredith. You've not heard from him?'

'No, sir. We wrote a few times. The last I heard was that he was out East——'

'I remember. I fear he—His ship was torpedoed. Away, bleak thoughts! Go and drool to your trawler types while I batten on to the Micky lads for a while.'

Finally Haley caught Mahoney's eye and walked over to him.

'I think I'll go now, Haley, before some of these young blades embroil me in an all-night session at some night club. That is what they threaten, but I'm too old in the tooth for that. By Neptune himself, a few years ago I would have taken them on the razzle and had them hollow-eyed by dawn. Oh yes, I knew my way about in my youth, Haley.'

With Mahoney at his side, Haley circulated once more saying farewells and together they walked to the door of the restaurant.

'Come and stay with us for a few days in the summer, Haley. Bring the missus and the lad. Mrs. Mahoney will be delighted. She feels she has a vested interest in your family. Is that a promise? I'll keep you to it. Good night, my boy. Good night.'

Haley stood on the step and watched his former senior officer roll off into the night and once again he found himself feeling the deeply rooted warm affection for the older man which he had felt during the war years when Mahoney had stood behind him, guide, philosopher, always there when courage was ebbing, always with a quiet word of advice and encouragement.

Haley stood irresolute, wondering whether he would go back into the laughter-laden room or would collect his coat and leave.

'Haley, isn't it?'

Haley spun round swiftly. Before him stood a short, squat figure. A smile spread over the man's face. Recognition came almost instantly.

'Meredith! By all the——You weren't in there, were you?'

Meredith found his hand taken and clasped tightly.

'No. It was just by the slimmest chance that I knew the dinner was on. I had to meet somebody here earlier and saw a notice on the board in the hall.'

'Why in Pete's sake didn't you come in? The Old Man asked about you. He had the idea you were—we thought—— Well, come in now and meet the fellows. Not that you will remember many of them. But, by gosh, they'll know you! They heard enough about you.'

Meredith grasped Haley's arm.

'I've been sitting here in the corner wondering whether I would go in, but—funked it, I guess. I saw you and The Old Man saying good night—and decided to say "how-do" to you. No! You go back and we'll meet again sometime.'

Haley looked keenly at him.

'I wasn't going back. Wait until I collect my coat and we'll push off somewhere quiet. I wish you had come forward when the Old Man was saying good night.'

Haley collected his coat and together they breasted the crowded pavement until a discreetly lighted door offered them what they wanted. Soon they were seated nursing a drink each.

'Well, who is going to start?' Haley asked with a smile. 'I'll open the conversation. What are you doing these days? Back in the Merchant Service?'

'No. I've got a nice job with a tug concern, sort of personnel manager-cum-assistant marine superintendent. I try to pick the right man for the right job and look after the tugs. I get in the odd trip round the coast when I get fed up with an office chair.'

'Good enough! And the family?'

Meredith cupped his hands round his glass and looked down. 'I—er—a buzz bomb dropped on the farmhouse where they were living—and——'

'All of them?' Haley whispered it.

Meredith nodded.

'Good God! How awful.'

There was a silence, then Meredith lifted up his chin.

'It knocked me over for a while. I was out East when I heard. . . .'

He lifted his glass and tossed back the contents.

'At first I couldn't grasp it. When I did, it became unbearable. A Jap sub got my ship; we lost quite a few and I ended up in hospital, down in the West Country.'

Meredith signalled to a waiter hovering near.

'And your family?'

'Full of beans. He's rising six, now. We've only the one. You must come and see us. Let's make it a hard date, shall we?'

'I'd love to. In one way I'm sorry I didn't barge in tonight. But I wasn't certain who would be there. How many would I know? Of the old crowd who were at the Base in '40 and '41, how many are there left?'

'Two or three. But the Old Man was there. And I was there.

176

'I didn't know that earlier tonight. I'll come next year if you hold another.'

'We've decided to make it an annual do.'

'And watch ourselves wither, and listen to the years condemn, eh?'

They sat in silence and Haley covertly studied the man in front of him. He suddenly realized that the Meredith facing him was no longer the volatile, explosive Meredith he had known in the earlier war years. His face was set in taut, immobile lines. Whereas once his lips were full, almost pouting, and his eyes were lively pools of animation, now there was a frozen look about him. The lips had fined down, the mouth was level, straight-chiselled, thin, and when he talked the top lip scarcely moved. His voice, which once had the lilt of Welsh and soared over the best part of an octave, was now clipped, devoid of any variation, without that rising note at the end which Haley had found so attractive. Above his ears the hair was generously flecked with grey.

Haley broke the silence.

'Were you—did you get knocked about when the sub got you? You say you were in hospital?'

'Six months. Physically not at all.'

Haley nodded slowly. 'I think I understand.'

There was a flash of the old Meredith as he sat upright.

'Like hell, you do! You haven't a clue in the world. Neither has anybody else unless they've been through it, or are doctors working at it.'

He stood up abruptly. 'Do you want any more, or shall we walk a bit?'

'I've had enough.' Haley looked at his watch. 'And the night is young. I expected to be gassing away until about midnight.'

Meredith chuckled. 'I know. "Do you remember?" and "Do you remember?" and fight the good fight all over again without boring other people who either were not in it or have a better fight to tell. C'mon, let's take a turn along the Embankment.'

They walked in silence until they reached the broad pavement of the Embankment. The dark, silent waters of the Thames slid past like black glass. Lights threw their reflections on to it and let them wriggle like glowing snakes imprisoned by the head. Together they leaned on the wall.

'Fascinating, isn't it?' Meredith said. 'I often come here and just lean over the wall looking into the water. At first the policemen used to stand near and sooner or later they would start a conversation, trying to find out whether I was contemplating taking a header or not.'

Haley laughed.

Meredith went on as if he had not been interrupted.

'I've talked to policemen who were in bombers, in tanks, and in the Navy. Bless my soul, I've fought the war over again half a dozen times just leaning against this wall.'

He stood upright and rested his fingers on the wall. 'But people do come here and lean against it; then there is a splash, and somebody has ended all their troubles.'

'A cowardly way out, surely? And what a gloomy line of talk.'

Meredith turned until his elbows were resting on the wall.

'You asked me a while ago if I was knocked about when the sub got us. I said not physically. All the damage was done when I—got the news. Things can become too big for you to carry, Haley. They can become so big that they hold you, possess you every waking hour. And the waking hours are too long. There comes a moment when you want no further part in the world. You don't even want to know yourself; you try to refuse to acknowledge that you ARE you—even the sight of your own written name drags you back into that world you want to forget. That is the moment when. . . .' He jerked his head towards the river. 'That can spell everlasting peace from it all.'

Haley remained silent for a few moments.

'I think I begin to understand.' He paused. 'I can't imagine you contemplating that.' He made a gesture towards the dark, gliding river.

Meredith gave a short laugh. 'That was the first question they asked me in hospital. The opening gambit.'

'Did they, by Jove!'

'I think my answer reassured them.'

Haley threw back his head and laughed. 'I can almost hear you saying it.'

'I told them, "Not any longer. That moment has passed,"' Meredith said in a flat voice. 'It had. I fought that one out alone.'

Meredith linked his arm in Haley's. 'I have a train to catch, into the wilds of south-east London. Walk to the station with me. Now, when can we meet again?'

'How about Sunday? Come to lunch and stay as long as you like. I'll give you my address.'

A little later he stood at the barrier and watched the train pull out.

He entered his home quietly, sat for a spell smoking a cigarette, his thoughts mainly on Meredith, then turned out the light and crept upstairs.

He peeped round the door of The Boy's bedroom and listened to his steady breathing. There was no light showing beneath the door of his and his wife's room, and after opening the door silently he stood framed in the doorway. Suddenly the room blazed into light and he saw his wife sitting up in bed, a broad smile on her face.

'Let go the door, darling. I'll pick you up if you fall,' she laughed.

'Chump! I'm stone-cold sober. Why aren't you asleep?'

'I wanted to see what you looked like after letting your back hair down. Was it a nice dinner? Did you see lots of men you knew?'

As he struggled out of his clothes he said, 'Seeing that I've spent the last four months writing to all of them I expected to see them.'

Soon he was seated on the side of the bed in his pyjamas.

'Do you know who showed up? Not at the dinner, but afterwards?'

He told her about Meredith and their meeting. Of Meredith's loss.

She looked at him with chin tilted and a quizzical look on her face.

'So that was why you stopped to peep into His Nibs's room, was it?' she said softly. 'It must have been awful for him.'

'It has changed him. He's quieter, and struck me as being sort of brittle-hard, somehow. I've asked him to lunch on Sunday. Is that O.K.?'

'Bill! What will I give you to eat? On six ounces of meat?'

He reached up for the light switch.

'Go shopping in that black market you seem to know so well. Get into touch with—Emily, was it?'

'You're nearer the truth than you know.'

A little later he felt her snuggle up close to him.

'How awful,' she whispered, 'to lose them all like that. Imagine how you would have felt if. . . .'

'I have been thinking of it.'

Meredith paused outside the gate. It was not too late; he could still turn and walk away. A couple of nights ago it had been so easy to say, "Yes, I'll be delighted." But this was the moment. In a minute or two he would have to meet somebody who would talk to him, who would know all about how They died. He would meet a wife who was helping her husband to pick up the ravelled threads of what was left for her husband after the war—and there was nobody to pick up his shredded remnants. Even if she didn't mention his family he would know that she knew all about them and would be tight, restrained, longing to bring them into the conversational orbit.

Meredith thrust the gate open. Before he could put a finger on the bell push the door opened and Mrs. Haley stood facing him.

'We never did meet, but I know you from what Bill has told me,' she said, a glad smile on her face. She extended her hand and Meredith took it. 'Gosh, the number of stories he has told me about you! I feel I ought to slam the door in your face and scream for the police. But I won't.'

Meredith found himself taking her cool, firm hand.

'Don't believe half of them. Your husband lies in his throat, as he ever did. And where is the brave lad? Cowering in the cellar?'

As they talked she walked beside him until they reached the attractive, compact lounge. There, something akin to a giggle escaped her.

'Early this morning, when I was dead asleep, Bill jabbed me in the small of my back and broke the news that we had only four tots left. "Tots" is right, isn't it? And today being Sunday he had to wait until the local opened before he could buy some. He's gone there with The Boy to see if he can spell-bind them into selling him a full bottle.' The giggle became more pronounced. 'It should be fun. He'll leave his son on a seat outside while he bargains in the market place for a bottle of mother's ruin.'

Meredith felt the tautness at his shoulders disappearing. This was a woman of the salt.

'Before Bill comes back I want to hold the floor,' she continued. 'But in the meantime I can manage one for you and one for me. If he doesn't strike oil—or gin—it's just too bad.'

She poured out two drinks, handed one to Meredith and lifted her glass.

'Down the hatch!'

'You've learned all the depraved wardroom phrases, I see. But down the hatch!'

'I can even offer you cigarettes.' She handed a box and he took one.

Meredith sat relaxed in a chair while she occupied the arm of a settee.

In a few moments she stood up. 'If I squeeze the bottle hard under my armpit I can get two more. May I have your glass?'

Meredith nursed the glass on his knee and watched her as she settled herself opposite him. There was a wife, there was what he had wanted, there was what he would have had if it had not been for that buzz-bomb. . . .

He found that she was looking at him with a steady, unwavering look.

'Bill told me of your dreadful loss.'

It came like that, like a soft ball coming through the air, small, round, something from which to flinch, but which sinks into the hands without a shock.

'It was—was. . . .' Meredith paused and tried to find a phrase.

She leaned forward. The smoke from her cigarette went upwards in a thin stream and Meredith watched it.

'They were all together, and there was no pain,' she said softly. 'It would have been more dreadful if you had gone and they had been left without you. I've tried to imagine what it would have been like if Bill had. . . .'

Meredith nodded. 'I—I suppose so.'

She leaned back. 'Bill told me you were in hospital for a long time. He said something about you being torpedoed. That must have been dreadful.'

'It wasn't funny.' He scratched his ear, searching for words. 'That wasn't the worst part. I—I. . . .'

Before he could finish the sentence he heard a slight commotion in the hall and she climbed to her feet.

'There are men in the house,' she said solemnly. 'Heavy-footed men. I hope they have been successful.'

Haley came in triumphantly carrying a bottle in one hand and the other clutching his son.

'Hullo, Meredith! We made it, but only just. While I was haggling with the laddie behind the bar His Nibs wandered in and threatened their licence. I think his presence swayed them and they let me have a bottle to get rid of us before the police showed up.'

Meredith grinned. 'You've got the wrong technique. You want to breeze in and yell in no uncertain voice that you want a bottle, and if you don't get it you'll tear the place apart.'

'Not in our circumspect local. It's the sort of place which

remained open throughout the war, offering chromium plating and sky-high prices for the gentlemen who had weak hearts and Government contracts.'

'And bulging note cases. I know—don't tell me!'

Meredith dropped his eyes and saw The Boy regarding him gravely in an unwinking stare. Gently he extended a hand until it hovered over the child's head. He lowered it until his whole hand rested on the boy's hair. His thumb moved in a stroking motion.

'Quite a boy,' he said, scarcely above a whisper. 'Quite a boy.' A smile crept over his face. His fingers ruffled the boy's hair. Haley and his wife exchanged swift, smiling glances over the child's head.

'Have a noggin for the road,' the youngster said solemnly.

Meredith's head rolled back in laughter. It was a sound which startled him; it had been so long since he had laughed out loud.

'A true son of his father. "How are you? So long,"' Meredith chuckled. 'After that I can't say "no".'

And they went in to an uproarious lunch before which Mrs. Haley had whispered to her husband, 'If you say grace don't forget to include Emily.'

'Thanks be unto Thee, O Lord, and to Emily,' Haley had whispered back.

11

HALEY'S MEETING with Meredith was the foundation of a renewed friendship which grew and expanded between the two men.

'The odd part is,' Haley said to his wife one evening, 'we were not particularly drawn towards each other during the war. He was a first-class officer and we used to visit each other's ship, but. . . .' He ran his hand through his hair. 'We just didn't get close. When he left us, I was sorry to see him go, but that's all there was to it.'

She lifted her eyes from the book she was reading. 'Maybe if he had stayed you would have become as fond of him as you are now.' She turned the book face down on her lap. 'When you met him on the night of your dinner you said he struck you as being hard, brittle. I saw some of it the day he came to lunch for the first time. That is going away now.'

'I—I don't quite know how to say this, but—er—I hope he isn't going to spoil The Boy. He makes an awful fuss of him when he comes here, and The Boy looks forward to seeing him.'

'Jealous?'

'Don't talk rot.'

'I've no doubt he would have shamelessly spoilt his own family if they had lived. Do you think he is getting over it?'

'I've never discussed it with him since I met him after the dinner. He seems to be going along all right.'

'Sometimes, when he thinks I am not looking, and you are fussing with The Boy, I see an odd little look come into his eyes. It lasts only a second or two, but—it's there. I can't define it more clearly—but it's there.'

'Oh, I expect he has his memories. But nobody can live with them for ever. Even if they don't fade, they lose their sharp outlines.'

She lifted her book, turned a couple of leaves until she found her place.

'Yes, I expect they do, in time.'

He looked at her, trying to assess the significance of her remark, but her attention was on her book.

Several pages later she lifted her head. 'Of course, the solution is for him to marry again.'

'Good Lord! Do you think that is the answer to all problems?'

'No. But there are some men who should be married, for their own good and peace of mind.'

'For instance. . .?'

'As you are doing nothing you can make tea,' she said with complete irrelevance. 'And if you search in the larder you might find something passable.'

He climbed to his feet with exaggerated weariness.

'I see what you mean, but I'm wondering who is getting what out of this married-life racket. And am I to thank Emily for anything I may find?'

'No, darling. My own sweet smile and a few judiciously bestowed packets of cigarettes.'

'Thank heaven there is somebody in this family with a sense of moral balance.'

'Who could that be, I wonder?' she asked sweetly.

A little later he resumed. 'I suppose I should consider the privilege of washing up another married-life blessing.'

'Not on your life! Men drop empty cups, but not full ones. They are too hard to replace. You bury your nose in your paper.'

She was putting the crockery away when she heard him say sharply, 'Good Lord—it can't be!'

He was standing, the newspaper clutched in his hand, pointing to a news item.

'It's—it's unbelievable! How did he come to be mixed up in that business?'

'What is it, darling?'

'Read it for yourself.'

She took the paper and read aloud a long item at the bottom of the page:

'"RIVERSIDE GANG BROKEN UP.

"At South Side Police Court today police officers of the River Police related how they had captured three of a gang of river thieves in the act of breaking into a warehouse full of foodstuffs. Two of the men, William Curtis, aged 38, lorry driver, and Edwin Senior, aged 34, a painter, who had both pleaded not guilty, were sent to prison for nine months. The third man, Thomas Clay, aged 39, a labourer, who pleaded guilty, was put back for forty-eight hours, Mr. Launcelot Martin, the magistrate, saying he wished to consider the circumstances before sentencing Clay. Inspector Harold, of the River Police, said they received information that a gang would endeavour to break into the Sunrise Wharf warehouse and police were concealed about the premises. Immediately the police revealed themselves Curtis and Senior, with other men not in custody, put up a fight and it was only after a prolonged struggle and a chase over the roofs were they arrested. Clay made no attempt to escape, neither did he struggle. Inspector Harold said he was satisfied that the three men were not the prime movers in the raid. . . .'"

'I wonder if it's my Clay? You know—my old leading hand. He lives down there somewhere. I wonder how I can find out?'

'Well, if it is, darling, there is not much you can do. He pleaded guilty, the police caught him, and that's all there is to it.'

'I could speak to the magistrate. I could say something. He was a first-class man. There must be something I could do.'

She rested her hand on his arm. 'Listen, darling. He might have been a good man for you, a good leading seaman, but——'

'Clay was a good man by any yardstick,' he snapped. 'You don't live in close contact with a man for five years and not learn most there is to know about him.'

'Perhaps the magistrate will talk severely to him and let him off.'

Haley flicked his fingers irritably. 'Magistrates don't do that sort of thing. They listen to the evidence, find a man guilty or not guilty, and act accordingly.'

She finished wiping the plate she had in her hands, disappeared into the scullery, then put her head round the corner.

'Why don't you write to the magistrate and tell him what you know about Clay? That he was a good man, that you think he has been led into trouble.'

Haley smiled thinly, 'Nobody leads Clay into anything he doesn't want to do. And I've no doubt the beak has already made up his mind. He would read a letter, toss it to one side and sentence Clay without giving it a second thought.'

'Well, why not go to the court and ask to speak on his behalf?'

He thumped a clenched fist into the palm of the other hand.

'I will! It can't make it any worse. I'll go tomorrow morning to the police court and ask if it is possible.'

The tall inspector at the police station was helpful. After Haley had explained his reason for coming the inspector leaned back, holding a pencil delicately between finger tips.

'The case is really a River Police job, but I'll have a few words with my opposite number down there, and speak to the inspector at the court.'

Haley watched him as he used the telephone. The inspector was quite impassive as he talked, giving no clue of what was being said at the other end.

'Well, sir,' he said finally as he replaced the telephone, 'this, of course, is off the record. The River lads have been after this particular mob for a long time. The other two who were caught with your man are old-timers although they are small fry. What we were after was the king-pin, or somebody near to him. The two who have gone down will keep their traps closed, and take their sentence knowing that their folks will be looked after. The River Police inspector hopes that Clay will be able to help them with some information. That could make his sentence lighter.'

Haley shook his head.

'Not Clay, I'm afraid. He won't give anybody away as he would consider it disloyal.'

'Anyway, there it is, sir. If you go to court tomorrow morning ask for Inspector Cummings and he will put you right.'

'Thank you, Inspector. Thank you very much.'

'No trouble, sir.' He stood up to shake hands. 'You weren't up Iceland way at all during the war, were you, sir?'

'No, I missed that. Were you?'

'I had a son who was. He was on a corvette. He—it was in 1942. A torpedo, we understand. It took his mother a long while to get over it, he being our only son. Good luck, sir.'

The following morning Haley sat at the back of the court listening to a series of drab stories of drab people who had broken the law. Drunks, street walkers, grey, withered men who had been found wandering abroad without visible means of support passed through the dock in an almost endless procession. The grey-haired, alert, poised man on the bench dealt with them conversationally.

'Evidence, Officer.'

The policeman droned out the details.

'Five shillings or one day.' 'Two pounds. Seven days to pay.' Justice was dealt out in crisp, cool words.

'Call Thomas Clay.'

Haley heard it like a slap. It echoed down a corridor, a door slammed and in a few seconds Clay came into the dock.

It was his Clay, his leading seaman, and all at once Haley realized that it might not have been.

The magistrate rustled some papers, read them, then lifted his head.

'This man was put back for forty-eight, your worship. He was found guilty with two other men now sentenced for breaking into a warehouse.' The clerk intoned it like a lesson.

'Yes, of course. I remember.'

"How could you forget?" Haley thought impatiently. "It's only two days since you saw him."

The magistrate leaned back in his chair. Haley caught the swift glance he threw towards the police inspector and saw the officer slightly shake his head.

'Clay, I delayed sentencing you because I wanted to consider your case apart from the other men I sent to prison. You have no police record—in fact, I understand you have a good war record. Yet you made this attempt to steal foodstuffs, which are in short supply. In other words, you were stealing to feed the black market. In these days of strict rationing in this country there is just so much for everybody—and no more. Had you been caught stealing food for your family which was starving there might have been some excuse. I wish I knew whether this was your first excursion into this form of crime. But you seem not anxious to help.'

He turned to the police inspector.

'There is nothing at all known about this man, is there?'

The inspector cleared his throat.

'Nothing at all, sir. He worked regularly before the war. Joined the Navy and—I understand—was a first-class man. Up to a few weeks ago he worked as a labourer on building sites and we believe got in with this gang because he can handle a boat quite well.'

The inspector caught Haley's eye and moved his head slightly. Haley stood up.

The inspector continued. 'His old commanding officer is in court, sir, and would like an opportunity of speaking for him.' He extended an arm. 'This way, sir.' He lifted his voice slightly. 'Lieutenant-Commander Haley, D.S.C., your worship.'

Haley climbed to the witness box. He saw in front of him a card bearing the words: "I swear by Almighty God that the evidence I shall give. . . .' He picked it up, but a police officer standing below tapped the ledge.

'You won't want that, sir.'

Haley lifted his head and found himself looking into a pair of grey eyes. The magistrate nodded slightly and waited. For a long time before he had gone to sleep the previous night Haley had gone over and over in his mind what flight of eloquence he could use, how he would string together a flawless, irresistible appeal for Clay. Now he found that the words failed to come.

'This man was—was'—the magistrate leaned forward and read from a paper on his desk—'your leading seaman at one time during the war. How long was he with you?'

'Five years, sir—your worship.'

'What was your task.'

'Minesweeping and patrolling, sir. In the Channel.'

'He had some authority as a leading seaman?'

'Oh yes! But over and above that whenever there was a spot of trouble Clay was always in the forefront. The crew sort of looked to him for a lead.'

'I see.' The magistrate drummed silently on his desk. 'Have you met him at all since the war ended?'

'No, sir.'

'You know now, of course, that he has departed from that trustworthy regard you held, or hold, for him?'

'So it seems, sir.'

'Do you think that if this court dealt leniently with him that he would refrain from any further similar crimes?'

Haley opened his mouth to speak, then stopped. "How can I answer that?" he thought. "When I was his commanding officer I could order him to do things. I can't do it now. Yet this is such an important question. What can I say?"

'. . . and he has, furthermore, shown a reluctance to assist the police in their investigations. I must take all those things into account.'

Haley heard the dispassionate voice breaking through his thoughts. He smiled. 'I have known him decline—or shall I say be unable to help?—vested authority in the past, and deal out justice in his own way. And it was effective, too, your worship.'

The magistrate concealed a smile with elegant fingers.

'Thank you, Commander Haley. You have been very helpful.'

Haley walked from the witness box miserably aware that the flights of eloquence he had imagined had remained imagination. He felt a sense of frustration, a feeling of complete failure. As he passed the dock he looked at Clay for the first time. He stood there to attention, chin out, immovable. Only his eyes moved until they met Haley's.

Clay smiled and lifted his chin slightly.

The magistrate leaned forward. 'Your old commanding officer has taken the trouble to come here this morning because he felt, from his knowledge of you, that you were trustworthy and honest. The evidence we have heard points to the contrary. It was my intention to give you a salutary sentence. I am determined to deal harshly with thieving to supply the black market. Something your commanding officer said has modified my intention. You will go to prison for three months. Take him away.'

Haley drew in his breath sharply. He had hoped against hope that Clay would be let off. He watched his one-time shipmate turn smartly and disappear through the door.

'The Old Man will let you see him, if you ask,' a police officer whispered out of the corner of his mouth. 'He'll be down below for a couple of hours before they take him away.' The police constable whispered to the inspector who, without waiting for Haley to say anything, spoke to the magistrate.

'Commander Haley would like to have a few words with the prisoner, your worship. The police have no objection.'

The magistrate inclined his head. 'Very well. You will arrange for that, inspector.'

Haley was taken through white-tiled corridors by the inspector who walked by his side without speaking. He halted at a door, opened it and showed Haley in.

'Bring Clay in,' he ordered a warder. 'You must stay the other side of the table; you mustn't try to pass him anything, or shake hands. You've got five minutes.' The inspector paused before closing the door. 'Try to talk some sense into him. That mob won't do anything for him.'

Clay halted at the door when he saw Haley waiting for him. He took a step forward and his arm began to rise.

'This side,' the warder said shortly. 'You've got five minutes, and no whispering.'

He stepped back and stood with his back to the door, his face completely impassive.

Each waited for the other to start talking. It was Haley who began.

'Hullo, Clay! I came along to see if there was anything I could do.'

'I was pleased to see you this morning, sir. How's things?'

Haley felt a surge of urgency. This was not the time for small-talk exchanges.

'Clay, when you come out—in three months isn't it?—come and see me. I'll get my address to you. Somehow we'll square things up. It isn't long, three months, I mean.'

Clay grinned. 'I can do it on my head, sir.'

'You are not married, are you? Is there anybody I can see for you. Anybody I can help?'

Clay's eyes flickered towards the impassive warder. 'I am married, sir. Got two kids. One nearly two and the other three months old. I got married just after I come out.'

'Where does she live? I'll go and see her.' Clay's lips tightened into a line.

'We—she's got a room in 14 Zenith Street, Southwark. She's a good girl, sir. She'll stand by me.'

Haley reached into his pocket for his diary and started to write.

The warder stepped forward. 'No passing notes,' he barked.

'I'm not. I'm taking down his wife's address. Is that all right?'

'You could have got it from the charge sheet,' the warder said, as if explaining a simple lesson to a child. 'You've got two minutes more.'

'How did you know I was coming up?' Clay asked.

'I read it in the papers a couple of day ago. I—I—had sort of lost touch with you since we came out. I had thought once or twice of trying to look you up, but I couldn't remember where you said you'd be. Perhaps it would have been better if I had.'

'Maybe, sir. But I've shifted about a bit since I took my demob.' He looked down at his hands spread wide on the plain table. 'They was good days, sir. She was a good ship, the old *Arandite*. Better days than now.' He lifted his head. 'It always seems that, looking back. There were times when it looked and felt pretty grim.'

There was silence between them but they looked steadily at each other. Haley managed a smile.

'I'd like to be making a drop of special coffee right now,'

Clay grinned, 'to bring one up to the bridge with a spot of you-know-what in it. I always slipped a tot or so in the coffee.'

'Which I always knew, of course. It tasted good.'

'We often wondered how much you did know, sir. Often.'

The warder stirred, pulled a watch from his breast pocket and looked at it.

'Time's up. C'mon, Clay.'

They stood up. Once again a smile passed between them. Clay came smartly to attention.

'Thank you, sir. I'm glad you're going to see my missus. She'll be looked after, but she's heard me talk about you.'

The warder touched his arm firmly.

'Good-bye, sir.'

'See you in three months, Clay.'

A spasm crossed the warder's face which Haley recognized as an incipient smile.

'If Clay keeps his nose clean and doesn't step out of line, he'll have three weeks knocked off that carpet.'

The door clicked heavily behind them. In a few moments it opened again, and a police officer beckoned.

'The inspector would like to see you before you go, sir. This way, please.'

The inspector was relaxed behind his desk with a cigarette glowing in his lips.

'Well, could you get some sense into him?' he asked.

Haley shrugged. 'I wouldn't like to say. He gave me his wife's address. I'll see her. And I'll meet him when he comes out. Inspector, what is a carpet?'

The police officer smiled.

'Crooks' jargon for three months' imprisonment, why do you ask?'

'I understand Clay will be out in two months and a week if he behaves himself.'

'That's so.' The inspector leaned back. 'If I thought he would tell you anything I could arrange a visit for you, in, say, a month or so. He'll be at Wormwood Scrubs. We don't want small fry like him. We want the Big Nobs—the king-pins. And, Commander Haley, you would be surprised if you knew who some of them are. Apparently it's big business men who finance this thieving, who have the market all ready before they organize a big steal.' He looked critically at his glowing cigarette. 'We even thought you might be part of the organization, until we made an inquiry or two.'

'Good Lord! Me a big-time thief? I wouldn't know how to steal a bottle of milk.'

'You wouldn't. You would have somebody else do it.' The inspector stood up. 'And the jargon for "thief" is "tea leaf". Your education has been broadened this morning, Commander.'

'Indeed it has, but I think I could have done without it.'

As they said good-bye the officer again offered to arrange for Haley to visit Clay.

'I think not. He wouldn't tell me anything about his—his gang boss—is that right? And——' Haley paused, looked straight at the officer. 'And I wouldn't be inclined to ask him.'

'As you wish. I'm glad we were able to help.'

Haley found Zenith Street after diligent searching. It was a narrow, grey-black street overshadowed by lofty grey warehouses. As he walked along even the people seemed grey. The houses, three and four storeys high, opened right on to the pavement. Here and there were gaps where bombs had demolished houses, and those which still stood looked battered and cracked. Number 14 had solid baulks of timber shoring up its side.

Haley took a deep breath and reached up to the rust-encrusted knocker. It rang hollowly through the house and Haley heard a shuffling inside. The door opened and a middle-aged, slatternly woman, her hair straggling and escaping from her head in untidy wisps, partly opened the door.

"Good Lord," Haley thought, "surely not the spruce, tidy Clay and this woman."

'Mrs. Clay?'

She peered at him round the door. 'Who wants her?'

'I do. I want to see her about her husband. Are you Mrs. Clay?'

'Blimey, no!' The door closed to a mere slit. 'Are you a bogey?'

'I want to see Mrs. Clay. Her husband and I were in the Navy together. Is she at home?'

The door opened slightly. 'You looks like a bogey. Them lying so-and-so's. Lying their souls away just to get a man sent down. What did he get?'

Haley struggled with rising impatience. 'Clay was sent to prison for three months. I WOULD like to see Mrs. Clay.'

'Lumme, they let him orf light, didn't they?' The door started to close again. 'I'll see if she'll see you. All upset, she is, poor thing, her old man being took like that, and on his first job, too.'

The door closed with a decided click. Haley heard the shuffling dying away inside and looked down the street, fighting against a sense of futility. Idly he watched a long, sleek car roll past and draw up against a mean, drab-looking public-house on the corner. "Somebody around here has money, anyway," he thought.

The door opened and the slatternly woman beckoned. 'Third floor. Don't fall over the barf. It's dark on that landing. She's been washing the kid. Washes him every day,' she said, slight awe creeping into her voice.

Haley climbed the bare stairs, his nose wrinkling in distaste. He stopped on the third, noisesome, landing and regarded the three doors which opened on to it. As he pondered, one opened. It swung open purposefully, wide, and a young girl stood framed in it.

'Yes?' she said crisply. Her chin was lifted up defiantly. She kept her hand on the door.

'Mrs. Clay?'

'Yes.'

'My name is Haley. I was your husband's commanding officer during the war. I've just left him. He—he has gone to prison for three months.'

The defiant chin dropped a little.

'I know. Mrs. Quale just told me. She seemed to think he would have got much more.'

Haley heard the stairs creak a floor below and guessed that Mrs. Quale was there listening.

'Could I come inside, please? I want to talk to you.'

She stepped back. Haley followed her and she closed the door.

The contrast between the drab, unkempt house and the room struck Haley forcibly. It was a small room, but it was bright. The walls were coloured with a light distemper; the window-frame was brightly painted and some of the furnishings were coloured to match. Along one wall was a double bed and near it a cot.

In the cot stood a small child, wide-eyed, looking at Haley. He was struck by the resemblance between the child and the mother.

'He follows you rather than his father, doesn't he?' Haley said with a smile.

'So they say. But he has his father's temperament.'

She glanced towards the double bed. 'The baby looks more like——' She paused. 'I've just finished bathing and feeding him,' she finished lamely.

'I'm not in the way am I? I would like to talk to you. Is there any way I can help? Are you—you short of money? Or——'

She smiled, stepped to the table, lifted up an envelope, opened the flap and pulled out a thin package of pound notes.

'This came this morning. There was only a short note with it. Just the envelope, the money and the note. Do you think it is safe? Is it stolen?'

Haley took the note. It was written in a broad, flowing hand, on good-class notepaper. "This will help. There will be more. You will be looked after." There was no signature.

'I shouldn't think it was stolen. From what I've heard this morning, I rather fancy the—the gang sent this because your husband didn't split on them.'

'Do you think I should take it to the police—or at least tell them it came?'

"I should say 'yes,'" Haley thought. "Perhaps the police can trace the notes and so find the gang. Possibly they know all about it already."

'I wouldn't,' he said aloud. 'You probably need it. If the police come here asking questions, then tell them. Otherwise, stick to it.' "And perhaps I'm persuading you to break some law or other, but does it matter?" he concluded inwardly.

'I should have kept in touch with Clay after we parted, but there were problems, and——Well, I didn't. If I had perhaps this wouldn't have happened.'

She pointed to a chair and when Haley was seated she followed suit.

'He did it for us,' she started abruptly. 'He had been badgering the housing manager on the Council about a house. This'— she looked swiftly around the room—'this was all right when we were first married. Then the children came—and Tom started to talk about a house with a garden somewhere. It was hopeless. The housing manager got nasty one day and told him he would have to wait ten years, and to be thankful he had a roof over his head, and one or two other nasty things were said.'

Haley's eyebrows climbed.

'What happened?' He knew his Clay and how he would react to such treatment.

She smiled. 'Some of the other people in the office got him out. There wasn't any damage done. But he came home furious. "We'll buy a damned house," he said. "It will be our own house." I thought it was just talk and asked him what he would use for money—matchsticks? He went out that night and when he came home he said, "I'll get that house." He went out two or three nights and was out until early in the morning. Then one day last week, after he hadn't been home all night—the police came—and——'

Her head dropped.

Haley stood up.

'I think I understand, Mrs. Clay. Try not to worry too much about it. He will be different when he comes—when he comes home. I'll try to do what I can, and I'll keep in touch with you. I'll leave my address. Please let me know if there is anything you want, or anything I can do.'

She lifted the envelope. 'It looks as if I shan't want anything, doesn't it?'

'I suppose it does. I'll come and see you later in the week.'

'Thank you, Mr. Haley. I'll get by.'

Haley stumbled down the dark staircase to find Mrs. Quale standing at the foot of the stairs.

'Pore, pore thing,' the woman whined. 'It's always hard the first time your old man is took. Mine went away for a niner the first time they nicked him. When he was in he hit a bloke in the workshop and they hooked another three on him so he did twelve moons before he was out. All the boys gave him a party.'

She stood on the doorstep, obviously anxious to make conversation.

'She'll be all right. I'll look after her. Fanny Brain will sit in with the kids one night, if we give her a couple of bottles of stout, and I'll take Mrs. Clay along to the boozer. It will brighten things up for her. The boys will buy her a few drinks.'

Haley looked towards the dingy public house on the corner, and at the flashy American car outside it. He imagined the slim, attractive Mrs. Clay being entertained. There was a distinct grate in his voice as he growled, 'I advise you to leave her alone. If she wants to go out, I will see to it.'

Mrs. Quale bridled for a moment, then simpered, 'Like that, is it? The price of a couple of bottles of stout and I'll watch the kids.'

Haley snorted and walked away from her.

As he reached the car a man stepped from the side of it.

'You been seeing Clay's missus?' he asked coldly.

'I have.'

'Friend of his?'

'We were shipmates for several years, I was his C.O.'

Haley studied the little group intently. They were hard-faced, sharp-eyed men, all of a similar age, in the late twenties.

On an impulse he asked, 'Are you the boss of the gang?'

The one who had barred his path smiled slightly.

'No.'

'Can I see him?'

The men exchanged glances. One opened the door of the car.

'Sure. Get in.'

The car sped through back streets and in a few minutes Haley found himself climbing steep stairs in an old building given over to offices. On one door he read: South Side Importers Ltd.

He was ushered into an outer office and with almost no delay was taken in to the boss.

A youngish, clean-shaven man rose to meet him. He was quite unlike the gang boss Haley had visualized.

He rose and held out his hand.

'How do you do. My name is Wendall. Like you I'm an ex-lieutenant-commander R.N.V.R.'

12

'LET ME MAKE one point clear, Haley,' Wendall said later, 'I did not directly employ your man, Clay. I had never heard of him until this unfortunate affair blew up. He was incorporated, shall I say, by Dickie, the man who asked you to come here.'

'Dickie being one of your fellow-directors?'

'Scarcely. More of a personnel expert. Do have a drink, Haley. It puts me off my shot seeing you standing there like a request man. No?'

He poured himself a drink and splashed it.

'What did you get out of the war, Haley, apart from temporary acting rank of lieutenant-commander? The same as me, about sixty quid gratuity?'

'Roughly. But I didn't go to war to get anything out of it except to come out alive and—and——'

'Go on, say it—"To do your bit for freedom and democracy." Strike up the band while the heroes march by in threes. What ships were you in? Minesweeping! A lousy game. I was in M.G.B.s and M.T.B.s until I was switched to a special job following up the Germans. Then I got into the real cash.'

'You weren't alone in that.'

'I'll say I wasn't. And the Yanks had us beaten to a frazzle. Why, they had colonels in rimless glasses with bulging brief-cases really on the make.'

He tilted back his chair and crossed his arms. 'Oh, I did the naval job I was sent to do. Got a Mention in Dispatches for it, too. But I salted away a fair amount of cash. Never mind how. I was looking around for an opening to start a business of some sort and. . . .' He waved his arm expressively round the expensively furnished room.

'So you went into the black market,' Haley sneered.

'You are an irritating man, Haley. Let us say that I appreciated the difficulty of supply and demand.'

'And you meet demand by gulling some fools to break into a warehouse so that you can supply.'

Wendall's face hardened. 'I take it that anything we discuss here today remains between the two of us, Haley?'

Haley smiled thinly. 'Like Clay, I won't talk.'

Wendall nodded. A grin creased his lips.

'So I understand. Well, if it makes you feel any better the warehouse we were—shall I say prospecting?—was full of stuff earmarked for the black. I was twisted in a deal and was, in actual fact, merely trying to collect what was rightfully, if not legally, mine.'

'And three men have gone to prison because the raid failed.'

'An occupational risk, my dear man. You took far greater risks, so did Clay and the others, for much less money. Clay stood to get two hundred pounds down for a couple of hours' work. Did he ever receive even two pounds for two hours' minesweeping? Of course he didn't. Look, Haley, the black market is here; it prospered while we were scrapping during the war and it's here to stay, at least for the next five years or more.' He leaned forward. 'And I propose to cash in as much as I can to try to catch up on the fraternity who were piling it up for nearly six years.'

'That is between you and your conscience, if you have one. But let us get down to the matter of bringing me here.'

'Very well, but as for your damned conscience, or mine, answer one question, Haley. Have you never bought the odd coupon, or the pair of nylons, or a tin of something for your wife?' He watched Haley's face and chuckled. 'You see, the only difference between us is that you are looking through the wrong end of the telescope and the picture is small. Furthermore, you are demand, I am supply. See?' He pushed the cigarette box over and Haley took one.

When it was glowing Wendall chuckled.

'And they came through the black, too. Would you like a nice American ham? Can do!'

He poured a drink into a glass, looked inquiringly at Haley

with his thumb on the siphon and splashed a little into the glass. He pushed it towards Haley.

'That's not black. It's Black and White, to be exact. Honest, but expensive. It cost the earth. Like a case delivered at home, as a gesture?'

'No thanks. Do you know why I'm here? Why was that car there?'

'That's simple. Clay saw some of the—er—importing organization. If he talked to the police it would be awkward—and perhaps expensive. I said expensive,' he repeated, having caught Haley's look. 'Poor policemen have to live, you know, and the higher they are the more expensive it is. You were in court and saw Clay afterwards. Then you went into the head copper's office. I had to know what went on.'

'Was it you sent the money to Mrs. Clay?'

'I can only say, with a show of virtue, it was. And she will get some more, too. If it is of any comfort to you, when Clay comes out I propose to use him on a job which is not quite in the front line.'

Haley leaned forward and frowned.

'When Clay comes out he will have nothing more to do with you, or your organization. I'll see to that.'

Wendall smiled gently. 'No doubt you will have that little house with a garden all ready and waiting. Be your age, Haley, and leave Clay to me. I'll look after him. In passing, this touching solicitude for him is quite new, isn't it? You hadn't bothered about him from the day you parted. He's grown up and has got what I want.'

Wendall stood up. His hand disappeared beneath the edge of the table and as he heard the door click open behind him Haley guessed there was a bell push there.

'Right, Dickie. See Mr. Haley gets away nicely. Run him to where ever he wants to go in the car. The front way. Dickie.'

'Right, Boss.'

He stood with his hand on the open door, his face completely expressionless.

'It's been quite a naval re-union, hasn't it, Haley? Have dinner with me one night. Bring your wife. You'll like mine; she's quite a—gangster's moll!'

Haley grinned. Despite his repugnance for the work Wendall was doing he liked him and his engaging manner.

'We'll leave it at that. I reclaim Clay. You can try otherwise.'

Wendall nodded. 'We'll see. For the time being, *au revoir*. Remember, bring your wife. Mine is staying this week with Lord and Lady Fordmantle at Basset Ford. They are her grandparents and brought her up. I met her when she was a Wren.'

Haley smiled wickedly. 'I'll concede you the blue blood.'

Haley spent the remainder of the day in a thoughtful, introspective mood. Some of Wendall's shrewd arguments kept recurring to him. A backlog of work awaited him at his office but he found it difficult to concentrate. He found himself looking at a trim typist, at her nylon-sheathed, shapely legs.

"I wonder if you bought those in the black market?" he thought. He was gazing out of the window when somebody put a cup of tea at his side.

'Oh, thank you, Mrs. Loughton. I wanted that.'

'Comes nice, a cuppa' in the afternoon, doesn't it? You can have a spot of sugar, too,' the middle-aged woman said. 'We're all right for tea and sugar this week. My Ernie knows a man who can get it under the counter. Two quarters of tea and half a pound of sugar as easy as kiss me hand.'

Haley shook his head. 'It's all wrong, Mrs. Loughton, isn't it?'

'Lor' a' mercy, Mr. Haley. If it wasn't for the black we'd all starve. Do you know who is my Ernie's best customer, for tea, sugar and the odd steak now and then? Why, our vicar. Never misses a bet, he doesn't. "Ernest," he says in my hearing, "Any time you have anything and it's honest come by," he says, "I'd like to hear about it. Honest, mind."' She stood with her hands crossed over her ample middle. 'If it's good enough for the vicar, it's good enough for me, I says.'

Haley nodded. 'I suppose so, Mrs. Loughton. Thank you for the tea.'

He looked about him, at his colleagues. One of them, he

knew, had bought sufficient coupons to enable him to buy a suit. Another occasionally had mysterious parcels left there for him which, he explained with a wink, were from "a pal in the know".

Haley tried to concentrate again, and failed.

The introspective mood lasted him until he arrived home.

His wife clutched the neck of her dress when he told her what had occurred.

'Oh, Bill, anything might have happened, and I would never have known. Why didn't you shout for a policeman when that horrible man forced you into the car?'

'He didn't force me into the car, my dear. I asked him to take me to see his boss.'

'I've seen it happen on the films, and the man is always dead afterwards. Don't see him again, please, darling.'

'I don't suppose I ever shall. But I'm worried about Clay. You see, he wants a house away from that slum. And the only way he can get it, so he thinks, is by joining that organization. There must be another way, somehow.'

He moved to the sideboard and looked bleakly at the bottle. 'I'll have to go easy on this. About four tots left and Meredith is coming tonight.'

She put her head round the kitchen door.

'Perhaps they'll have some in over the week-end. They promised to keep a bottle for you when it came.'

Haley grinned. 'Believe it or not, I firmly refused a gift of a case of this today.'

'Then you want your head reading. Tell your friend to try me with a box of nylons, or anything else. He wouldn't hear me say "no".'

'He is not my friend and I don't think nylons come into his scheme,' Haley said with a tinge of irritability in his voice. 'Shall we change the subject?'

'Yes, dear,' she replied demurely. 'What time is Owen coming? For dinner or after?'

'Oh, afterwards.'

She looked archly at the ceiling. 'He's never any problem.

204

In fact, he often helps out with a couple of chops, or something. He seems to have a fairly fat meat ration.'

'You're impossible and quite unmoral.'

'Is that the same as being immoral?'

'Worse.'

'Interesting, isn't it, though? Scarlet woman will now prepare dinner.'

'Not scarlet, darling. Just plain, dingy black. Black as soot.'

'Can't I settle for grey?'

'Black it is and black you remain.'

'Then I should have pearls to match,' she said mischievously.

'I am offering you pearls—pearls of wisdom, and you are throwing them away.'

'Keep at it, Solomon. You're wearing me down.'

Haley found himself in a minority of one when Meredith arrived. Meredith was almost glowing when he came in. He slipped a packet into Mrs. Haley's hands and grinned.

'That will help out with the breakfast,' he said. He turned to Haley and continued, 'And I have something for us. From a friend of a friend of a friend.' He pulled from his hip pocket a half bottle of whisky. 'One of my tugmen gave me this. Probably pinched from a cargo. But that won't stop it from tasting good.' He sparred for an opening with the younger Haley, swept him up in his arms and swung him high. The boy yelled with delight and took a good handful of Meredith's hair.

'Did you say "pinched"?'

'Ouch, leave me some hair, youngster! I said "pinched". Cargo pilfering is almost a major industry at the docks these days—that is, if the railway thieves leave enough to steal. It's Big Business, Bill.'

'So I learned today,' Haley said drily.

'Bill was taken for a ride today, by a big gangster, Owen, and was nearly bumped off.'

'Not so easy as it sounds. People spent years trying to bump him off. If it comes off, I put in the first claim for the attractive widow.' He wrestled with the boy for a few seconds. 'That is, if it includes The Boy.'

'There are moments when you could have him for nothing,' she laughed. 'You tell him Bill while I put the finishing touches to the dishes. You've eaten, by the way, Owen?'

'Like a king, with a beautiful lady, too.'

'That I must hear in detail. Wait until I finish off. You tell him about your gangster, Bill.'

'Knock the top off that bottle,' Meredith said, seating himself in an armchair with The Boy on his knee.

Haley related the events of the day. He expected Meredith to bridle and flame and outline what punitive action he would have taken. Instead, Meredith was quiet.

'Just as well you didn't get tough. Those boys are deadly. You wouldn't be the first to be found at low-water mark. I'm told the favourite method is a few large lumps of rock salt chained to a man's feet. When the salt melts he comes to the surface. "Found drowned" is the usual verdict.'

'Great Scott, I wasn't quarrelling with him.'

'Lucky for you.'

'I've been thinking, Meredith. Clay was a good seaman, one of the best. Could you find a billet for him on your tugs?'

'No,' Meredith said shortly.

'Why not?'

'Because he now has a criminal record. The police would be round to us every time there had been a big steal at the docks, asking "Where was Clay?" "What job was he on at the time?" It wouldn't work, Bill. Sorry!'

'But you've just said that half your tug and lighter men know about this stealing, and buy some of the goods. You do yourself.' Haley held up the bottle Meredith had brought with him.

Meredith pondered. 'True. I hadn't quite looked at it from that light. But so far as I know none of my men have records.'

'But some of them are, according to you, in league with the river thieves if they are not actual thieves themselves. Like you—and me, for that matter—we receive, which is, in the eyes of the law, akin to stealing.'

'I refuse to be drawn into an argument. You produce too

206

much pitiless logic for me. The short fact remains that I cannot fix up Clay when he comes out.'

Haley breathed deeply as a feeling of resentment stirred inside him. Before he could pursue the point his wife came in.

'Now tell me all about the beautiful lady. Where did you meet her? Who is she? Why have you left her so early?'

Meredith leaned back, his hand fondling The Boy's hair.

'The first time I ever saw her I disliked her intensely. Not strange because at that time I disliked everybody, including myself. She was the ward sister in the hospital where I was. Now she is at a hospital down in Kent somewhere. I met her at Charing Cross. She was very early for a date so I persuaded her to have a quick dinner with me.'

'Are you meeting her again?'

Meredith grinned.

'I've got her phone number and address if that is any criterion.'

'It will serve for a start. Tell me, is she beautiful? What colour is her hair?'

'She's extremely attractive. I found that out even when she was in hospital and wearing that starched and stiff uniform. Her hair? Oh, sort of tawny gold.'

'And blue eyes?'

'I didn't notice. I think they are.'

'You spend an hour with a girl and notice nothing. Marjorie would look at her for five seconds and could spend the next hour telling you in detail all about her,' Haley grinned.

'You'll have the chance to look at her for longer than five seconds. I hope you'll meet her in the near future.'

'Oh, oh!' Mrs. Haley made it sound significant.

' "Oh, oh!" nothing. She's married. At least, she wears a wedding ring,' Meredith countered with a smile.

'Time for small men to go to bed,' Bill's wife said, capturing The Boy, who was led off, protesting.

Meredith tilted the bottle over their glasses.

'Women are marvellous, aren't they? Give them a fragment and they build up a detailed whole from next to nothing.'

Haley nodded. 'I begin to understand now why the French

207

women are such incredible experts at making do with so little and making that little go a long way. After two major wars, with the effects of the Franco-Prussian war still hanging on their necks, they had no choice. British women are in the same boat now.'

Meredith sampled his drink, added a little more water, tasted it again and nodded.

'There's something in that, Bill. Look, I know you hold some decided views on this, some odd views, I consider them, but there is no need for you and the folk to live on the edge, you know. I get all sorts of things offered to me, things I have no use for, but I'm sure the missus could——'

Haley looked at him unsmilingly. ' "*Et tu, Brute ?*" ' he said.

Meredith grinned. 'I think that means, "so you are in the racket, too?" doesn't it?'

'Broadly.'

Meredith finished his drink and put the glass down with a smack.

'If I could stop this black market and buying of unrationed stuff, I would. But there is no man breathing who can do it. Abroad it has become an accepted part of life. I'm afraid we will have to adjust ourselves to a new sense of values. You were talking about Frenchwomen a while ago. I had to go to Calais recently to discuss a towing job. The Frenchman I had to see is a stout, upright citizen who fought like hell against the Germans in the Resistance. He counts himself fortunate that he earns enough to enable his wife to go out and purchase things in the black market—quite openly—which officially are in short supply. He told me that even Ministers of State do it. It's a business.'

Haley drove his fist into an open palm.

'Probably so, and what is it doing to the moral fibre of France? What has it done already? Look at it—a mass of people which was once a nation is now a—a—rabble without backbone, leadership, or a code of honour. Youngsters are growing up accepting that twisted code as the correct thing. I'd hate it like hell for my kid to grow up with that outlook. And this country is shaping that way.'

'Things will improve. Once we get this Red rabble out of power and get Winston back the country will come back to normal.'

'You should meet Captain Mahoney. He holds the same views as you about the men who rule us.'

'Rule be damned! This mob impeded every effort we made to prepare for the war; when we were in it they did nothing but yowl about the lack of preparation—that is, when they weren't squealing for us to launch a second front to take the pressure off their Russian pals.'

'There's a touch of the old Meredith. Don't forget, the head shouter, or nearly the head, is a countryman of yours.'

'All flocks have their black sheep,' Meredith growled. 'Let's talk about something more cheerful. 'Nother drink, Bill? There's more where this came from.'

Haley accepted.

'I'll make one more point, then we'll talk about ships, or shoes, or sealing wax. . . .'

'. . . or cabbages and kings,' Meredith completed with a laugh. 'It's a long time since I heard you say that. Regan always claimed that when you said that you were entitled to two more drinks, then you were tiddley.'

'Nonsense!'

'Well, go ahead, make your point.'

Haley plucked at his bottom lip.

'It's about Clay. If you—if we,' he amended, 'if we accept the black market and accept what it provides as a substitute code why shouldn't we extend a helping hand to a man who has been—unfortunate, shall I say?'

Meredith frowned. 'You help him all you can. I'm not stopping you. But I can't.'

'Won't,' Haley interjected.

'No, Bill, can't. I've told you why. If I hear of anything which might suit him, and it doesn't come within my job, then I will tell you.'

'We'll leave it at that. I find it odd that men who wouldn't think twice about going back through a minefield, or under shell fire to help another man, can't find the same spirit in peace time.'

'I could pick a quarrel with you on that point. One was a duty. We were all comrades together, a sort of——'

'I know—one for all and all for one. Strike up the band while the heroes march by in threes.'

'Bit cynical for you, isn't it?'

'I was quoting something I heard earlier today.'

'Your racketeer pal?'

'My black market acquaintance.'

Marjorie Haley bustled into the room. 'There! He's asleep and there is peace in the house. What have I missed? And when are you seeing your nurse friend again, Owen?'

'Your wife has a one-track mind, Bill. Soon, I hope. I was figuring on making it a four-handed dinner somewhere, and a show afterwards. You can fix a sitter-in for the lad?'

'Easily! I'd love that. You fix the date.'

Meredith wrote to Sister Payne and wound up his letter:

You will like Bill Haley and his wife. He and I were together in the early days of the war. I met her but recently and the more I see of her the more I like her. Please say you can come.

Sister Payne replied promptly:

I will be delighted. I do not get out often enough. Your friends sound as if they are very nice.

At the end of her letter she wrote:

I have to be in London next Wednesday morning for a conference. I will be clear by half past twelve. Could we meet for lunch?

Meredith met her and took her to one of the few remaining genuine chop houses in the City.

'This is one way of getting a lunch on the cheap,' he said brazenly. 'Get your business over and foist yourself on a friend. What will you have? The menu is all yours. There are some good items about a couple of bob lower down the list.'

210

'I've got a jolly good mind to soak you for a steak, with all the trimmings——'

'And a half bottle of burgundy. You're a good judge. This place still does the best steak in London. But think of your curves. You'll creak at the corset for hours. It takes three men to carry one of their steaks.'

'Bring on your three men. After a diet of mincemeat and bacon and beans I could eat the men as well.'

The meal continued in the same light-hearted vein until Meredith lifted his glass of rich red Burgundy.

'And they're a sort of violet-blue. Now I can answer that,' he said.

'What on earth are you talking about?'

'Your eyes. Mrs. Haley asked me what colour they were. I couldn't tell her, not with any certainty. I knew they weren't brown.'

'The way you men walk about three parts blind makes me despair for you. And what was your thumbnail picture of me, may I ask?' She was all feminine.

Meredith leaned back, put his elbow on the arm of his chair and propped his chin on his hand.

'I'm abridging now, of course, but I touched on the outstanding features. Let me see, now. I said, "a bit hatchet-faced, chin like a tombstone, dyed hair—'carroty' was the nearest I could get".'

A twinkle showed in her eyes.

'Oh, and the eyes. I couldn't recall the colour but I touched on the merciless glint.'

'Just you wait until we women get together and I'll give her a detailed picture of you. And I mean detailed. You forget I had you for a long time under my charge.'

'Under your thumb, you mean. I must have been the world's worst patient.'

She shook her head. 'Not quite. But you were stubborn.'

'I have frequently wondered exactly what it was I was supposed to be suffering from. I find it difficult sometimes, when

I mention I was in hospital, to explain to people. Haley and his wife, for instance. Could you put a name to it for me?'

'I could, but you wouldn't understand it. It means, roughly, carrying a too heavy a load for too long.'

'Men carried bigger loads than I, and didn't crack.'

'It is all relative. In all probability you would have absorbed severe physical wounds with an almost carefree attitude. Yours was a long accumulation of strain, mental of course, with'— she paused and looked steadily at him—'a sudden and devastating increase when you were at the limit of your endurance.'

'Go on.'

'So nature said—and nature always has the last word— "this lad has had enough". It folded you up.'

She lifted her arm and looked at her wrist watch. As she did so Meredith again noticed her wedding ring.

'I said it was all relative. A load for a carthorse which would be well within its power to carry for a long time would break a donkey's back in half the period.'

'An entertaining comparison. Donkey will now get the bill.' He signalled to a hovering waiter and collected his check.

'Chump,' she chuckled. 'If you like, I'll amend it and talk about eagles and sparrows.'

Meredith changed the subject.

'What time does you train go?'

'I have a choice. I don't have to be back at the hospital until five o'clock.'

'Then Old Father Thames, and the tugs which chug on him, will have to get along without me for a couple of hours. Do you mind putting up with a donkey for a bit longer?'

'I love them. They look so patient and long-suffering.'

'Wait until you hear me bray.'

'I've heard you. It's horrible.'

They stood together on the pavement outside the chop house. A warm sun battled through the perpetual haze which hung over the city.

'Like to see a part of the Thames which is different from Westminster Reach?'

'I would.'

They walked through the narrow bomb-scarred streets of the City, breasting against the hurrying, harassed people until they found themselves standing on a curved stone forecourt which looked almost like a battlement. The wall dropped down sheer to the water. Behind them was a solid-looking house, its small, paned windows also curved.

'Years and years ago this was a merchant's house. His ships tied up alongside this wall and the cellars were his storerooms and warehouse. Didn't somebody once call the Thames "liquid history"? This is part of it. Down in one part of the cellar you can still see the chains in the walls where men—and women—waiting to be transported were chained up until the ships sailed.'

'And what is it now?'

'Partly offices; one floor is a small club. I belong, but I won't take you there. We would find it full of maudlin men, having spent a couple of hours drinking after a morning's so-called work. They'd tell you their troubles.'

'Commander Maldon holds the theory that a good—what did he call it?—a good sozzle occasionally does a man the world of good. He proved it once, if I remember,' she concluded, looking innocently up at the grey-blue sky.

'Bull's-eye,' Meredith chuckled, sitting on the broad stone wall. 'I remember.'

They sat in silence, watching the river traffic on the yellow water. Finally Meredith touched her hand lightly.

'Wake up. You're miles away.'

She turned with a slight start. 'I was,' she confessed.

'I've spent enough on you today, filling you with horse-flesh, so I won't offer a penny for them. You'd probably take it.'

'A bit too mixed to sort out at the moment.'

'I see.' He kept his hand on her fingers. She made no attempt to pull them away. 'As we will be meeting again—more than once, I hope I can call you something else besides "Sister Payne".'

'My name is Jean. You can't shorten that any more, can you?'

213

'Indeed not. I was afraid it might be Eliza. And my name is Owen.'

'I knew that.' She stood up.

Meredith touched the wedding ring. 'There is something I want to ask you. Your husband—will he—does he mind if you——?'

'He's dead. He was a bomber pilot. It was one of the big raids over Berlin.'

'I'm sorry,' Meredith said.

'I'm not. And I wasn't when I heard that he was dead. I hated him and hated every minute he was with me.' Her voice was emotionless, calm.

'Good God!' Meredith exclaimed.

She took a deep breath, looked out over the river, turned to him and smiled.

'Did it shock you? It's not an original story. He was handsome, much too handsome. It was one of those whirlwind romances that are so frequent in war time. It took me just two days to find that he was a sadist, that he had not the slightest love for me. All he wanted was me in bed. Maybe the war had twisted him. I'll never know. I think not. Cruelty was his passion. And I—I learned that he was happiest when he was being cruel to a woman, more so when she was his. I used to dread his leaves and prayed that one day he wouldn't come on leave. It came. People thought I was breaking my heart. I wasn't. I was crying from sheer relief.' She started to walk away from the wall. 'I have thirty minutes to catch a train. How long will it take me to get to Charing Cross Station?'

Meredith fell in beside her.

'Fifteen minutes, less in a taxi. I'm sorry.'

'Sorry for what?'

'Mentioning your—your——'

'My late husband? There is nothing to be sorry about. A similar sort of man was hanged a few weeks ago. I was lucky. The girls that one killed were unlucky.'

Meredith waved a taxi to a stop and during its journey to the station he was silent.

214

As he waited for the guard to signal the train away he stood outside the window.

'I'll fix up a show and a dinner and you'll come?' he asked.

'Be delighted. Not next week, the week after. On my day off next week I'm meeting Clint.'

Pheep pheep. The guard's whistle shrilled.

'Clint? Who in hell is Clint?'

'A nice American officer I've got to know.'

'To the devil with Clint! Make it next week.'

'Sorry—can't. The week after. Write or phone me.'

The train started to move.

'I will. And I hope that Clint man falls and breaks a leg.'

He was walking with the moving train.

'Better still, his neck.'

He watched the train out of sight.

And for no reason that he could define he felt glad that there was no husband.

"Damned Yanks," he muttered. "Why the blazes don't they go back to their own country?"

13

In the succeeding months a rich and understanding friendship sprang up between Jean Payne and Marjorie Haley. The nurse formed the habit of calling on afternoons when she had her weekly day off. Once she confessed to a feeling of slight guilt.

'I sometimes wonder if I am imposing, dropping in on you like this. But you don't know how refreshing it is to meet somebody who doesn't want to talk shop all the time.'

Marjorie Haley smiled at her. 'You come whenever you like, my dear. I look forward to seeing you. The day gets a bit long at times with only The Boy to talk to.'

One afternoon Jean Payne brought with her a friend.

'I'm not stopping. I've just called to say "hullo" and "good-bye". Clint is taking me to a show tonight. Just fancy, I've got all of twenty-four hours' leave. I'm not due back until midday tomorrow. Gorgeous!' She waved a hand towards a young American army officer.

'May I introduce Clint? Clinton West, this is Mrs. Haley. You've heard me talk about her.'

'Sure is a pleasure to meet you, ma'am.' The officer extended his hand. 'There have been times when I figured Mrs. Haley was a secret boy friend she had hidden away. When I couldn't get her to make a date.'

Marjorie Haley chuckled. 'She probably has, if she's clever. But I assure you we just sit with our knees up, drink tea and gossip about unimportant things.'

'Men not being one of them?'

'I said "unimportant things". But speaking of tea——Hang on until I get a pot and you can listen while we gossip.'

As they sat drinking tea Marjorie Haley quietly studied the tall, lean young American.

"He looks like the young men I see in the films, and he talks like them," she decided. "Most attractive. I wonder if she is in love with him?"

A little later, when they had gone and Haley had arrived home, she told him of their visit.

'And that American is very much in love with Jean, Bill. It stuck out a mile.'

'How did you guess that? Did he lean up against her? Or stroke her arm? That's what most of them do when I see them with a girl.'

'He did nothing of the sort. He's a very nice boy, extremely good-mannered. I caught the way he looked at her occasionally.' She stood with her lower lip held lightly between finger and thumb. 'I wonder—is this going to hurt him?'

'Who? The Yank? More likely the other way round.'

'No. Owen.'

Haley paused with a cigarette half way to his lips. His eyebrows registered surprise.

'Owen? Meredith? Why in the name of Pete should it hurt him because a Yank soldier ogles Jean Payne?'

Marjorie Haley's head came forward. She spoke each word slowly and distinctly. 'Because Owen is in love with her, too. Has been since he first met her again in London.'

'Nonsense!'

'You walk about with your eyes shut three-quarters of the time. It's been obvious for months now.'

'Well, why hasn't the clown said something to her? She could only say "no" and that wouldn't kill him.'

'How do you know he hasn't?' She amended it rapidly. 'No, he hasn't, not yet. But he will.'

'Gracious me! The romances you women build up from nothing. From nothing at all.'

'From nothing at all is right.' She looked scornfully at him. 'You men don't know how much fantasy, how much romance, we build around what we have.' The beginning of a smile quirked at the corners of her mouth.

Haley took one step and put his arm round her waist.

'All right, I'm Gregory Peck or Gary Cooper in disguise.' His arm tightened. 'But I'll settle for what I have.'

She leaned back against his encircling arm until she could look into his face.

'Me, too,' she whispered.

It was Meredith himself who brought events to a head. He had taken upon himself the role of baby sitter for The Boy when Haley and his wife wanted to go out on an odd evening or two. Haley had protested when Meredith first mentioned it, but Marjorie Haley brought to it a wealth of understanding.

'He likes doing it. To begin with, it is somewhere for him to come where he feels he is at home,' she urged. 'He plays with The Boy until the child is tired, then he puts him to bed. Maybe he remembers his own children. Maybe it is just because he likes Terence. You see, dear, all he has when he has finished his day's work is his digs, or to go out for the evening, or to come here.'

'You win,' Haley said. 'But glory me! Owen Meredith, tough fighting man baby-sitting just makes me chuckle.'

'Hold your giggles until you work out who is doing the baby sitting. Weren't you ever lonely?'

Haley looked at her, his head on one side, the tip of his tongue on his lips.

'I think I know what you mean. I think I do.'

'And don't you dare say anything to him about it. If you do, he'll slip back into his shell.'

'I won't.'

Meredith arrived earlier than usual one evening. He had promised to sit with The Boy while Haley and his wife went to a show at the local cinema.

'A spot of fog around, Bill. The lower reaches of the Thames are blacked out. I've got tugs stuck all over the place, and there they'll stay until it lifts.'

'Do you think we ought to go?' she asked with a tinge of doubt.

'Oh, it's not so bad here,' Meredith said. 'You can see fifty yards. And in any case what's a spot of fog to a man who could shove a ship through the Goodwins in a fog like a wet blanket?'

Haley chuckled. 'That wasn't choice; it was necessity.'

Marjorie Haley still had her doubts. 'It's not only the fog. Terence hasn't been too well during the day. He seems to have a sore throat. I think perhaps we had better stay.'

'Nonsense! I'll whip him off to bed early. You get out and enjoy yourself.'

She looked at Meredith. Then she shrugged.

'All right. But we'll make it early home. Isn't Jean coming up to Town tonight? This is her day off.'

'I wouldn't know,' Meredith answered shortly. 'She said she had a date so I didn't ask any further questions.'

For once The Boy did not take uproarious and rapturous advantage of Meredith. Shortly after Haley and his wife had left he crept whimpering on to Meredith's lap and crouched there. He seemed to breathe with difficulty. To breathe in he had to lift his head with a jerk and the breathing was accompanied by a harsh whistle. He was like a boy who had run too far. Meredith tried giving him sips of a drink, but the child just turned his head away. Gradually the little lad's face turned a purplish blue and his head lay back jerking convulsively as he tried to breathe.

Meredith became deeply worried. He tried looking down the child's throat, depressing his tongue with the handle of a spoon. He could see that the back part of the mouth and throat was an angry red flecked with streaks of white but beyond that his examination told him nothing.

He had just laid the boy on a settee and was watching him writhing and twisting in his efforts to breathe when the door bell jangled stridently. He opened the door and stepped back from the billowing fog which swirled in through the door. A shadowy figure stood on the doorstep.

'Mr. Haley?'

'No.'

'This is the Haley residence? I think I've got it right.'

The young man on the doorstep stepped into the hall, closing the door behind him.

'We can keep some of this darned fog out, anyway. My name is West, Clint West. Is Mr. or Mrs. Haley at home?'

'They're out. Gone to a show.'

'I've got it! You're Meredith. I've heard Jean talk about you.' He held out his hand.

Meredith took it and looked at the youngster. Although he was in civilian gear it was easy to detect the American cut of his clothes.

'Come inside,' Meredith said, and turned to make his way back to the lounge.

'Would Jean be here?' Clint asked. 'We had a date but the darned fog made me more than an hour late. She wasn't there so the only place I could figure where she might be was here. I came near to buying the taxi which got me here. But it was worth it. How in Hades that driver found his way beats me.'

'Mrs. Payne isn't here. If she had any sense she wouldn't have started out. The fog has been bad over Kent all day.'

'Mrs. Payne? Oh, you mean Jean. I keep forgetting her other name. Hullo! What's up with the lad?'

He bent over The Boy and studied him closely.

'I don't know,' Meredith said. 'He was a bit off-colour when Haley and wife went out, but it was nothing much. He got much worse about half an hour ago.'

Clinton West stood up.

'I figure a doctor is wanted. Can you get one?'

'What is it?'

'I'd guess diphtheria or something like it. This kid will choke if we don't get a doctor.'

'There's no telephone in the house. I'll have to find one outside. Are you certain?'

The young American stood up. 'I only got part way through medical studies before that man-sized war interfered. But I'd yell "doctor" every time at the top of my voice for this.'

Meredith shrugged himself into a coat. 'Haley and his wife will have a blue fit if they come home and find a doctor here. I'll try phoning; if I don't get any joy I'll ring the police for an ambulance or something.'

'Sure, sure! If we don't get somebody it's this kid who'll have the blue fit. Why in hell didn't Jean show up here?'

Meredith shrugged. Resentment still rode him roughly as he stepped out into the swirling fog. He hadn't the slightest idea where to start looking for a telephone box and he wandered rather aimlessly into the opaque darkness, his footsteps echoing hollowly as he walked.

"Surely one of these houses must have a phone?" he thought. He groped his way through a front gate, found a bell push and kept his finger on it. When no reply came he thudded heavily on the knocker. Still there was no answer.

Slight panic began to grasp him. He realized that he wasn't certain of his way back. He stepped out of the gate and a deep voice startled him.

'What's going on? Where have you been?'

A tall figure loomed in front of Meredith. It was a policeman. Hurriedly Meredith explained.

Only slowly did the policeman's doubts vanish.

'That's an empty house. Has been for weeks. You passed a telephone box fifty yards back.'

Impatiently Meredith asked where it was and the policeman explained.

'I'll come along with you,' he said. His torch glowed and he examined a small book.

'We've got Doctor Robertson and Doctor Lloyd near here. We'll try them. What did you say the address was where the child is ill?'

Neither doctor was at home and Meredith slammed the receiver down.

'Now what?'

'Ambulance.' The policeman's doubts had now evaporated. 'I'll meet it here and bring it along to the house. It's a bit hard to find. You get back. You are about half a mile away. Straight as you go until you pass the third turning on the right. Then cross the road and take the second left. Got it?'

Meredith nodded. 'Yes, but I didn't cross any roads getting here.'

'You came a long way round. Now, the third turning on the right, straight across the road and second left.'

Meredith stepped out into the fog, leaving the policeman at the telephone box.

And in one minute he was completely lost.

"This must be the third turn right," he thought. He stepped away at right angles to cross the road, expecting to come to a kerb in a few yards. There was no kerb. Then he realized that he had been walking along a road which joined at an angle. Carefully he retraced his steps, once more re-crossed the road until his foot touched the pavement. He found a gap. Then doubts arose. Was this the third turning? Or had he crossed at an angle? He decided to go back to the telephone box and meet the ambulance. He walked for a while without success. Then he stopped dead and listened.

Muffled through the fog he heard the clang of an ambulance. It stopped momentarily; he heard its engine softly rev up and the clanging bell dwindled away.

"Was it in front? Or at the back? Or. . . ." Meredith felt rising panic taking over.

"Easy now, easy," he whispered to himself. "Keep going, you'll meet somebody who can tell you where you are. Easy now."

He plunged off again into the fog, trying desperately to get a bearing. Despite his effort to keep it under, panic began to assert itself. He had been left in charge of the child and he had gone dashing out into the fog because a young shavetail of an American officer had practically ordered him to do so. Why hadn't he sent the American out while he stayed with The Boy? Why hadn't Jean come along? He swerved away from a dark shape which loomed up, found it was an electric fuse box. He leaned against it, his breath coming in deep gasps.

"Jean, Jean, why didn't you come? I wanted you—we wanted you."

There built up in his mind a picture of what would have happened had she been at the door instead of the American. She would have taken over coolly, calmly. He could almost see her competent hands coping with The Boy. They were trained hands, soft, gentle yet firm. Even the mere touch of them was comforting. He remembered how their gentle pressure had brought to him a slight glow when he was a patient in hospital.

Meredith straightened up, squared his shoulders and stepped off once more into the fog. He had got a grip on himself. "Decide on a line and stick to it. It's bound to bring you out somewhere where there are people." He found himself longing desperately for the sound of a human voice, the echo of a footfall.

His resolve to stick to one line of direction was soon abandoned. He saw a faint glow a few yards ahead and at an angle away. He hurried to it. Above him glowed a light. It was fixed at the top of a wrought-iron archway. Meredith wrinkled his forehead. This was a gateway, but leading where? He turned inside the gate. Beneath his feet he could feel rough gravel. The loom of the light disappeared behind him and ahead was the wall of fog. Twice he turned in an effort to re-locate the light, and each time he failed. His foot caught in something low down and he fell, hitting his shoulder a sharp rap. His hands searched for the cause of his fall. He had caught his foot in a loop of wire border. His shoulder had struck something solid. It was a gravestone.

"This is wonderful!" he cried, standing up. "I'm in a church-yard." His voice rose sharply, wildly. "A bloody churchyard! I'm looking for a doctor and I find gravestones."

Meredith reeled away, felt the gravel under his feet once more and staggered on. His breath was coming and going in heavy gasps.

Ahead of him he saw a faint oblong of light. He staggered to it. It was an open door. The open door of a church.

Meredith stood with legs apart and shoulders hunched.

"Now belay panic," he almost snarled at himself. "Pull yourself together. Where there's an open door and lights on there are people."

He moved into the dimly lighted church. The fog swirled about inside nearly as thickly as outside. Little haloes of diffused glow showed where lights high in the church were on.

'Is there anybody here?' he called.

223

He heard the rustle of an echo of his own voice. He called louder.

'Is there anybody here?'

He took a few steps further into the church and rested his hand on the back of a pew.

Suddenly something inside him snapped. In a plunging, scrabbling run he reached the front row of seats.

'There's got to be somebody here,' he shouted. 'Somebody answer! Somebody answer!'

Meredith hit the back of the seat time and again as he called. His head dropped forward, his hand slid down from the back of the seat. He took one step sideways and sat down. His head shook from side to side dully as would an animal punished by persistent flies.

'There's nobody,' he whispered. 'Nobody.'

He leaned forward with his head in his hands.

'There's nobody to answer.' He lifted his head and looked wildly about him. He caught sight of a large crucifix, a glow of light making play with the features.

Then he sprang to his feet, his arms wide apart.

'Why isn't there somebody?' he shouted. 'Why isn't there somebody in this house? This is God's house, but He doesn't answer. He doesn't answer because He isn't here.' He stumbled into the aisle again. 'If there were a God He would answer. If there were a God he wouldn't have let my family die. He wouldn't let The Boy die. There isn't anybody here. There isn't any God here. Nobody. . . .'

His voice broke in a sob; he dropped to his knees in the aisle and rested his head against a pew. The sobs increased until they shook him from head to toe.

A hand rested gently on his head.

'You called, my son. You are in trouble?'

Meredith jerked himself upright. He swept away the priest's arm.

'Why didn't you answer before? I've been calling—and calling——I wanted a doctor—The Boy—but nobody answered. Nobody answered in this, God's house.'

The priest firmly but gently took him by the arm and led him to a seat.

'One need never fear to call in this house,' he said. 'There is always an answer, but sometimes we don't hear it.'

With infinite patience the priest guided Meredith back from the realms of wild, savage panic. Gradually he pieced together the whole story.

'And this address is where?' he finally asked.

Meredith told him.

'Just two hundred yards from this church,' the priest smiled. 'Come, I will guide you.'

'It's as thick as a yard up a chimney. It's impossible to see ten yards, let alone two hundred.'

The priest slipped an arm over Meredith's shoulder. 'Then we will go out into the darkness together, you and I, and place our trust where it will not be forgotten.'

Meredith twisted his shoulder away.

'Now would be the time for a couple of full-sized miracles,' he said savagely.

'The whole of life is a miracle, my son, and the course it pursues is hidden from us, perhaps mercifully, but it is a miracle.'

By this time they were walking towards the door. In the porch the priest paused, wrinkling his forehead.

'It is thick, isn't it? I was in the vestry. I heard you call and came out. I, too, have my problems. I was seeking the solution of them in prayer.' He peered into the fog.

'Let me see. We turn right at the gate, then right again. And then it is straight ahead. Come.'

Meredith stood irresolute.

'I'm sorry, Father. I sort of blew up when I found I was completely lost. I said things—shouted them out—I'm sorry.'

'I understand. Here's the gate. Turn right and we follow the wall.'

They strode into the darkness together in silence for a while.

It was Meredith who broke it.

'I've remembered something you said a few minutes ago. Early in the war my wife sent me a text. I kept it hanging on

225

my bulkhead until——' He paused, then went on. 'It ran something like: "*I said to the man who stood at the gate of the year: 'Give me a light. . . .'*" I—I forget, now, quite how it ran. But it was something similar to what you said.'

The priest softly quoted: '*And I said to the man who stood at the gate of the year: "Give me a light that I may tread safely into the unknown. . . ."*' It's not a text, my son, but it should be.' For a few seconds he stood still.

'Now turn right here, I think. And the number is—what?'

Meredith struck a match and peered at some numerals on a gate.

'Two houses away,' Meredith said jubilantly. He hurried along, found the gate to Haley's house and raced up the short drive, the priest following.

Meredith thrust at the bell push. He heard the clang of the bell, and heard footsteps.

Haley stood framed in the doorway. 'Where the devil have you been?' he snarled, peering over Meredith's shoulder at the dim outline of the priest.

'How's The Boy?' Meredith snapped it.

Haley stood aside for them to enter, looking questioningly at the priest.

'I'm Father Cranley. That is my church on the corner. I found your friend somewhat lost so I guided him here. He has told me something of the crisis.'

As Haley shook hands he explained.

'Terence has gone to hospital. If you hadn't put a jerk into it and organized that ambulance it would have been a bad show. But where have you been since? Marjorie and West have gone to the hospital. West took a devil of a chance, but it came off. It gave him—The Boy—a fighting chance until he got to hospital.'

'What happened?' Meredith asked impatiently.

'West says that after you went out to phone the kid really began to choke. He thought it was all over.'

Haley stepped over to the sideboard and picked something up.

'West cut a slit in The Boy's windpipe and inserted a piece of

226

this. It enabled him to breathe after a fashion and the ambulance men said it was the best thing he could have done.'

'What is it?' Meredith took it from Haley.

'Part of the handle of a silver fruit dish. It's tubular. It served.'

Meredith held it in his hand, then tossed it on to the sideboard. He started to laugh, jerkily, wildly.

'There's one of your miracles, Father. Right out of the bag. No wonder—no wonder I couldn't hear your God answering. He talks American.' His voice became a sob.

'Owen! Meredith——!' Haley took a step towards him, snapping the words out.

'You wanna miracle? Sure thing, kid. How wide an' how handsome? The biggest an' the best.' Meredith's eyes were wild and staring as he spoke.

Haley slapped him sharply across the face and the near-hysteria stopped. For a few seconds there was silence in the room, broken only by the low whine of a motor car grinding along in low gear outside.

'Sorry, Bill. Sorry, Father,' Meredith whispered.

Haley looked critically at him. He poured out a generous drink and thrust it into his hand.

'You look like the morning after a rough night on the bridge, Owen.' He lifted the bottle towards the priest, who smiled and shook his head.

'We wondered what had become of you. The policeman who came with the ambulance said you had come on ahead. We thought perhaps you were still trying to rustle up a doctor.'

Meredith shook his head, regarded the remainder of the drink, tossed it back and blew sharply.

'I lost my bearing completely. I—I——'

'And came to the church for re-direction. I think that points a moral somewhere,' the priest chuckled. 'But I won't pursue it. I'm glad your little boy is now safely in hospital. No doubt. . . .'

He trailed off as they heard the front door open and voices came to them. Marjorie Haley and West entered. On her face there were still signs of tears.

'Oh, Bill!' she cried and ran over to her husband. 'It

was just in time. And the sister said Clint did the right thing. It gave him a chance. Owen! When did you get back? We were worried to death when you didn't return.'

'We sure were. And you organized that ambulance in one quick time, pronto,' West added. 'You had me worried. The top nurse said people were being lugged into the hospital in a steady stream after falling under cars or walking into buses. We thought perhaps——'

'I was all right,' Meredith said shortly. 'I just missed my bearings.'

'One good thing, the fog is lifting now,' West said. 'You can see fifty yards or more. Is this what you call a pea-souper?'

Marjorie Haley had been dabbing hastily at her tear-stained face and she looked questioningly from her husband to the priest and back.

'Oh, this is Father Cranley. He guided Owen back. Found him wandering in the fog.'

'I feel as if I've been dragged backwards through a hedge,' she said. 'I'm going to make some coffee.'

Father Cranley started buttoning his coat round his throat.

'Not for me, Mrs. Haley. I have much to do. I would like to call on you again to ask after the child, if I may.'

She nodded her head and held out her hand.

'Please do.'

'You go freshen up your face,' Clint said. 'I'll make the coffee. I'll make it American style and, believe me, it will be good.'

Meredith laughed. 'It will! I'll see Father Cranley to the gate.'

A few minutes later Marjorie Haley re-entered the room as Clint West came in with a jug of coffee.

'You try this. It's made the way Mom makes it. A cup of this and you won't mind whether President Truman is Republican or Democrat.'

Marjorie Haley sipped it. 'Hm. You must teach me how to do it this way. Which is he, by the way? Republican or Democrat?'

West laughed and handed a cup to Haley. 'He sits on the

fence just whittling.' He paused with the jug hovering over a cup. 'Where's that Meredith fella?'

Haley placed his cup of coffee on the table. 'He went to the gate with Father Cranley. He should have been back by now.'

West moved towards the door. 'I'll give him a shout.'

'No.' Haley stopped him sharply. 'I think I understand. He won't be back.'

'But why?' Marjorie asked. 'But why?'

'I'll explain later. He won't be back.'

A couple of hundred yards away Meredith followed Father Cranley into the dim church and stopped by a front seat.

'I'll sit here, if I may, Father.'

'So long as you wish, my son.'

And Meredith was again alone in the church. He sat with his head bowed in his hands. Gradually he became aware that tension was slipping from him, like the shedding of a heavy coat. A feeling of calm came over him. His memory took him back over the recent events, back beyond the moments which had led him to hospital, back to the moment when a padre had first broken the news to him that his family had been wiped out. He found that he could dwell on it without a stab of acute pain.

How long he sat he could never recall.

He came out of his calm reverie when he felt a hand on his shoulder, and a quiet voice started speaking. '*And I said to the man who stood at the gate of the year: "Give me a light that I may tread safely into the unknown." And he replied: "Go out into the darkness and put your hand into the hand of God. That shall be to you better than light and safer than a known way."* It came back to me, my son. You stay as long as you wish. I never close the door until after midnight.'

And Meredith sat on, alone and unafraid.

OWEN MEREDITH sat opposite Jean Payne at a small table in a quiet restaurant. He had written to her asking her if she would have dinner with him on her next evening off and she had replied immediately accepting and saying:

I don't want to go to a show afterwards. I have to be back at the hospital fairly early in any case. Could we have dinner somewhere quietly where we can sit and talk? Do you know a place where they will not put the bill in front of us as soon as we finish eating?

Meredith did, a small but efficiently run restaurant on the fringe of Soho in which the lighting was subdued and the service discreet almost up to pre-war standard.

They had eaten their way leisurely through dinner and were at the coffee stage.

'I know it is useless asking you for an opinion,' he grinned, 'but what will you take for a brandy? If it were methylated spirit you wouldn't know any different.'

'Part of the act of being a woman is to pretend to know nothing. Bring on your meth.—I'll know that by the smell.'

Meredith leaned his arms on the table, a matchstick in his fingers tracing a complicated pattern in the ashtray. It was a complex design of intersecting curves.

Jean Payne watched him from beneath lowered lids for a couple of minutes. Then she broke the silence.

'I know a few people who would profess to tell you a whole lot about yourself from just watching you make shapes in cigarette ash,' she told him.

'Can you?'

She shook her head. 'I'm keeping up the act. I'm just a woman.'

Meredith lifted his eyes and looked steadily at her. 'Yes. So you are. All woman.'

She felt a curious little tremor run through her as he spoke.

"In a few seconds he's going to say something else," she thought. "I want him to say it. And yet I don't. At least, not now." She stirred in her seat and turned the talk off at a tangent. 'Seen the Haleys recently?' she asked as she stubbed out a cigarette, demolishing his intricate outlines.

He moved the cigarette butt to one end of the ashtray and began again his elaborate design.

'No.'

'Why?'

Meredith shrugged. 'I've been rather busy. I did make a call or two at the hospital to inquire about young Terry.' He looked up again. 'He's going to be all right?' It was both a query and a statement.

'Of course he is. It meant only a comparatively minor operation and then isolation until the diphtheria ran its course. He'll be out and full of beans in a fortnight at the most.'

'I thought he was going to die that night.'

'He probably would have if he hadn't been whisked away.'

'For all I did, he would have died. It was West who saved him. He took the chance while I wandered about in the fog like an hysterical child.'

'You found somebody to get an ambulance. That was vital.'

Meredith frowned, shook his head. 'Sheer chance that I found a policeman. He got the ambulance. It took some guts to do what West did.'

'Any second-year nurse would know how to do it. Don't forget, he is half way to being a doctor.'

'I wish he was half way to hell.'

'May I?' she asked, helping herself to another cigarette. She accepted a light carefully, then blew a cloud of smoke towards the ceiling. 'If he were half way there you would still be a long way ahead of him. Well on the way to a little hell of your own making,' she said calmly.

Meredith sat bolt upright.

'The conversation was bound to get into this channel tonight so we might as well let it run,' she continued.

'Both the Haleys are puzzled. They know you went out into

the fog and that is all. Would you care to tell me what went wrong? If anything did go wrong.'

Meredith took a deep breath. 'There is no reason why I shouldn't tell you.'

He described how he went out in search of a doctor, of the rising tide of panic when he found that he was lost. She watched him narrowly as he told her of the moments after he had reached the church and nobody seemed to hear him calling.

'Now you know,' he finished quietly.

'Where did you go after you left the house with the clergyman? Bill Haley was certain you would not be back. He isn't certain but he has an idea that he knows where you did go.'

'Has he?' Meredith made an intricate pattern even more complex. 'I went back to the church. Father Cranley walked in with me and left me alone there. I sat down for a while and . . . and. . . .' He looked up at her and smiled. 'Somehow I felt a wonderful sort of peace come over me. I don't know how long I stayed. It might have been a few minutes, or an hour. I only remember Father Cranley touching me on the shoulder and saying, "Stay as long as you like. I never close the door until midnight."'

'You know, Surgeon-Commander Maldon had a theory about you. You remember him, don't you?'

'Indeed I do.' A small smile hovered at his lips. 'For a long time I hated his innards.'

'He meant you to. In the state you were in when you arrived resentment was the easiest emotion to start moving.'

'Overcoming initial inertia, eh?'

'Largely. His theory about you was that, being a Celt, you were nearer to primitive man than were perhaps a lot of others he had. He argued that because you were afraid of things in the dark you drew endless drafts on your basic courage to prove to yourself—to kid yourself, if you like—that you were not afraid of being afraid.'

'I haven't quite unravelled that, but I think I know what you mean. But tell me, why should a grown man, with a fair amount of experience of the world, be so unreasonably scared all of a sudden in the darkness? I've had it come over me at sea when I was on the bridge, or in my berth, and it would take all I had to keep it under control. Sometimes I couldn't do that.'

'And then you would dash off and do something audacious, or brave. That was Maldon's theory again.'

'Sometimes.'

'I know that horrible feeling. You want to spend a night shift in a hospital. I've been walking along corridors and all of a sudden I've wanted to run and scream.'

'You! I can't imagine you getting into a panic over anything.'

'I said I often feel like doing it. I usually end up in a ward patting a pillow or straightening the bedclothes of a patient who doesn't want patting or straightening.'

'That explains the passion nurses have for doing that sort of thing. I thought it was merely a craving for neatness.'

'A bit of each, possibly.'

She looked at her wrist watch.

'Time flies, and so must I.'

In the taxi she laid her hand on his arm. 'You'll go to the Haley's soon, won't you?' It was almost an order rather than a request.

'Yes. I have something to tell Haley.'

'They're feeling puzzled, and just a little bit hurt.'

'Haley isn't. He understands.'

'You were friends during the war, weren't you?'

'We were together. Haley's great friend was Regan, another commanding officer. Regan was killed after I left the base. Haley was quite cut up about that.'

The taxi pulled into the station and conversation lagged until she was in the train and leaning out of the window.

'I know some of the story of Bill Haley and his friend Regan,' she said.

'How come? He doesn't often talk about it to—to——'

'To strangers?'

He shook his head. 'I wouldn't call you that. I meant to people who didn't know us at the base. How did he come to talk to you about it?'

'Promise you'll keep it a secret? Bill Haley is writing the whole story of that base you were at. He started it a while ago

233

after he had tried to help one of his men who was sent to prison. Marjorie let me read some of it one afternoon. It's so simply written, no epic highlights. It's a sermon on comradeship, the part I read. It's about men going back to help one another when they were in trouble.' She turned her head sideways. 'You're in it, too.'

'I'll sue him for libel.'

She chuckled. 'I don't think you will.'

A strident voice shouted up the platform. 'Stan' clear! Stan' clear of the doors!'

'See you next week?' Meredith asked.

'I'll decide during the week. Clint has asked me to come to Town for the day.'

Pheep—phee-e-e-p. The whistle shrilled.

'Put him off. We'll make this something special.'

'It will be something special that day.' She stood with her hand on the window. The train gave a preliminary jerk. 'He has asked me to marry him. He wants an answer next week.'

Meredith felt as if he had received a blow. Before he could speak she shot the window up and sat back in her seat. She waved gently with her fingers shoulder-high and the train moved away.

Meredith watched the end of the train disappearing along the platform. Through the turmoil of his thoughts he vaguely surrendered his platform ticket and a little later climbed into a taxi and gave Haley's address.

'That's a long way out in the sticks. I might not get a fare back,' the driver objected.

'Get cracking!' Meredith snarled.

'O.K. mister.'

'And speak English for a change.'

The driver grinned.

Meredith stood irresolutely outside Haley's front door, then he pressed the bell push.

'Long time no see,' Haley said. 'Come in. I've got a wee drappie in the house.'

'Where's Marjorie?' Meredith asked when he was settled in a chair with a glass in his hand.

'Oh, your preacher pal, Father Cranley, has roped her in for something. She'll be home about ten.'

It was characteristic of Haley that he posed no question about Meredith's long absence.

'Where's your man Clay?' Meredith started abruptly. 'Fixed up now?'

Haley shrugged. 'A job of sorts. It's still too near that black market crowd he was caught up with. He assures me it is on the level, but he's still living in that slum and sooner or later money will talk. He's desperately anxious to get out of it.'

'Would he go to New Zealand? Up sticks, lock, stock, barrel and family and go out there?'

Haley was gathering together some papers covered with writing as Meredith spoke. He dropped them and turned. Again it was characteristic of Haley that he wasted no time with questioning.

'Tell me more.'

'Briefly, it's this. If he is interested I can put him forward. Three of our smaller tugs have been sold to the New Zealand Government. There is an almighty big project on out there. The tugs will be towed out by a deep-sea tug—remember them, Bill? I have been asked to find crews for them. Some of the crews will sail on the towing tug, the rest will go out on assisted passages with their families. It's a permanent job, Bill. If he agrees I will put him forward.'

'He's a tip-top man, Owen. Just the man for the job. I'll contact him tomorrow and give you an answer. My bet is that he will take it.'

'You can make it clear that for the next few years they will live in prefabs provided by the Government. But they'll be somewhere which is growing healthily, not decaying from the inside outwards, like this country.'

Haley stood in front of his friend. 'You're wrong, Owen. I used to think like that one time, just after I came out of the Service. There was no pride; everybody seemed too tired to be anything but dishonest.' He poised the bottle over Meredith's glass. 'I've been changing my views recently.' He sat down opposite Meredith and crossed his legs.

'I always remember something Regan said to me once when things were very tough at the base. We were being licked to a frazzle at the time. Chased out of everywhere, the Japs belting us at one end of the world and the Hun was triumphant all along the line.' Haley sipped his drink. 'Old Regan said, "Nothing can lick a nation of people who have the faith to plant an acorn and wait for it to grow into an oak tree." He's right, you know, Owen. We still have that unshakable faith. There is no nation in the world which could have taken the beating we took and come up for more.'

'Maybe you're right.'

They sat in silence, each with his thoughts. Suddenly Haley stretched forward and picked up his pile of papers. Almost shyly he held them out.

'You'll probably think I'm daft, but I've been writing the story of the base. Of Regan, Mahoney, Clay, of all the ships and of the job we did. Just sweeping mines. No glamour, no fast-moving fight. Just sweeping mines every day. It began to grow on me. Like to look at it?'

'I knew that——' Meredith bit it off; he had nearly given away Jean Payne's secret.

'You knew what?' Haley said sharply.

'I knew that somebody some day would start writing about it. Why not you?' Meredith craftily went on.

'I've finished it. I'm going to have it typed.'

'And then?'

'Maybe I'll send it out to a publisher.'

'And if he doesn't take it he'll be a B.F.'

'Who wants to read war stories?'

Meredith tipped his glass back. 'The people who are planting the acorns you talked about. They know about the R.A.F. and the Army. Let 'em hear about us.'

'Take it with you. But you are the last dog I should try it on. You were there.'

'I sometimes think I would have been happier if I had stayed at the base with you. A larger ship turned me into a remote man when really I wanted the intimacy of the small ship. Bill,

I'll bet you that after a few minutes' thought you could give me the name of every man who served on *Arandite* with you. Not only their names but a picture of their characters.'

Haley studied the glowing end of his cigarette.

'I think I could, at least of the men who stayed any length of time.' He pointed to the manuscript which Meredith was nursing. 'I haven't consciously done it, but you will find it is part of the pattern of that.'

'On fleet sweepers and frigates they were just men, just numbers. If there was a job to be done Number One, or another officer, detailed a man for it, and a petty officer saw that it was done. I was interested only in ultimate results, no matter how well a man did the job. I wouldn't even know his name.'

Haley watched the smoke climb up from his cigarette.

'Now you know why I so badly wanted to help Clay. To me it had become almost a piece of symbolism, a sort of carrying on the—the comradeship. It's a clumsy word, but you know what I mean.'

'I do. By the way don't worry about Clay having been in the can. I explained it to the New Zealand man who is fixing things and he laughed. "Look where Australia got on a foundation of convicts," he said. "In any case, I did sixty days cells for being rude to some Italian generals and for pinching their watches and binoculars." ' Meredith stirred in his seat. 'Do you think Clay will accept?'

'A hundred-to-one on he will.'

'And that makes me feel good. I was toying with the idea of giving him a job on the tugs on the Thames and damn the police and the other men. But this is a better proposition. A clean start in a clean country.'

Haley held up a restraining hand. 'We've been down that road; don't let's begin again.'

'All right. You find the acorns, I'll make the holes and push 'em in. But you'll have to furnish the faith.'

Haley turned and looked at a photograph of his son.

Meredith followed his gaze. He breathed deeply once or twice.

'That was quite a night, Bill. I—I—went over the top when I found myself lost in the fog. I——'

Haley smiled gently. 'I can guess. Forget it. We're having him back next week. He looks splendid now. Would you like to——'

He broke off as a key rattled in the front door and in a few seconds Marjorie Haley walked in. She stood before Meredith, an accusing finger waving in front of his nose.

'Not before time,' she said in mock severity. 'We had almost forgotten what you looked like.' Her voice softened. 'Has Bill told you that The Boy comes home next week?'

'He has. And I've promised to come along and help to collect him. Bill asked me.'

Haley looked slightly surprised.

'Did I? I meant to, but didn't have time before you came in.'

'I read your thoughts.'

'The mystic Celt, eh?'

She bustled about the room. 'You'll have to have coffee without sugar. I'm out of it until——'

'Go on, say it! Until you see Emily's mother again,' Haley laughed.

'Or until I arrive tomorrow evening,' Meredith grinned.

Haley shook his head in disapproval. 'Complete moral collapse, and over sugar.'

'Didn't you ever snitch some from your steward for Mahoney's Wren?' Meredith asked. 'Of course you did! And so did I.'

'And so did Regan. It was he who first found out that Mahoney liked a lot of sugar in his tea.'

'So he provided the tea as well.' A far-away look crept into Meredith's eyes. 'In some ways they were good days, Bill. Good days.'

'Because we remember the good parts more easily than the other bits.'

'Maybe.'

Marjorie Haley had been listening to their conversation as she prepared cups and saucers. She saw Bill's manuscript on Meredith's chair and glanced swiftly at her husband, then back to Meredith.

'Have you been looking through Bill's story? I think it's wonderful. Parts of it made me cry. It's bound to be accepted.'

'Let him do his own reading,' Haley said brusquely. 'And I haven't made up my mind about sending it to a publisher. I doubt if people want to read war stories yet.'

'Of course you'll send it to a publisher.'

Meredith and Marjorie Haley said it simultaneously. Then they looked at one another and smiled.

'Two-to-one. You're overruled,' Meredith added.

'We'll see.' Haley pulled a wry face. 'Without sugar this coffee is dreadful.'

'Floreat black market,' she laughed triumphantly. 'I'll have him inviting his gangster friend here yet. You'll see.'

'Over my dead body!'

'I'll help you to wash up. I'll wash, you wipe,' Meredith said. 'And Bill can pack up the story of our cold endeavour.'

'What did you call it?' Haley asked sharply.

'Cold endeavour. It was that, wasn't it? Just plain, soul-searing hard work.'

Haley ran his hand through his hair. 'I've been trying to think of a title for weeks. Now you come out with one just like that.' He clicked his fingers. '*Cold Endeavour*. That's the title.'

Meredith was drying his hands as Marjorie artlessly asked, 'Seen Jean recently?'

'Tonight.'

She lifted one eyebrow at him.

'She had to go back early,' Meredith continued. 'So I came round to see you. Look, Marjorie, I—I——'

'I know what you're going to say. Don't! We understand. All we are thankful for was that you found some way of getting an ambulance in time. Now that's all over. When are you seeing her again?'

'Couldn't say. Never, probably. She's going to marry that American fellow, West.'

'Wha-a-a-t!' Her voice climbed sharply.

'Apparently he has asked her to marry him——'

'And what did she say?'

239

'She's going to give him his answer next week. My bet is she'll say "yes". He turned to see Haley standing in the doorway leaning against the wall. 'You'll have to fork out for a wedding present. Get your black-market pal to produce something exotic in nylons.'

Marjorie Haley placed the last cup down with deliberation. She grasped Meredith's arm and marched him into the lounge.

'Now,' she commanded firmly, 'you tell me exactly what she said, where she said it and why she said it. Exactly, mind.'

Meredith gave a more-or-less detailed account.

'Good!' she said decisively.

Meredith paused with the packed-up manuscript under his arm.

'I expect so. See you soon.' He moved towards the door.

'Tomorrow night. Don't forget.' She smiled sweetly at him.

'Don't forget the sugar,' Haley said wickedly. 'And do me a favour. Leave that manuscript in a bus. Lose it.'

When Meredith had gone Haley grasped his wife by the arm.

'What did you mean by saying "good" when you heard Jean was going to marry that American lad?' he asked sharply.

She shook her head at him. 'To begin with, she hasn't said she's going to marry him. It's he who has asked her. Secondly, she hasn't given him an answer.'

'And if she says "yes"?'

'Then you'll have to get your friend to smuggle you something nylon for a wedding present, as Owen says,' she answered with disarming detachment. 'Expensive ones, and some for me, too, to wear at the wedding.'

Haley grasped her by both arms. He remained on the true course.

'I still want to know why you think it is a good thing for her to marry West.'

With exaggerated patience, as if explaining something to a child, she went through the points once again.

'He has merely asked her. She hasn't given him an answer. That's all.'

'It's not all, by a long chalk.'

240

'Bill, darling, if Jean were going to marry Clint West she would tell me first and she most certainly wouldn't break the news to Owen just as a train was pulling out, and after they had been together most of the evening.'

Haley digested that slowly. 'But why?'

She moved up close to him.

'You wouldn't understand. Now, what else did Owen tell you? Any news worth while?'

He told her about the offer to get Clay to New Zealand. 'That's wonderful. He'll take it, won't he, my dear?'

'Almost certain to. In fact, it was one of the things he used to talk about on board. He liked the sea, even though it was war time.'

Later she listened to his steady breathing after they had gone to bed and knew that he was still awake.

'If she says "no" to this American fellow will she say "yes" to Owen?'

She produced a well-simulated, long-drawn-out snore.

Carefully he drew one arm from under the clothes, selected his curved target and slapped sharply.

'Ouch! You beast!'

'I knew you weren't asleep, or anywhere near it. Do you think she would marry Owen if he asked her?'

'He'd have to ask her, wouldn't he?'

'I'll jog him into it.'

She sat bolt upright.

'Don't you dare, Bill. Don't you dare say a word to him. That would ruin it for ever. You stick to getting your old seaman shipped to the far corner of the world.'

'And no mean achievement, that, either.'

She wriggled down under the bedclothes again.

'Wonderful, darling. In fact, I think a lot of you is wonderful. The book, the title—all wonderful.'

'And the parts of me that are not wonderful?'

An arm crept over his shoulder.

'There aren't any. Not any at all.'

'Good night, darling.'

'Good night.'

15

CLAY SURPRISED even Haley by his prompt acceptance of the offer to emigrate. Haley had written to him telling in detail of the job Meredith had to offer. Haley had scarcely reached his office before Clay was speaking to him on the telephone.

'Who do I have to see about it?' Clay asked, coming to the point at once. 'I'll go along this morning.'

Haley was struck again by the deep resonance of Clay's voice. It was a powerful bass voice with a curiously curt, commanding ring about it. He explained to Clay that he would have to contact Meredith first for particulars.

'It didn't take you long to make up your mind, Clay.'

'About twenty seconds after me and the missus had read your letter, sir.'

'And how does she feel about it?'

'Almost too excited to breathe. You see, sir, we had talked it over, I mean about going abroad—Canada, Australia or somewhere. I was going to put my name down, but I waited. I thought perhaps they would ask questions about that time I was inside. Now you say that doesn't matter. We just looked at one another.'

It was fixed up in a few days. The New Zealand Government official was most impressed by Clay.

'Find me a hundred like him and I'll find them jobs,' he said. 'Our trouble is we get too many applications from misfits and work-shy types who think that emigrating is the answer to all their problems.'

On his advice Clay decided to sail on the liner with the other family parties, leaving the single men to go out with the tugs.

The days sped by until one morning Haley and his wife found themselves at Tilbury on the liner quay, talking to Clay and his wife on sailing day.

Marjorie whispered to Bill, 'She's beautiful. Isn't it wonderful that they are going to have a chance like this? I'm certain they'll be so happy.'

There were but a few minutes left before the emigrants would have to be on board when Meredith joined the group.

'I had a job to do at Gravesend, just the other side of the river, so I got one of our tugs to drop me over.'

Clay looked at him.

'I remember you, sir. You were C.O. of *Jacinth*.'

'Indeed I was. And I remember you.'

Clay thrust out his hand.

'Thank you, sir,' he said simply. 'I won't let you down.'

A harsh, metallic voice rang out through the loud speakers on the ship.

'All visitors ashore. All passengers aboard, please.'

Clay looked round him at the scattered parties making tearful going of the farewells.

He squared his shoulders, lifted his head.

'Now, come on, my lucky lads. Get the kissing over, gather up your bits and pieces, wives and kids, and nip smartly aboard. Smack it about a bit.'

As if by magic a dozen men were drawn from the bewilderment of farewells. They shepherded tearful wives and excited children towards the gangways.

'O.K., "Killick",' one grinned at Clay as he ushered his wet-eyed flock aboard. 'Starboard watch all present.'

Haley and Meredith exchanged glances. Haley felt a glow of reflected pride steal through him.

'Once a leading hand, always a leading hand,' Meredith murmured. 'He'll be bos'n of one of those tugs before he's out there a month. He'll have that little lot nicely organized before they reach Ushant.'

The New Zealand official had joined them in time to hear Meredith's comment.

'He's mate of one of them before he leaves Tilbury. Remember, it's coastal work so he won't want a ticket. Only common sense and one or two other qualities. And he seems to have those.' The official looked at Meredith. 'I could use a captain or two if you could find them for me.'

His significant look included Haley.

'Get to work on Meredith,' Haley laughed.

'You won't get Haley; he's too busy planting acorns in this country,' Meredith said without a smile.

'A private joke,' Haley explained.

The liner's deep-throated siren boomed twice in throbbing notes.

'That's the lot, sir.' Clay and his wife stood at the foot of the gangway. 'I'll write, sir.' He slipped an arm over his wife's shoulder. 'Me and the missus—we aren't taking much with us. Didn't have much. I've got a picture of—the old ship. Could —would you send us one of you, and your family?'

Haley held out his hand.

'That's a promise. And you send us one of you.'

Marjorie Haley suddenly kissed Mrs. Clay.

'Look after him, my dear, won't you?'

Mrs. Clay tearfully nodded. She turned towards the gangway.

Clay suddenly came smartly to attention and his hand slipped upwards in the old familiar salute. Without another word he wheeled and followed his wife.

'Not all your oaks will grow in this country,' Meredith said.

'If you'll promise to tell me what this is about oak trees I'd be delighted to buy you all lunch,' the New Zealander smiled.

When he had heard he leaned back reflectively. 'I have an idea I can turn one of my high-pressure writers loose on that theme. It should go down very well with the papers at home. We are all very sentimental about England down there.'

Meredith leaned towards Marjorie Haley.

'You know, Marjorie, these boys are born in New Zealand, grow up there, yet when they come to England they talk about coming home. I used to hear them saying it when I met them during the war. "I hope I get a chance to go home before I go back" used to puzzle me. That is so, isn't it?'

The New Zealander nodded his head.

'I suppose it is because we consider ourselves just a younger

244

member of a big family and—— Well, England is the sort of home, or headquarters, of us all.'

Meredith snorted.

'By the time this bunch of red-hued yobs in power finish with the British Empire it will be only New Zealand—and Wales—left. Look at them; they are giving it away port, starboard, for'rard and aft. Oh, I know they call it "self-government within the framework of the Commonwealth" but that's all my eye and Betty Martin. I've talked to some of them and I know. South Africa is more pro-Nazi and more anti-British even than the Germans. Canada, or at least large slabs of it, would go over to the land of the Almighty Dollar like a shot if given the choice. In a couple of years India will be attached in name only. And who built it up? Answer that. As for Australia, it only wants somebody to spill a case of tea in Sydney Harbour and it would follow America's example and bust clear.'

'A long speech, and perhaps a bit biased,' the New Zealander said, catching the waiter's eye. 'It must have made you thirsty. One for the road and then I must fly.'

Marjorie Haley managed to get a few minutes with Meredith alone as the party broke up.

'Have you seen Jean lately?' she asked, pretending to search in her handbag.

'No. When is she getting married?'

Marjorie smiled sweetly. 'I don't think she's made a final date yet.' She found what she was searching for and promptly thrust it back into her handbag.

'Do we see you tonight?'

'I'd like that. About seven o'clock?'

'Earlier if you can. Terence likes to see something of you before he is shot off to bed.'

'Say half past six.'

Meredith, Haley and his wife stood in the forecourt of the hotel looking down the river. Half a mile down, attendant tugs, bustling ahead and astern, moved the emigrants' liner.

'There go the beginning of a thousand dreams,' Meredith said.

245

'Why don't you have a stab, Owen?' Haley asked. 'New places, new faces, new—ouch!' He rubbed his ankle where her foot had caught it sharply.

'Sorry, darling. Did I accidentally kick you?' Her smile was sugar-sweet.

'You nearly hacked my ankle off.'

Meredith saw and heard nothing. His eyes were on the liner.

'New everything,' he murmured. 'It's an idea.' He spun on his heel. 'See you folk tonight,' he added abruptly and strode off towards the quay.

'Now see what you've done. You've put ideas in his head. I'll never forgive you if he does it.'

'Why not? It's a good idea for him.'

'Well, I say it's not. And we must get back. I have things to do.'

Meredith was considerably earlier than half past six when he rang the bell.

He stopped short with a jerk as he entered the lounge. Sitting in a chair facing the door was Jean Payne.

'Hullo, Owen! I haven't seen you for months. How are you?'

'Three weeks precisely.' He held out his hand.

A curious dryness afflicted his lips and he licked them briefly.

'It seems longer.'

'It seems years.'

The Boy claimed his attention for a boisterous romp until finally they subsided into a chair, in their favourite position, The Boy sitting across one of Meredith's knees, his head on one shoulder with the man gently running his fingers through the child's hair.

'Now I am in a spot,' Marjorie Haley said, offering the cigarette box. 'I haven't a thing in the house to eat. I didn't see Emily's mother today,' she added, with a wicked look at her husband. 'All I can suggest is that Owen takes Jean out and buys her a dinner. She looks starved.'

'Get Mrs. Carter to keep an eye on The Boy and we can all go,' Haley said brightly. 'And I'll toss you for the bill.'

'Oh, I've got enough for a scratch meal for us,' Marjorie inserted hurriedly. 'But not enough to spread to four.'

She signalled swiftly and covertly to Bill to agree.

He shrugged, a puzzled look on his face.

Jean Payne stood up. 'I feel rather guilty about this,' she said, 'but I happened to be near so I dropped in.'

Bill Haley caught his wife's warning eye and said nothing.

Meredith lifted The Boy down, ruffled his hair and stood up.

'If you haven't another date I would very much like to take you out to dinner. Have you?'

Jean smilingly shook her head.

'I haven't. Could we go to that little restaurant we went to the last time you took me out? I liked it very much.'

A little while after they had gone Marjorie asked Bill, 'What is "a fall guy", Bill?'

Haley frowned in concentration. 'A fall guy? It's an American expression. The nearest I can get to it is this. A confidence trickster has a smooth pal who gets a victim up to the point where he is ready to fall for the trick, whatever it is. Does that explain it clearly enough?'

'Admirably.'

'Why do you ask?'

'Bill, get me that large dish out of the larder. I'm starving.'

Bill Haley surveyed the large oval dish on which rested five chops.

'Either you are an infernal little liar or you have some deep plot afoot,' he said severely, holding up the dish. 'You could have put on a meal here quite easily.'

'Yes, Bill, darling. But there would have been too many of us.' 'Two is a nice neat number, don't you think?'

He placed the dish firmly on the kitchen table, grasped her by the arms and said, 'Now talk, unless you want your son to see you being spanked. Go on, start talking. And while I am on the subject, why did Jean say she had just dropped in? You knew three days ago that she was coming.'

'Oh, Bill! You are so blind. I sometimes wonder how you ever got a ship into harbour.'

'That was because I was handling a predictable thing.'

'Which you call "she". Don't hold my arm so tightly. You're stopping the blood.'

He tightened his grasp. 'Start talking.'

She leaned back against the grip of his hands. 'You see, Owen couldn't propose to Jean in front of us, could he? So I had to pretend I had nothing in the house to get them out somewhere to dinner. If that hadn't come off I had another plan. I would have fed them, then you and I would have left them baby-sitting while we went out to the pictures, or something.'

He released his grip and held his arms upwards, his eyes closed in long-suffering bewilderment.

'Look, woman, let's start at the beginning, shall we?'

She shook her head impatiently. 'I've told you as clearly as I can. Owen is going to ask Jean to marry him tonight——'

He sighed heavily. 'He can't marry her tonight. It takes weeks. You should know that. And how do you know he is going to ask her? And how do you know he wants to marry her? And how do you know she wants to marry him? And what about that young American, Clint West? Answer those questions in that order or take the spanking.'

'Oh, Clint West—he's just the "fall guy". He asked Jean to marry him, but she said "no" and he got shirty. He said she had just been using him for a "fall guy". That's why we, Jean and I, wanted to know what a "fall guy" was. Now we know. But Owen thought she was going to marry Clint just because he had asked her. She's going to marry Owen.'

He thrust the dish at her.

'Get on with those while I think this out. I have two cardinal points cleared up. One is that she is not marrying West. The second is that you two women between you have got some scheme cooked up to hook Owen Meredith.'

'That's what I've been trying to tell you all the time. But it isn't to "hook" him, darling. It's to help him.'

248

A few minutes later he added, 'It will be a good thing if it comes off.'

She jabbed dexterously at the cooking chops.

'You stand by, sailor, to buy me something really thrilling for the wedding. Something really whooo-whooo.'

'It's a deal.'

Owen Meredith held the stem of his wine glass lightly between finger and thumb. Gently he revolved the glass, watching the ruby wine. Suddenly he looked up and found her gaze fixed on him.

She shook her head. A smile came, then disappeared.

'I said "no".' It was so quiet that Meredith scarcely heard.

The wine glass jerked convulsively and some of its contents spilt over the edge, starting a widening stain on the table-cloth.

Meredith's throat tightened; his lips dried and he helped them with a quick movement with the tip of his tongue.

'You are not going to marry him?'

Again she shook her head.

'Why?'

'Simple. I'm not in love with him.'

Meredith pushed the glass out of the way. He rested both his elbows on the table and held his head in his hands. His face had a taut, almost agonized, expression when he lifted it. One hand dropped to cover hers resting on the table.

He swallowed convulsively. 'Jean.' It was a hoarse whisper.

'Owen—Owen, darling.'

His other hand helped to imprison her fingers.

The head waiter watched them benevolently. 'Do not—I say again—do not take the bill to table nine yet,' he instructed the young waiter who hovered near. 'Not for a long time yet. Then tell them we have a nice brand of champagne. You understand?'

The young waiter nodded reluctantly.

The head waiter spun and faced him. 'You know no more than enough to lay a table. You just say "hullo", pinch them on the derriere and you call that romance.' He snorted. As an afterthought he continued, 'And add an extra ten shillings. He won't count the bill. No, make it fifteen shillings. After all, we are losing the use of number nine for a long time.'

It was some while before Meredith turned and signalled to the waiter to bring the bill.

As the head waiter had predicted, he glanced at it for a second and put some notes on the plate.

Jean pulled her gloves through her fingers. 'Owen Meredith,' she said primly, 'you haven't even asked me to marry you and here you are talking about wedding plans.'

He grinned. 'Here goes!' The grin disappeared. 'Jean, will you marry me?' A hand stroked his forehead. 'It seems as if I have always loved you—— I can't seem to get things into sharp focus before that——'

'Don't try.'

He shyly took her fingers in his hand. 'I know it is the bride's prerogative to choose the church, or wherever it is. Have you any choice?'

'None.'

'Would you like to be married in Father Cranley's church? I feel that it was in there that I——'

She nodded. 'I would love it.'

He leaned back. 'Then that's settled.'

16

BILL HALEY was as delighted as his wife was when he heard that Owen Meredith was to marry Jean.

'But what puzzles me is how you knew it would work out the way it did,' he remarked. 'After all, Owen might not—I repeat might not—have been in love with her. And she might not have been in love with him.'

'How much does it cost to have a seeing-eye dog? You know—a trained dog which takes you about at the end of a lead.'

He looked suspicious. 'Somehow I'm at the end of the plank but I refuse to be pushed off. I still maintain it might not have worked out like that.'

'But it did, so why talk about it?'

'You women are inclined to take too much for granted. Nobody knew when I had screwed up courage enough to ask you to marry me. I didn't know myself until a few hours before.'

She looked demure. 'No, darling. Nobody knew. Only me. And I knew weeks before.'

Jean Payne stayed with the Haleys for a day or two before her wedding, and the night before the marriage Haley met Meredith for what he called 'the last supper before the execution'.

'I have the idea it is breakfast at that ceremony,' Marjorie smiled. 'You have a good time. And when you get home just kick the door and lean against it.'

'I'd give a five-pound note to be here to listen in to the conflab between you two,' he chuckled. 'What will you talk about?'

'Men,' they chorused.

'And how stupid they can be,' Marjorie added.

'And how slow,' Jean contributed.

'And how blind.'

'Stone-blind, and deaf.'

'And often dumb.'

'Enough—I give in! I did have an idea of sneaking back and listening. But not now,' Haley laughed.

When he had gone, and The Boy had been put to bed, the two women sat in silence, cigarettes glowing and a couple of Haley's precious drinks balanced on their knees. It was Jean who broke the silence.

'There's something about this house, Marjorie. Something comforting. It's a feeling I had when I first came here and it has grown more on me ever since.'

Marjorie Haley smiled. 'A nice, friendly house. Does that fit what you are trying to describe?'

'It does indeed. Is that what you think about it?'

'There have been times when I've hated it, not for itself but for all the things people did to us when we first bought it.'

She told Jean of the troubles they had experienced, of the surveyor, of the builder, and the frustrations they had had. Of how they had come near to defeat, to selling it for what it would bring and leaving it behind for ever.

'But there is one old chap, a one-armed man who is a sort of handyman. He told us about the people who had it years ago. And it was he who said "it was always a friendly house, a nice, friendly house".'

'It fits.' Jean leaned forward and her hand rested on Marjorie's arm. 'It fits the people who live in it, too. I shall always be grateful to you and Bill. More so for what you have done for Owen. He wanted somebody like you two so badly when he came out of hospital.'

'My dear girl, we have loved having you come here, both of you. He was very ill in hospital, wasn't he?'

'No. He was just willing himself to die. And nearly did.'

Later that evening Meredith and Haley sat nursing drinks.

'Everything all set, Bill?'

'Sure! We've got her in captivity and only a war will stop Marjorie getting Jean to the starting post tomorrow. I've arranged a cylinder of oxygen for you at the church in case you feel faint.'

'Ass!'

Meredith finished his drink.

'Feel like a walk, Bill? Shall we go down the Embankment? Remember we took a walk down there the first night I met you?'

'You're not contemplating a jump at this late hour, are you?' Haley grinned. 'You merely have to say "no" tomorrow.'

They leaned against the wall, watching the play of light on the water.

Meredith's cigarette described a long, glowing arc as he shot it into the river.

'That always reminds me of a tracer, Bill. All that seems a long way back, doesn't it? And it was all so futile. Where are we? How much better off are we?'

Haley let his hand rest on Meredith's shoulder.

'Some of this you read in my novel. Believe me, I don't often talk in this strain, but I am one of the people who believes part of it, at least, was worth while. Look, Owen—before the war we had lost spirit; even our courage was a doubtful quantity. Remember that Hitler and his gang used to start off scares every week-end and the world would quiver, wondering whether he meant it or not. When he finally did mean it we found that we had got those qualities.'

He stared out over the dark, glistening water.

'I shall always remember a soldier we lifted off the beach at Dunkirk. He was so tired he couldn't stop his legs from buckling. He hadn't shaved for a week, and he and his crowd had fought a running fight almost from Metz. We hauled him over the side, with others, and he stood there swaying. Then he turned to our Number One and said, "We ain't licked, sir. By cripes, we ain't! Just let us get our second breath." I watched him as he gazed at the beach full of troops. "I'll be back, you square-headed so-and-so's. Me and all them there on the beach. You just watch out when we do."'

'What point are you trying to make, Bill?'

'Just this. That soldier had nothing except what he stood up in, and that wasn't much more than his rifle and a couple of rounds of ammunition. He represented the whole country at that moment. We had just nothing. But he—we, if you like—had that basic something which we had thought we had lost. The war has left us as poverty-stricken as beggars. But on the other hand we have the knowledge that we fought on alone, taking a terrible licking, for more than a year when other countries—the whole world—thought we had had it. That has given pride a root which will stay put for a couple of hundred years, Owen. I always remember that soldier and consider him sort of symbolic. I wonder if he got through long enough to go back.'

'You could interpret that as meaning that we were too daft to know we were licked.'

'You and cynicism don't made a good team, Owen. Cynicism is the weapon of the defeated. You were never that.'

'Indeed I was—all along the line. I didn't want the to-morrows, not even the todays, and the yesterdays were full of pain.'

'Yet you stood it off and licked it. And tomorrow for you is something—— Well, you know what I mean.'

'Indeed it is.' Meredith took a deep breath. 'This is something I haven't talked about much to you, Bill. But when my family was wiped out it seemed the end of all things. There just didn't seem any point in going on living. Then I met Jean again and somehow I found it became a little harder to keep the memories sharp and clear in my mind. At first I thought I was being disloyal to them; I even fought against it for a while. But now they are something apart. I can recall many, many moments with them, happy moments, but the feeling of incredible loneli-ness because they are no longer with me doesn't affect me now.' He paused, then went on rather shyly, 'I have even persuaded myself that she approves of me marrying again.'

Haley pushed with his hand to turn Meredith to face him.

'I'm certain she does, Owen. I used to wonder sometimes during the war what Marjorie would do if I hadn't come back. Human beings are not meant to live alone.'

'Thanks, Bill. Come on, let's have one more for the road.'

A few minutes later they stood facing each other in a quiet bar.

'I can never remember it, but that speech Diana Wynyard made in Noel Coward's *Cavalcade* just fits. Remember it?'

'Yes, but not the words. As you say, it will do. And to the years ahead, Bill.'

Meredith lifted his glass.

'And confusion to the years which have past—at least, to some of them, the more recent ones.'

'Confusion to the bitter years, the brittle glass years.'

Meredith caught his breath when he turned and saw her coming up the aisle with Marjorie Haley a step behind. She was dressed in a soft shade of grey with a saucy hat atop. In her arms she had a small sheaf of flowers. But it was her face, her eyes, which made Meredith catch his breath. From them seemed to come a radiance, a smile without the use of other features. He felt his heart give a thump, then take up the load from the laggard beat.

Her hand trembled slightly as he slipped the ring on her finger.

'Do you, Jean, take Owen to be your lawful wedded husband. . . ?'

'Do you, Owen. . .?'

But dimly he heard the priest speaking the words of the ceremony.

Then a phrase came to his mind.

'Until death do you part.' He seemed to hear it echo again and again faintly through the church. He held her fingers tightly and whispered them to her.

'Until death do us part . . . and afterwards.'

Her fingers tightened on his. He looked up. She was gazing at him, lips slightly apart. Almost imperceptibly she inclined her head.

And they became man and wife.

A couple of hours later Bill Haley lifted a flat, shallow glass and to the small group of people he said, 'We'll drink to Mr. and Mrs. Owen Meredith. And that's all the speech you'll get from me. But, if you insist, I'll add I have known the bridegroom a long time. I have had many opportunities for judging the

255

qualities I know he possesses. I have not known the bride so long, but the longer I have known her the more I have grown to like her. Owen and Jean!'

Meredith's return speech was equally short.

A little later Bill got Owen into a corner.

'This came this morning. I'd like you to read it.'

Owen looked at him wonderingly and opened the letter. It bore the name of a large publishing concern.

... *After receiving reports from my readers I am pleased to inform you that we will be delighted to publish your novel, 'Cold Endeavour'. Perhaps you would be good enough to let me know when it would be convenient to call so that we can discuss terms.* ...

Meredith lifted his head.

'This is wonderful, Bill. Not that I had any doubts. It's the best wedding present we could have had. Does Jean know?'

'You tell her.'

'It's bound to be a best-seller. And I want a signed copy when it comes out,' Jean said.

Haley smiled. 'I doubt if it will be a best-seller. But if it tells a few thousand people of our part of the war, then I will be satisfied.'

When they had departed on their honeymoon, and the few guests had gone, Marjorie Haley said, 'Light me a cigarette, Bill. I don't know whether I have been on my head or my heels all day.'

She sat on the arm of his chair, ruffling her fingers through his hair.

'They'll be happy, won't they? He'll be kind to her. She wants it, Bill.'

'They will, and she'll be kind to him, too, won't she?'

'They'll be like us, darling. Just going on being in love.'

'In a nice, friendly house. Like ours.'

'With nice friendly people living in it, like you.'

'Like you, too.'

She dropped her head until her lips were within reach. She closed her eyes and waited. And she did not wait in vain.